Annja hung back

More than his physical size, the rock musician's sense of *presence* loomed like a skyscraper and warmed like the sun. He seemed wholly aboveboard. Despite the unsolicited contact, his manner seemed totally correct and friendly. Charisma emanated from him like heat from a forge.

Annja had not been born yesterday. "What exactly did you whisk me here for, Sir Iain?"

He smiled a lopsided smile and bobbed his head once. "Fair enough question," he said. "Permit me to answer with one. How would you like to save the world?"

"That's not an offer an archaeologist hears very often," she said. "But I'm afraid I can't make much of a donation to any of your causes."

"It's not money we want," he said, "but your courage, your skills—your soul."

She looked at him and he grinned.

"Now, how would you like to see an authentic cursed tome?" he asked.

She grinned back. "You do know the way to a lady's heart, sir," she said. "Lead on!"

Titles in this series:

Destiny
Solomon's Jar
The Spider Stone
The Chosen
Forbidden City
The Lost Scrolls
Secret of the Slaves

ROGUE Angel

Alex Archer

SECRET
OF THE SLAVES

A GOLD EAGLE BOOK FROM

WORLDWIDE®

TORONTO • NEW YORK • LONDON
AMSTERDAM • PARIS • SYDNEY • HAMBURG
STOCKHOLM • ATHENS • TOKYO • MILAN
MADRID • WARSAW • BUDAPEST • AUCKLAND

First edition September 2007

ISBN-13: 978-0-373-62126-2
ISBN-10:   0-373-62126-4

SECRET OF THE SLAVES

Special thanks and acknowledgment to
Victor Milán for his contribution to this work.

The
LEGEND

...THE ENGLISH COMMANDER TOOK
JOAN'S SWORD AND RAISED IT HIGH.
The broadsword, plain and unadorned,
gleamed in the firelight. He put the tip against
the ground and his foot at the center of the blade.
The broadsword shattered, fragments falling
into the mud. The crowd surged forward,
peasant and soldier, and snatched the shards
from the trampled mud. The commander tossed
the hilt deep into the crowd.
Smoke almost obscured Joan, but she continued
praying till the end, until finally the flames climbed
her body and she sagged against the restraints.

Joan of Arc died that fateful day in France,
but her legend and sword are reborn....

PROLOGUE

The Upper Amazon Basin

With a growl of its potent diesel engine, the 124-ton bulldozer rumbled into motion across the clearing. Riding outside the enclosed and air-conditioned cab despite the sweltering wet heat, Henrique da Silva felt the power surge through his legs and spine and exulted. Hanging on with one hand and with the Uzi submachine tipped skyward in the other, he felt filled with power, like a conqueror of old. He could even ignore the seismic jiggle the massive engine's vibration induced in his substantial belly fat, straining against the already sweat-soaked front of his white shirt.

The workers driving the heavy machinery wore coveralls. The heavily armed mercenary force, riding inside and on top of the armored cars that rolled forward flanking him to either side, wore camouflage. But Silva affected dark trousers, shirt and a tie flung rakishly over his shoulder. He was Amazonas State associate secretary for environmental protection. He had an image to project. While some men in his position were only too willing to tart themselves up in rain-forest-pattern battle dress, Silva preferred to distinguish himself from the men he had hired to protect his workers. They too were mere hirelings. He was the man in charge.

Not that that meant he would willingly relinquish his grasp on his submachine gun.

"Your Excellency." His assistant's voice crackled with worry as much as static in Silva's headset. Silva was hardly an excellency. But he seldom reproved his assistant for using the title. He liked its ring. And once they received the returns for the hardwood from the virgin stand of selva on the clearing's far side—not to mention certain discreet bounties for dealing with native populations that stood in the way of progress—*excellency* might apply. He knew a number of enterprises where he could rapidly leverage his newfound wealth.

"Excellency, are you sure this is wise? Many men have been lost in this region." They had landed from a flotilla of riverboats far up the Amazon Basin, distant from anything either man would recognize as civilization.

"Carelessness, Ilyich," Silva said. "Augmented by silly superstition. Doubtless some earlier parties got themselves ambushed. But we're not going to be put off by a handful of naked savages, are we?"

"But there are stories—the hidden city of magicians."

"Fah. You're a government employee, Ilyich. An educated young man. Not a stupid and ignorant dockhand in Bahia, ready to scuttle off at the first rumor of Indian witchcraft."

Silva considered himself above all that. The little deer-hide pouch of chicken bones, tobacco and certain other none-too-clearly specified substances he carried inside his watch pocket was merely a memento.

"I'm concerned for our work schedule," his assistant said. "And costs. Costs, of course."

"Then let's not delay. Soares? Are your men in readiness?"

"Yes." The work-gang boss rode another huge bulldozer. He most closely resembled a brick, in shape, complexion, and consistency. He was a man of medium height with dark reddish brown skin, a curly fuzz of red hair brushed with yellowish white around the fringes of a dome of skull, even slightly reddish murky eyes. The single affirmative was all Silva needed or expected of him—he spoke about as much as a brick. He allowed no nonsense, which recommended him highly for his task, where neither sloppiness nor malingering could be tolerated.

"And you, Colonel Bruckner?" Silva asked.

The security chief was a real German, not a second- or third-generation Brazilian German from down south. He was a veteran of the former East German National People's Army and a thoroughly work-hardened mercenary—or private military contractor, as he preferred to be called. He was a short man, precise and slim as an ice pick, with a prematurely white buzz cut and coal-black eyebrows over bright blue eyes.

"Yes," Bruckner replied. "My men champ at the bit. Let's go kill some savages." His notion of how to deal with indigenous peoples accorded well with Silva's.

"Go," Silva commanded. With a hand on top of the cab, he waved his Uzi in a rough circle in the air. Few actually saw the gesture; they were either sealed into metal boxes or peering intently at the jungle lying ominously in wait. But it made Silva feel like a conqueror.

The vehicles swept forward. The mercenaries mostly rode in their six-wheeled armored cars, the workers clinging to the bulldozers or banging around like loads of papayas in stake-bed trucks. Silva rode a precarious perch just behind the monstrous, hot engine. But as the machine's treads bit into the black soil and the great blade began to shove down the tall yellow grass in front, he knew it was worth it.

This land was low but only submerged when the rains caused the great river to rise over its ill-defined banks. The path from their river beachhead led across a wide clearing, with its high grass and anomalous black soil. The rich topsoil was called black Indian earth. Found throughout the Brazilian Amazon, it was supposedly a special soil artificially created by the inhabitants. The undersoil of the Amazon Basin was poor, weak and thin. He believed it had to be some kind of unexplained natural phenomenon. Who could believe ignorant savages could create something modern science was unable to duplicate, and so much of it?

The stink of diesel overpowered even the jungle reek of wet and rotting vegetation. The roar of big engines overpowered everything, enclosing Silva in a microcosm of noise and power. A heavy warm wind blew against Silva's plump face.

Ahead and to the left, a flight of small blue birds rose from the high grass and swirled up chittering in the air, as into an inverted invisible drain. After a reflexive glance at the sudden movement, matched by a sort of interior jerk, Silva ignored them. He was a progressive, a man of the modern world. As far as he was concerned any bit of nature he couldn't bend to the use of the state—with a bit of profit on the side for him—was just clutter.

The associate secretary assumed the white smoke that puffed into the heavy air ahead was some kind of primitive signal by the savages to alert their friends and relatives to the mechanized doom rolling toward them. Then a fierce crack stabbed his ears right through the engine's roar.

The hatches of an armored car just four vehicles to his left flew open. An astonishing quantity of black smoke erupted from them. Men scrambled out, shrieking. They burned with flames that were almost invisible in the bright sunlight.

The associate secretary heard Bruckner curse in his earpiece.

"You said these were just Indians, Silva. Where did they get MILANs?"

Silva was still blinking in amazement at the stricken armored car. It had rolled to a stop. Orange flames jetted from the open hatches. Yellow explosions crashed and flashed through them like fireworks as ammunition belts cooked off inside. The vehicles immediately behind it had stopped, more in response to the sudden attack than any obstacle the wreck posed. The word at the end of the German's sentence made no sense to Silva.

"I hired your men to fight," Silva replied. "So fight!" As he gave the brusque command machine guns began to snarl from vehicles to either side of his. It made him feel on much firmer ground. He was in charge.

The German had his white-fuzzed head down and was talking into his mike on a different frequency. Over the grumble of engines and the wind-roar of the flames they heard distinct pops from the woods behind them. Having read reports of prior expeditions to this rich virgin district, they were prepared as well as possible. Their 82-mm mortars would clear out any ambushers the machine guns couldn't deal with.

Beyond Bruckner's command car, a yellow bulldozer rolled. It was still immense at half the size of the machine Silva rode.

The laborers riding it wore overalls with no shirts beneath, and hard hats. As Silva watched Bruckner give commands he saw a worker simply slip from the dozer and disappear into the grass. A moment later a second followed, and a third.

The bulldozer stopped. The remaining two laborers

riding it jumped off and ran. One screamed horribly as the dozer immediately behind, which had swerved to avoid hitting its suddenly stalled mate, sucked a boot into its treads. His leg was twisted off at the thigh.

More pops from overhead, surprisingly flat sounding, drew Silva's attention upward. He saw dirty gray puffs of smoke unfold against the blue sky overhead. He realized he had not heard the slamming cracks of mortar shells among the trees ahead. Could the savages have somehow exploded the shells in air?

"Impossible!" he exclaimed.

Around him he heard explosions, screams, the rippling of machine-gun fire. The bulldozers had all stopped. Even the armored cars had halted, three of them including Bruckner's out in front of the rest of the mass. The machine cannon in Bruckner's cupola fired, its sound like the fabric of reality tearing right across.

Silva felt his own machine slow. He pounded on the top of the air-conditioned cab with a palm. "Go! Go, you cowardly piece of shit! Or I'll have you and your whole worthless family sent to the gold camps!" He did not have to tell the driver a steady stream of humanity flowed into the camps. And almost none returned.

Lights flickered among the trees, still over two hundred yards ahead. Silva had never been under fire before but he couldn't help recognizing muzzle-flashes. These savages were well-armed. The evil small-arms merchants had much to answer for.

Yet despite the screams and blasts all around he felt no fear. This wasn't real somehow. He could feel nothing, not even the Amazon heat. He was just barely aware of shock waves drumming against his cheeks. Besides, he was prepared—he was the master of the situation. So the savages had gotten guns from some traitor. He had a preponderance of force. He had Germans, damn it!

"Bruckner," he shrieked. The German showed no reaction. Though he was barely twenty yards away he couldn't hear the associate secretary over the head-crushing racket. Silva fumbled with the channel setting on his communicator. "Bruckner, deploy your men! Attack, damn you! They're nothing but a handful of primitives."

"Ja," the German replied. Silva was outraged. He resolved to see to Bruckner when this was done. The man was incompetent, and trying to cover it with impudence in the very belly of battle!

"Soares," Silva commanded his labor chief, "keep your machines moving forward. If they fear danger, there's more of it here in the open." And even more if they fail me! he thought furiously.

There was no response. Just a crackle in the headset.

"Soares!" he shouted in his microphone, as if that would help. "Answer, damn you."

"He can't, Excellency." He heard the voice of Ilyich Chaves, his personal aide. It shook so badly he could barely wring sense from it.

"Why not?" Silva shrieked.

"He's dead."

"Dead?"

"An animal," Ilyich said. "Some horrid beast—it leaped from the grass."

"Get hold of yourself, imbecile! Speak sense!"

From the right he saw a sudden flicker of yellow—

It emerged from the grass and sprang from the black Indian earth. A great cat, thick bodied, spotted with black rosettes, ears pressed flat to a skull that gleamed like gold in the sunlight. It hit Bruckner in a sort of flying tackle, rocking him back in his seat.

"An *onza?*" Silva breathed. "A golden *onza?*" It was a jaguar—and more than a jaguar. A huge golden one. An almost mythic beast of the great Amazon woods, seldom seen but always feared.

The German's gloved fists beat against the great cat's shoulders as it sank huge yellow fangs into his neck and dragged him out of the hatch onto his back atop the armored vehicle. The beast pounced and raked open Bruckner's camouflage battle dress and the Kevlar vest beneath as if they were wet tissue paper. Then it began to scoop the guts right out of the mercenary's living belly, kicking with its monstrous hind legs.

Bruckner's screams put the thunder of battle to shame.

More motion snapped Silva's attention away from the nightmare spectacle. His own machine lurched to a final stop.

A young man stood before him, fifteen yards away, clearly visible through a gap in the grass. He was nude, tall and lean and muscled like a god. His long, handsome, high-cheekboned features were impassive. Dark brown dreadlocks cascaded about his broad shoulders.

"Bastard!" Silva shrieked. He clutched the Uzi in both hands and ripped a burst from right to left. It should have stitched the man across his washboard belly. But even as the associate secretary brought his weapon up, the man sidestepped into the high grass and was gone.

Silva sprayed the grass with bullets. The tall stems might shield the naked savage from view, but they wouldn't keep copper-jacketed lead out of his golden hide. The Uzi's heavy bolt locked back as the magazine ran dry. Cursing, weeping in frustrated fury, Silva fumbled in his pockets for a backup magazine.

Triumph thrilled through him as his fingers closed around a cold steel bar. "Ha! Ha!" he shouted, pressing the latch and dropping the spent magazine from its well in the Uzi's pistol grip.

A figure reared up beside him as from the depths of his own nightmares. An anaconda, a huge serpent with mottled brown-and-yellow scales glistened in the hateful sun. Its head was as large as a bull mastiff's. The eyes were huge and golden and seemed to glow with terrible intelligence.

For a moment it stared straight into Silva's eyes. He tried to jam the fresh magazine home. Trembling hands could not find the opening. But he could not tear his eyes from that golden gaze.

The serpent opened its mouth. It was like some kind of trap opening. A pink trap, edged with yellow-white.

Silva screamed and tried to swing his otherwise use-less Uzi like a club.

The anaconda darted its head forward and crushed Silva's face with a single grip of its jaws.

1

Pain jabbed the muscle of Annja Creed's right forearm as she slammed it into the hardwood limb jutting from the trunk-like pole before her.

Good, she thought savagely. She slammed a palm into the slick-polished wood of the trunk itself even as her left forearm blocked into another protrusion.

Faster and faster her hands moved, in and out, over and under the blunt wooden posts stuck in sockets on the central pole. She practiced blocks, traps, strikes with stiffened fingers and fists and palms. A drumbeat rose as muscle and bone met wood with jarring impact.

Annja was a tall, fit woman in her midtwenties. She wore a green sports bra and gray shorts. The humming air conditioner kept her Brooklyn loft cool.

She paused to brush away a vagrant strand of chestnut hair that had worked loose from the bun she had pinned it in. Her scowl deepened.

The stout wooden apparatus rocked to a palm-heel thrust, despite the fact its wide base was weighed down by heavy sandbags. Annja's sparring partner was a training dummy used as an adjunct to *wing chun*–style *gongfu*. She had taken up the study because it was supposed to be highly effective and easy to learn, while giving her another option for nonlethal use of force.

She had plenty of lethal options available. The deadliest was currently invisible to the naked eye. But it was not intangible, not like her rapier-quick intellect or boundless resourcefulness, which she knew could be as deadly as any physical weapons.

She whipped the back of her right hand against a wooden arm. She let the hand flop over it in a trapping move, fired a punch that made the post rock. As she worked into a blinding-fast pattern of blocks and strikes, all oriented toward the centerline of the post, as they would be to the centerline of an opponent's torso, she found herself worrying about the turn her life had taken.

She thought about the sword—her sword.

She had learned that it had once belonged to Joan of Arc. And that she was the inheritor of the long-ago martyr's mantle. On a research trip to France she had, seemingly by chance, found the final piece of St. Joan's sword, broken to pieces by the English captors who burned her. At more or less the same time she had met the man named Roux. He was spry for his gray beard—and even sprier for the fact he claimed Joan had been protégée. He and his apprentice Garin Braden had failed to rescue her from execution. As a result they had been cursed—or blessed—with agelessness.

Roux had spent the half millennium since Joan's death trying to reassemble the saint's shattered sword. At first he'd regarded Annja as an interloper and tried to steal the final fragment from her. Yet when she came into the presence of the other pieces, in Roux's chateau in France, the sword had spontaneously reforged itself at her touch.

It was a bitter pill for a lifelong rationalist to swallow. Especially one who made most of her income as the resident skeptic on the notably credulous cable series *Chasing History's Monsters*, on the Knowledge Channel.

Her arms and hands now moved too fast for the eye to follow. The tough, seasoned hardwood creaked and strained to the mounting fury of her blows. Human bone would give way long before that old wood did.

The sword. It had come to dominate her life.

It rested now in its accustomed location—what she thought of as the otherwhere. It was not present in this world, except at her command. To summon it, she had learned, all she needed was to form a hand as if to grasp its hilt, and exert her will. And her hand was filled.

But her life, it seemed, had correspondingly emptied since the sword came into it.

Sweat soaked her hair and flew from her face. Her

wrists and knuckles and elbows sounded like machine-gun fire as they struck the *muk-jong*.

Orphaned at an early age, raised at an orphanage in New Orleans, Annja had always been alone. She was always apart, somehow, different, although she never tried to be. And it didn't often bother her.

She had never felt as if she couldn't enjoy companionship. But she didn't actively seek it. She'd had close friends at college, on digs, among the crew of *Chasing History's Monsters*. She had had lovers. But, she had to admit, no truly lasting loves.

And now she figured she never would. At least so long as she bore her illustrious predecessor's sacred sword.

She was an archaeologist. Her period of concentration was the later Middle Ages and Renaissance Europe. She spoke all the major modern Romance languages, and Latin, and studied any number of archaic forms—and weapons.

She wasn't sure why she was feeling a sudden gap in her life left by the lack of a lasting relationship. She had her mentor, Roux, and her sometime enemy, Garin. But she didn't really think those relationships counted. She didn't want them to.

Great, she thought as she slammed her forearms against the projecting limbs. She recognized the rare feeling she was experiencing.

"I'm lonely!" she said to her empty loft. She slammed an elbow smash into the upright on the last word. It broke free from its base and toppled backward.

"Nice," she said in disgust. She rubbed her elbow, the pain corresponding to her mood. "Those things cost money."

She stomped off to the shower.

ANNJA EMERGED from the bathroom wearing a long bathrobe swirled in patterns of green, yellow and blue. Her long hair was wrapped in a towel. She heated a cup of cocoa in the microwave and looked around her loft. While jobs were scarce for a freelance archaeologist, she had lucked into enough supplementary income from her television gig and some publishing deals to afford the space.

With Roux's assistance she sometimes accepted commissions to do special archaeological assignments around the globe—always consistent with her strict sense of scientific ethics—for employers who wanted them kept discreet. They tended to be a lot more perilous than the usual university dig, and accordingly well compensated. Sometimes only just slightly over the considerable expense such missions tended to incur.

Flopping on her couch in the space left by several piles of manuscripts various contacts had sent her, mostly dealing with her side interest in fringe archaeology, she made the key mistake of clicking on the television.

She was hoping for a distraction. What she got was Kristie Chatham, on location with some kind of cockamamy Knowledge Channel crossover production in

England. Annja was all too aware of not having been invited to take part.

"…standing here in front of Stonehenge," Kristie was saying brightly, "which as we all know was built by the Druids…"

Annja emitted a strangled scream and threw a cushion at the screen. "No, you bimbo," she shouted. "No, no, no. Stonehenge was built thousands of years before the Druids. Don't you bother to research anything?" A better question might've been, didn't the Knowledge Channel fact-check anything? But she knew the answer to that one, too.

"I'm here with Reggie Whitcomb of the South England Pagan Federation," Kristie bubbled on, "who's going to explain how the Druids levitated the huge cross-pieces, called sarsen stones, into place using their advanced psychic powers."

Annja grabbed the remote and clicked off the set just as Kristie turned her microphone toward a chinless guy wearing a white robe with a peaked hood that made him look as if he belonged to a middle-school auxiliary of the Ku Klux Klan. The skies were black over Salisbury Plain, and the wind cracked like wet sheets whipping on a clothesline. Annja hoped Kristie would get struck by lightning. Or at least soaked to the skin.

Of course that would make Kristie's sheer white blouse transparent. And Kristie would score another top-viewed video on YouTube. Unlike a lot of its media rivals, the Knowledge Channel never set its legal hounds to pull such videos down—the producers had noticed how ratings spiked for their repeats after one went online.

Annja slammed her remote on top of a stack of printouts on the couch beside her.

"It's not like I'm Ms. Establishment Science or anything," she muttered, with her chin down to her clavicle. "It's just that I don't open my mind so wide my brain rolls out my mouth."

Her cell phone rang and she frowned at it in suspicion. If that's Doug Morrell, his head's coming right off, she thought.

She picked it up, flipped it open. "Hello."

"Annja Creed?"

Whomever the voice belonged to, it was not her producer from *Chasing History's Monsters*. The voice was like liquid amber poured over gravel—deep, rugged, yet somehow flowing.

Her eyes narrowed. *I know that voice,* she thought. *It sounds so familiar.*

"Ms. Creed?" She was certain of the Irish accent.

"Oh. Yeah. Sorry. This is Annja."

"Ms. Creed, my name is Iain Moran. I'm a musician. You may have heard of me."

"*Sir* Iain Moran?" Annja asked. It couldn't be.

"The same." Her mind's eye could see that famous smile, at once roguish and world-weary.

"Publico? Lead singer for T-34?"

"The very one."

"Right," Annja was in no mood for pranks.

"Don't hang up! Please. I really am Sir Iain Moran."

"Sure. Multibillionaire rock stars call me every day. If Doug Morrell put you up to this, you're both way overdue for a good swift kick to the—"

"Please. I'd very much like to consult you on a professional matter, concerning your expertise. Would it help to assuage your doubts if my helicopter collected you on the roof of your flat in fifteen minutes?"

It *was* original, as pranks go. She had to give her caller that. "You're on," Annja said, daring her caller to push this as far as it would go.

Fifteen minutes later she stared openmouthed into the brownish haze of a hot Brooklyn day. Her face and hair were whipped by the downblast as a Bell 429 helicopter descended to the roof.

2

A man with long dark blond hair blowing out behind his craggy face was striding toward the helicopter as its landing gear bumped down into the yellow painted circle of the skyscraper's helipad. He wore a tan suit with a dark chocolate tie blown back over his shoulder.

Two men stood flanking the doorway the long-haired man had emerged from. Their hands were folded before them and they looked like slabs in black suits. Even from a distance Annja got the impression their musculature was the force-fed beef characteristic of U.S. ground-force soldiers, not the torturously detailed sculpting of weight-room juicers.

The pleasant young Asian woman in a blue-gray business suit who had originally squired Annja aboard the helicopter, and smilingly evaded the questions Annja peppered her with, helped Annja into the heat of the Manhattan summer morning. The man in the pale suit neared. His face split in a smile.

"I'm Sir Iain," he said, raising his voice to carry over the dying whine of the engine and the slowing blades. "Or Publico, if you prefer." He took the hand Annja extended in a dry, strong grip.

"It was good of you to accept my invitation on such short notice," he said. He put fingertips behind Annja's shoulder and applied gentle pressure. "I'm a huge fan of your work. Your writing, as well as your television career. Please, come with me."

She found, as he guided her toward the doorway, that she did not resent the physical contact. He was around her height, five-ten maybe five-eleven. His shoulders and chest seemed massive, which seemed unusual for a rock musician; she had them pegged as mostly on the weedy side. But his sense of presence loomed like a skyscraper and warmed like the sun.

There was no mistaking that this really was the famous Publico. There were those blue eyes, pale as the northern Irish sky beneath which he'd grown up. There was the famous craggy profile, looking more like a prizefighter's than a rock and roller's, thanks to the nose famously smashed by a British paratrooper's rifle butt during a Dublin demonstration. The voice, gravelly yet the more compelling for it, was compliments of an Ulster policeman's baton that nearly crushed his larynx.

Unlike a lot of celebrities, neither Moran nor his two longtime bandmates had any whiff of the poseur about them. They had been there and done that, protesting the

English occupation of Northern Ireland, as well as the bloody sectarian violence of both Catholics and Protestants. They'd earned the admiration of the world and the hatred of zealots on all three sides, and had paid their dues in real blood and pain.

The band's music reflected the socialist activism of its members as well as their fervent Christian convictions—decidedly less popular among their audience, which spanned the age range from preteens to baby boomers. But their sincerity won over even the most irreligious—as did their hard-rocking music.

Annja was intrigued. He seemed wholly aboveboard. Despite the unsolicited contact his manner was correct and friendly. Charisma emanated from him like heat from a forge.

"What exactly did you whisk me here for, Sir Iain?"

He offered a lopsided smile and bobbed his head once. "Fair enough question," he said. "Permit me to answer with one. How would you like to save the world?"

"That's not an offer an archaeologist hears very often," she said. "But I'm afraid I can't contribute much to any of your causes."

"It's not money we want," he said. "But your courage, your skills—your soul."

She looked at him and he grinned.

"How would you like to see an authentic cursed tome?" he asked.

She grinned back. "You do know the way to a lady's heart, sir," she said. "Lead on."

"IT'S IMPRESSIVE," she said.

With his two shadows drifting along behind—making little more noise than shadows—Moran had squired her down into the skyscraper and to a window he assured her was bulletproof polycarbonate, double paned.

It looked out, and down, on a cold room. In the middle of the sterile white floor, twelve feet below them, stood a large cylinder with what looked like a mirror-polished brass base and a similar cap. The cylinder itself was clear.

"It's Lexan, as well," Sir Iain said. "Treated with a special coating inside and out that resists corrosion."

On a gleaming chrome pedestal within the cylinder rested a book. It was certainly grand enough—the approximate size and shape of an unabridged dictionary. The cover was thick and cracked from what she could see on the open book. The pages were brown. She could just make out faded, crabbed brown writing on them.

"Nitrogen environment?" she asked.

"Of course."

She tried not to thrill at that rolling deep baritone.

She turned a raised brow to him. "I'm surprised you're interested in rare books."

"You think all rock 'n' rollers are illiterate, hell-raising dopers?" He shrugged. His shoulders rolled impressively inside his immaculately tailored coat. "I've been clean and sober since my well-publicized overdose. I've had to find something to do with my time since other than read the Bible."

IN A ROOM down a flight of stairs he gestured toward a large flat-screen monitor, hung above a modern workstation of stainless steel. Several other computers were set up at other stations. On the big screen two pages were represented many times larger than life. Here the ink looked purplish rather than brown.

"It's the journal of an eighteenth-century Portuguese Jesuit," Moran said, "recounting his journey up the far Amazon."

"A lot of Jesuits made the trip in those days," Annja said.

"Indeed. I rather suppose they did. Would you care to read it?"

"I generally prefer to read the original document when it's available," she said. "The camera so seldom catches everything"

She was a hands-on sort of woman where historical artifacts were concerned. It was a major reason she'd chosen to be an archaeologist as opposed to a historian. She didn't just want to study history. She wanted to *feel* history. To see where it had taken place, to hold in her hands implements—or documents—that had changed the world. She wanted to breathe the same air the heroes and heroines of history—unknown and world famous—had breathed when they performed their great deeds. She wanted to be part of history.

And I am, she thought. A lot more literally than I'm comfortable with.

"Not possible, I fear," he said.

"I understand," she said, unable to repress a little sigh

of frustration. "Obviously it's in an extremely fragile state to require such extreme preservation measures."

"You don't understand, Ms. Creed," he said. "Everyone who handles this book dies. Horribly."

She looked aside. A wall-sized window, waist high, opened into the cold room from the reading chamber. The book itself in its high-tech bell jar looked even more impressive closer up.

"I don't believe in curses, Sir Iain."

His laugh was short. "There's nothing paranormal about it," he said, "or not overtly so. The pages and binding are imbued with a hitherto unknown living organism that is not unlike slime molds. It attacks whoever touches it, both by means of airborne spores and by contact. The effect resembles a cross between flesh-eating bacteria and sarin gas. It isn't pretty. And it is extremely fast acting. As well as untreatable by any known means."

"Nice." She sucked in a sharp breath. The air was cool, smelled vaguely of ozone. "How did you get it back here?"

"Carefully. Very carefully."

She went to the workstation and sat in the chair. Reading was dead easy. A black wireless mouse controlled a cursor on the screen. She could point to icons around the perimeter of the image. When she ran the cursor over them, text tips popped up.

"Interesting," she said, frowning slightly in concentration at the huge high-definition screen. "Are these the pages it's currently open to?"

"Yes," he said, "although you can page through it. The entire volume has been digitized."

"I see. Well, it's open to a very dramatic passage. Our author's talking about what seems to be the end of his journey, of both the wonders and hazards he encountered—a colossal snake—had to be an anaconda. They're one of the world's largest. And, whoa, a golden *onza*. Hmm."

"You can read that? That easily?"

"I specialize in archaic Romance languages, Sir Iain."

"But the handwriting—it's all just spider tracks to my eyes. Worse than my handwriting, and that's saying a packet."

She smiled. "As I guess I hinted earlier, this isn't the first old Portuguese Jesuit diary I've looked at."

"What's a 'golden *onza*'?" he asked. "It seemed to strike you as significant."

"An *onza* is a jaguar. A golden *onza* is a particularly impressive specimen. Larger than life, you might say. Legend imbues them, some of them anyway, with incredible intelligence and sometimes outright supernatural powers."

"Indeed."

"Okay. Apparently our priest was captured by Indians, blindfolded and taken to something called *quilombo dos sonhos*," Annja said as she continued reading.

She sat back. "*Dos sonhos* translates as, 'of dreams,'" she said. "But what's a *quilombo*?"

He pulled a chair over next to hers and sat, leaning slightly forward, with his elbows on his thighs. "Have you heard of the Maroons, then?"

She turned to face him. "If I recall correctly, that was a name for escaped New World slaves who fought guerrilla campaigns against recapture—sometime with pretty significant success. Toussaint-Louverture ran the French colonial overlords clean out of Haiti. Of course, I suspect they'd be called *terrorists* today."

"These *quilombos,* I'm told, were settlements the Brazilian Maroons formed in the wilds, mostly along the coast," he said. "Some eventually became republics powerful enough to stand off their erstwhile oppressors for centuries. A few actually maintained their independence until the Brazilian empire became the republic in 1889. Several are still around today as townships."

He sat back and draped an arm over the back of his chair.

"The most famous of all was the Quilombo dos Palmares in northeastern Brazil. It held out against Dutch attacks, as well as Portuguese, until it was reduced by artillery in 1694." He frowned. "Curious, really. My researchers inform me they also traded quite frequently with the Dutch and the English, for arms to use against their former masters."

"Alliances were elastic in those days," Annja said, drawn irresistibly back to the big screen. "As well as these days, and all other days I've ever read about. This *quilombo* the good Father describes—"

"Father Joaquim," he said.

"The settlement was a sizable domain including rich farmland—which I thought was actually pretty rare in the Amazon Basin. It surrounded a fabulous city called Promessa—the Promise. There he describes himself as being treated as an honored guest by the inhabitants, whom he says are mostly intermarried Africans—those escaped slaves, I'm guessing, although they seem to have wandered pretty far from the Atlantic Ocean—and Amazonian Indians. He says the people are 'well-versed in all arts and philosophy.'"

The rock star said nothing. His gaze was so intent she could feel it on her cheek like sunlight. But she was engrossed in the ancient manuscript.

She read through several more virtual pages before surfacing, more to draw a breath than to report. "He speaks of meeting savants whom he claims come from Asia. He might actually know what he was talking about. The Jesuits loved the Orient almost as much as they did South America. He could have spent time in Asia himself. Claims to have witnessed miracles from artificial light to almost instantaneous wound healing and treatment for all manner of disease. And here he writes, 'Moreover the citizens know not aging, nor die, save by misadventure, or foul murder, or their own choice—wherein, sadly, they flout the Divine Will.'"

She gazed up at the screen a moment more. Then she sighed heavily.

"Okay," she said, turning around to face her host

again. This time there was an edge in her voice as chilly as the air in the room. "So this is a treasure hunt, right?"

The rough-hewed face split in a smile that had thrilled tens of millions of concertgoers—not to mention scores of CEOs and world rulers whom he addressed in his self-assumed capacity of global humanitarian activist.

"Imagine a world," he said in a low, compelling voice, "in which there's no disease, no suffering. No death.

"That would be a treasure worth hunting, wouldn't you say, Ms. Creed?"

3

"With all respect," Annja said, sipping green tea in a commissary appointed like a five-star restaurant, with dark oak paneling, bronze rails and ferns in place of the more traditional scuffed Formica counters and coffee machines, "Fountain-of-youth yarns have abounded in the Americas since, roughly, forever. As do fanciful accounts from the age of exploration. For that matter, the Jesuits have been known to bend the truth for their own purposes."

Ignoring his chai latte, Moran nodded encouragingly. "That's one of the reasons I contacted you," he said. "You obviously believe in reason, in evidence. You are also willing to keep an open mind."

"I did wonder," she said. "I'm not the most famous TV archaeologist on television by a long shot."

She smiled a bit lopsidedly. "Then again, if it was

boobs you were after, you'd have called Kristie Chatham."

"If you'll forgive a momentary lapse in political correctness, Ms. Creed," he said in that voice that had thrilled hundreds of millions, "you're a beautiful woman. At the same time I'm sure you appreciate a man in my position seldom lacks for attractive female companionship, should that be his intent. For my part I've tried to put my wild past behind me. So I also hope you'll understand that your striking appearance had nothing to do with my interest in engaging your services."

She set down her cup. Her cheeks felt hot. "Now you're flattering me."

"Not a bit of it."

"Well, after a speech that gallant, the least you could do is call me Annja."

"Done. If you'll consent to call me Iain," he said.

"It's a deal." She sat back in her chair, picked up her cup and regarded him through a curl of steam rising into the cool air.

"You don't strike me as the sort to fall for every goofy New Age notion to float past you in a cloud of pot smoke. I presume you have evidence more compelling than a wild diary, even if its pages are protected by a killer mystery fungus. Impress me."

"I'll do my best—Annja. In the *favelas*—the brutal slums—of northeastern Brazil they still speak of the *quilombo dos sonhos*. Legends still speak, also, of a magical city called Promise, where no one ever dies."

"Such legends aren't exactly uncommon worldwide, despite the inroads of science," Annja said.

"So I thought. Until a hardheaded German business associate of mine, an aggressive atheist and skeptic, began experiencing remarkable dreams. Of a beautiful city, hidden deep in Amazon rain forest, filled with beautiful, ageless people who combined indigenous lore, Asian wisdom and Western science to create a cultural and technological paradise. In these dreams he got flashes of psychic phenomena, of cars that fly without wings or even visible engines.

"Hypnotic regression seemed to substantiate that these were real memories, submerged and now attempting to resurface. I see you look skeptical. I hardly blame you. But when we dug deeper we found recurring spells when my acquaintance dropped out of sight during trips to Brazil. It's an aggravating thing. He cannot be *documented* to have ever gone deeper into Amazon than Belém, where the Amazon enters the Atlantic. He merely—vanished."

An aide appeared, a ponytailed young blond woman in jeans. She handed several manila envelopes to Moran. He thanked her with a smile.

Beckoning to Annja to come closer, he turned and opened one of the folders on the tabletop. "Here are the medical records for my friend," he said, setting out sheets of paper typed in English with names blacked out. With a forefinger he pushed a color photograph toward her. It showed the bare upper torso, from neck to just above the groin, with a puckered crescent from an appendectomy scar. She was glad the photo cut off where it did.

"Here's a 'before' picture," Moran said, tapping the image. "And here's the 'after.'"

He pushed another photo beside the first. Annja frowned. It showed the same pale, slightly pudgy torso as the first photo, with a distinctive reddish mole at four o'clock from the navel to clinch the identification. But the surgical scar was gone.

"You don't have to go to the wilds of Brazil to have cosmetic surgery to remove scars," Annja said.

"You rather make my point, I think," Publico said with a smile.

Annja shrugged. "I'm intrigued. I'll admit that much."

He showed her a frank grin. "So you're to be a hard sell. Well, I'd expect nothing less of you."

He braced hands on thighs and stood. "Well, come with me, if you will, and I'll see if I can sell you."

"Brazil has quite a history of widespread and well-documented UFO sightings, you know," Publico said. "What if some of the Maroons, retreating up the river from encroaching colonists, stumbled upon a crash site?"

They walked along the side of a sunken room Moran referred to as his "command center." Large plasma monitors hung from the ceiling over rings of workstations where staff wearing Bluetooth earpieces typed rapidly and spoke in earnest murmurs.

Annja chuckled. "I'm not sure that's the tack to take," she said. "You know I'm the show's resident skeptic."

"Ah, but you have an affinity for the strange, as well."

She crossed her arms and smiled tightly to hide the little shudder that ran through her. How true that was, she thought.

To divert attention from herself she gestured around them and said, "Where are we, anyway? What's this building? Yours?"

"In a manner of speaking. It's the New York headquarters of my eleemosynary network. It belongs to the institute, not to me personally. Although I admit I have freedom of the place."

"I'm impressed at the word eleemosynary."

"Not all my degrees are honorary, Ms. Creed. My MBA from Harvard, for example."

"A Harvard MBA? I thought you were antiestablishment, antiglobalization and all that."

"Ah, but running a humanitarian operation—actually a global network ranging from relief agencies to activists for a score of worthy causes—is an incredibly demanding task. So I learn the enemy's skills to use against him, as it were."

"If you say so."

He turned to face her. "Annja, I understand your skepticism. But why not go and see for yourself? That's what the spirit of scientific inquiry is about, isn't it?"

"Well…yes. And I have to admit you've at least given me enough to intrigue me."

"What do I need to make you passionate? I spoke earlier of saving the world. How about it? You can literally save the world—or many of the people who live on it—by helping track down the secret of conquering death. What else are you doing that's more exciting? More magnificent?"

"Well. Nothing. Since you put it that way," Annja said. She felt breathless, overwhelmed, needing to take back a little control of the conversation. "What if there's nothing to it? I can't promise results. It will probably turn out to be baseless."

"Then you'll do it?"

"I asked you first."

He laughed aloud. Some of the earnest heads down in the pit turned up to look at him, then back to their business. Annja supposed they were saving the world in the event eternal life didn't pan out.

"I won't ask even you to deliver what does not exist," he said. "But I suspect if I asked the impossible, in just the right way, you'd deliver."

"Flattery will get you—well, I guess it usually works in the real world, doesn't it?"

"I never flatter," he said simply. He took her gently by the arm. "Come and meet your associate."

"ANNJA, this is Dan Seddon," Publico said. "He'll be accompanying you to Brazil."

They stood in an echoing space beneath what appeared to be the interior of a pyramid of translucent white blocks. A young man stood in the center, next to a slowly rotating statue of dark metal, possibly bronze. The shape suggested a feather sprouting from the floor. He turned with a certain fluid, alert grace at their approach.

When he saw Annja he smiled. She smiled back and held out her hand. He took it and shook it firmly. He didn't seem the sort to kiss it.

He had a stylish brush of hair, either brown or dark blond, frosted lighter blond. His eyes were a green or hazel, not too different from Annja's own and alive with curiosity. His face was a tanned narrow wedge with dark brows. His nose had been almost patrician thin and straight, but had been broken at least once and had a bump in the bridge to give it character. His grin had a practiced flash to it.

"Good to meet you, Ms. Creed," he said, businesslike enough. He wore a lightweight jacket over a white shirt and blue jeans. His shoes were walking shoes, good quality. That scored points with Annja. An experienced field archaeologist who also tramped great distances in the course of her work with *Chasing History's Monsters,* she knew the value of good footwear.

"My pleasure, Mr. Seddon," she said. "So, you're an archaeologist?"

"No."

"Anthropologist?"

"No." His manner was relaxed. Perhaps even a trifle superior.

"Dan is a troubleshooter," Publico put in as smoothly as his gravelly voice would allow. "He's been a major activist for years, campaigning against globalization all over the world. Seattle 2000. Italy '03. Now he specializes in getting things done for me. He's proved himself a key part of my humanitarian operations."

Seddon smiled a lazy smile.

Annja frowned. "I'm sure Mr. Seddon has great abilities in his field," she said. "But I'm not sure what he brings to the table for an archeological expedition."

"It doesn't really rise to the level of an expedition yet," Publico admitted. "I hope it'll turn into one. In the opening phases, though, it's likely to entail a combination of intensive historical research and detective work."

"You've got the historical angle nailed," Seddon said with a grin. "I know you're good at that. Not like that bimbo Kristie."

Maybe this guy is okay, Annja thought.

"Mark's career as a campaigner has involved no small amount of investigative work," Moran said.

"Digging up dirt on exploiters and polluters," the young man said. "Also I might just be able to look out for you. I've been around some."

Annja had to press her lips together at the thought of his looking out for her. "I'd certainly appreciate your having my back," she said, truthfully if not so candidly.

He looked her up and down a little more deliberately than was strictly polite. "That I can do, Ms. Creed," he said. "That I can do."

4

"I said, Emo's for people not optimistic enough to be Goth," Dan said.

Annja laughed. On the long journey to Brazil from Publico's Manhattan penthouse her companion had proved consistently entertaining, with a sharp eye and facile wit. Those traits didn't exactly translate into being of perceptible use in fieldwork, but they did help to pass the time. And there was no doubt that his air of self-assurance, quite untainted by any hint of bragging over his own abilities or achievements, was an encouraging sign.

The Belém riverfront was splashed with noonday sun and alive with people as they strolled along it. It was hot, the humid air like a lead blanket that wrapped about her and weighed her down. The rain that had fallen as they ate a late breakfast at a café near their small but well-appointed hotel had done nothing to alleviate the heat. If anything the extra moisture in the air made it more oppressive.

The floppy straw hat Annja affected helped a little, but she still felt overdressed in sleeveless orange blouse and khaki cargo shorts. She had even forsaken her trusty walking shoes for a pair of flip-flops.

Her companion shook his frosted head. He wore a white polo-style shirt over khaki trousers, a surprisingly conventional upscale-tourist look. When she had called him on it at breakfast he had explained frankly that dressing like a more conventional college-age American, in jeans-and-T-shirt scruff, tended to attract a little too much attention from the local law enforcement.

"If there's one thing I learned from Genoa," he had said over a forkful of scrambled eggs and bacon—to Annja's relief he was no vegetarian—"it's to pick your battles with the Man carefully."

Genoa, she had learned, was the antiglobalization protest where police had killed demonstrators, resulting in a scandal that rocked the whole European Union.

"I wish I had a better idea where this shop we're looking for is," he said, waving a scrap of paper holding the address of their first contact. "Unfortunately it's not the sort of place you find in a clean and well-marked spot. Or even on Google Maps."

Feeling surprisingly rested after what amounted to a protracted nap, Annja was noticing how different Belém looked and felt than Rio de Janeiro, that gaudy metropolis sprawling like a drunken giant along the Atlantic coast far to the south. Tourists didn't come here as often as they did to Rio, or to São Paulo. It was hot as Dante's imagination, a degree south of the equator, and hadn't felt any cooler when they'd arrived at the hotel before sunup.

The esplanade where they walked was wide and bright and clean enough. But they were clearly in a poorer section of the city. Dan stopped and frowned dubiously down a narrow side street. "I'm sure it's down one of these alleys," he said. "But I'm afraid we could wander for days looking and not find it."

"I can't believe you're acting like a stereotypical man," Annja said. "Why not ask for directions?"

He raised both brows at her in an uncharacteristic and utterly amusing look of helplessness. "Because I can't speak Portuguese?"

"Fair enough. But you know some Spanish, don't you?"

"Enough to get by. But that's a different language."

She laughed. "So native Spanish speakers and Portuguese speakers are always trying to convince me. But if you just listen and try, you'll find you can make out a whole lot more than you think. Trust me—I did when I first started trying to learn Portuguese after knowing Spanish."

He set his chin in an expression she took for provisional acceptance. He seemed to cultivate a fashionable sort of perpetual three-day facial fuzz. She had to admit he wore the look well. Perhaps it was the underlying toughness he never alluded to in words, but was to

Annja's practiced eye unmistakable in the wary way he moved. He was always balanced and ready for action. It redeemed him from looking like some orthodontist's kid from Seattle rebelling against capitalism and the modern world on a five-figure allowance.

Annja spoke to a pair of middle-aged women wearing white blouses and colorful skirts. They seemed surprised to find an American speaking to them in good Brazilian Portuguese, but were as friendly as most Brazilians Annja had encountered, and quickly told her how to find the address.

"Watch yourself," the taller one suggested. "That's not the best part of town for a white girl." It was spoken matter-of-factly.

"I will," Annja said in response to the warning. "Thanks."

Annja led Dan away from the river down a relatively wide street.

"How many languages do you speak, anyway?" he asked.

"Several," she said. "I'm pretty good with the major modern Romance languages. Spanish, of course. Portuguese, Italian, French, Catalan."

He frowned. "Are you sure it's a good idea for you to be here?"

She laughed. "One of those nice women warned me, too. But why you? I thought you were used to knocking around the Third World. Emphasis on *knocking*."

"Yeah, I am. And one thing I learned early on—

sometimes it knocks back. There's a lot of resentment at Western colonialism and cultural imperialism. It isn't all just the wicked Muslims, the way the nutcases back home try to make it. And Brazil is kind of notorious for violence in its poorer areas."

She noted with approval that he didn't screw around with euphemisms. While she was no radical—she was pretty determinedly apolitical—Annja found herself more comfortable with the honestly hard core, as opposed to moderates, the mushy centrists, with their political correctness and nervous phrasing. She cared about words and what they meant. They were core to her professional discipline. She had little patience for people who muddied them with soft heads or hearts.

"*Favelas,*" she said. "Some of the Earth's most serious slums. You're thinking more of Rio de Janeiro. And yeah, that's full-contact poverty. There really are *favelas* in Rio where the police literally don't go except in battalion strength, the way they did in one of the worst districts just a couple of years ago."

"I read about that online," Dan said.

"I've been to Rio," she said, "and this place has a different feel. For one thing, food's a lot more readily available than it is in the middle of a huge urban wasteland."

By chance they had come into a little market square, lined with kiosks offering everything from live chickens in crates to bin after bin of mostly unfamiliar fruits and vegetables to big wheels of cheese. And everywhere fish, of a remarkable range of size and shapes.

"Look around you. The people are mostly smiling, happy," Annja said.

He shrugged. "Anesthetized to the realities of repression."

"Dan, that's not worthy of you," she said more sharply than she'd intended. "You know nothing about these people."

A man passed them with a cheerful nod and word of greeting.

"I stand corrected, Ms. Creed. "I confess I've been guilty of Western cultural imperialism and assumed superiority. *Mea culpa, mea maxima culpa.*"

"You know some Latin," she said. "That's a great grounding for Romance languages. And just for the record, I like the wiseass Dan a lot better than the doctrinaire Dan."

He might just as easily have told her off. They were, after all, contractors on assignment together. But he flashed a devil-may-care grin and said, "Noted. And maybe I do, too."

They wandered down a line of stalls, listening to the good-natured—mostly—bargaining. Sometimes the African dialects were so prevalent Annja understood little if any better than Dan appeared to.

"Whoa. Those are some ugly fish," Dan said, waving at a particularly formidable specimen, arrayed with armor and sinister spikes and barbs. "Didn't I see one of these eating tourists in Mexico on an old episode of *Outer Limits* on Nickelodeon?"

"It'd have to be a bit bigger and a lot more ambitious than that one looks," Annja said. "Of course, it *is* dead."

"Remind me not to take a dip in the river. Not that it looks that inviting—it's the color and consistency of pea soup." He shook his head. "Man spoils everything he touches, doesn't he?"

"Don't kid yourself. The crust of old plastic bags and junk is largely man-made. But the river's color and consistency are all natural, a combination of silt and things exuding into it from the forest all around," Annja said.

"Huh," he said, clearly unconvinced. She felt a flash of annoyance. He had a tendency not to see things that clashed with his preconceptions. She tried to let it go.

I have to work with him, she reminded herself. And anyway, for the most part he's a lot more fun than a lot of partners I've had…. She let the thought dangle, unwilling to follow it further.

They pushed on, turning into a narrow street where two-story whitewashed buildings seemed to lean toward each other overhead. They took a right turn into a dank, muddy path that it might have been a compliment to call an alley.

Dan hung back, frowning at Annja. "Uh—" he said.

She stopped and looked sternly at him. "Don't tell me you're going all male-chauvinist protective on me."

He shrugged. "It's my job to look out for you, Ms. Creed." She recognized he was in official mode.

"Hasn't it occurred to you I've looked after myself in some pretty rough parts of the world?" And more than that, of course, but she wasn't sharing that information. With any luck he'd never find out.

"Well—I don't see a film crew anywhere," he said. "Not to mention network security staff."

"You'd be surprised how sparse that is for our show," she said. "Anyway, look. If it makes you feel better, I happen to have long legs. I know you noticed."

To his credit his gaze never wavered from hers. "Yeah."

"So if anything bad happens I can run away real fast. Satisfied?"

He frowned at her a moment. Then his face unclouded and he laughed. "I get the feeling I have to be."

They stopped at a blue-painted door set into a wall missing some chunks of stucco. He nodded. "After you."

She pushed her way into darkness.

5

The first thing that hit her, along with the earth-burrow coolness, was the smell. It wasn't an unpleasant smell, particularly. But it was a complicated one. A skein of smells, a tapestry, woven out of elements familiar, hauntingly reminiscent and outright strange. Some were organic, some chemical and astringent.

"May I help you?" a voice said from the shop's dim depths.

A beaded curtain rustled. A woman emerged into the front room among close-packed shelves and counters. She was tall, possibly taller than Annja, although the red-and-yellow turban around her head added a few inches. In the gloom it was hard to be sure.

Annja glanced sideways at Dan. "We'd like to talk to the shop owner," she said.

"That's me," the woman said. She seemed to glide

forward without moving her feet, doubtless an illusion caused by her long skirts, which brushed the warped boards of the floor. "I am Mafalda. How may I help you?"

As she came close enough to distinguish detail, Annja realized that she was a very beautiful woman, seemingly no older than Annja, with mocha skin and eyes that might have been dark green.

"You're Americans," Mafalda said.

Annja smiled.

"What can I do for distinguished visitors from so far away?" Mafalda seemed to be slipping into a familiar role, which Annja guessed was half mystic, half huckster. She probably had one mix for the tourists and another for the locals.

Annja looked openly to Dan. Though never spoken, the arrangement seemed to be that while she was in charge of the scientific and research aspects of the expedition, he spoke for their mutual employer Moran. She wasn't entirely comfortable with the arrangement, but Sir Iain was paying her very well.

"We understand you might have some information about a hidden city," Dan said.

"Who told you that?" the proprietor asked. Shrewdly, Annja thought.

"Someone back in the United States," Dan answered blandly.

Mafalda seemed unimpressed with that response. "Lost-city rumors crawl all over the Amazon like bugs," she said, unwittingly echoing what Annja had told Sir

Iain in his Manhattan headquarters. "They have done so ever since the days of the first explorers. I don't deal in treasure maps. Perhaps you should seek elsewhere."

Shooting an exasperated look at Dan, who only shrugged, Annja said, "Perhaps if you'd be so kind as to show us what you do deal in, please, we'd better understand how we might help each other."

It occurred to Annja that their employer might be playing his cards too close to his well-muscled chest. Unless he simply had no better information to share. But he must have had some reason to send them here.

After favoring Annja with a quick, cool glance of appraisal, Mafalda smiled slightly. "Of course. If the lord and lady will follow me."

"Lord and lady?" Dan echoed quietly.

Annja sniffled. He cocked his head at her.

"I'm allergic to something in here," she said.

Mafalda, who had waited coolly for the whispered exchange to end—suggesting some experience with tourists—began her tour. "I serve the practitioner of *candomblé*. I have here everything needed for the *toques,* the rituals, whether public or private."

"What's *candomblé?*" Dan asked as Mafalda led them through narrow aisles with bins of sheaved herbs, colorful feathers and beads.

"It's a widespread folk religion in Brazil," Annja said. "It's basically a combination of Catholicism with West African beliefs."

"Like voodoo?" Dan asked.

"That's right," Annja said, nodding. She dabbed surreptitiously at a droplet that had formed at the end of her nose and sniffled loudly again.

"We believe in a force called *axe,*" Mafalda said, leading them into an aisle with a number of tiny effigies that reminded Annja of Mexican Day of the Dead figurines. There were also racks of odd, twisted dried roots and vegetables and sturdy cork-topped jars with not-quite-identifiable things floating in murky greenish fluids.

"Mind the *jacaré,*" Mafalda said as an aside.

"Huh?" Dan said. "What's *jacaré?*"

He bumped his head on something hanging from the ceiling. He did a comical double take to find himself looking into the toothy grin of a four-foot stuffed reptile hung from the ceiling.

"One of those," Annja said. She had found a travel pack of tissues in the large fanny pack she wore, and was in the process of blowing her nose. It made a handy cover for her grin. "An Amazon caiman. There's a specific species named *jacaré,* but people around here mostly call all crocodilians that."

Dan cocked a brow at Mafalda, who wasn't bothering to hide her own toothy grin. "Decorating with endangered species?"

"We're more endangered by the *jacarés,*" their hostess said promptly. "They eat many Brazilians each year."

"Is she serious?" Dan asked.

"Oh, yes," Annja said.

He shrugged, shaking his head.

"You were telling us about *axe*," Annja prompted
Mafalda. She had no idea if it had anything to do with
their mission—to find some lead, however tenuous, to
the mysterious hidden city named Promise—but she
was fascinated, personally and professionally, with the
local folk religion.

"Oh yes." The turbaned head nodded. "*Axe* is the life
force. It permeates all things."

"So your *toques* involve evoking this life force?"
Annja asked.

The woman led them on toward the front of the
cramped store. "Somewhat. Mostly we invoke the
orixás."

The word was unfamiliar to Annja. "What are they?"

Mafalda flashed a quick smile. "Our gods," she said,
"Olorum is the supreme creator, but he doesn't pay so
much attention to us little people. So we don't trouble
him. The *orixás,* though, they're the deities who deal
with us humans. So they're the ones we have to worry
about keeping happy."

"Makes sense," Dan said.

The tall woman had led them back to the cash register, which was a modern digital model, Annja noted,
Beside it stood racks of CDs with colorful covers. Dan
picked one up and scrutinized it. "You have a sideline
selling Brazilian jazz?" he asked. "These don't look
like New Age meditation CDs."

"They are for the *capoeira*," Mafalda said.

"The martial art?" Annja asked.

Mafalda laughed. "It's more than a martial art."

"What do you mean?"

"Do you know the story of the slaves?" Mafalda asked. Annja felt Dan tense beside her. Her own quick inhalation turned into a sneeze, only half-staged.

"Some," Annja said cautiously.

"Well, the slaves weren't happy being slaves. So they practiced to rebel. But the masters would not permit this. So the slaves had to create a way of training that they could practice under the masters' eye without their suspecting."

"Hiding in plain sight," Annja said.

Mafalda nodded, smiling. "Exactly. So they hid their warrior training as a type of dance used in religious rituals."

"And so in turn *capoeira* practice got worked into the actual rituals?" Annja asked.

"Perhaps. Today *capoeira* is all these things—a form of fighting, a dance, *candomblé* ritual."

"I see." Annja skimmed the rack until a cover caught her eye. A very dark, very skinny man was performing a trademark *capoeira* headstand kick in front of a rank of colorfully dressed dancers shaking what appeared to be feather gourd rattles. "I'll take this one, please." It seemed a gracious thing to do, a way to keep open lines of communication with their uninformative informant. Also she was curious.

Mafalda rang up the transaction. She wrapped the CD in fuchsia paper and taped it neatly.

"Some of the slaves did fight back, you know," she said as she handed the parcel to Annja. "They escaped and fled into the forest. There they fought. Some died, some won their freedom."

"The Maroons," Dan said.

"Yes," Mafalda said. Her manner was suddenly very grave. "The ones about whom you asked—they do not like strangers seeking after them. *Capoeira* was not the only weapon they created unseen beneath the world's nose. And their reach is very long."

6

"Was it just me," Dan said, sipping strong coffee the next morning at a green metal table at an open-air waterfront café near their hotel, "or did that woman seem scared to tell us about the Maroons?"

"It wasn't just you," Annja said. She took a sip of her own coffee. "But she seemed more scared not to."

"So did we learn anything?" he asked.

"They have a long reach."

Dan set down his cup, shaking his head. "This is all starting to sound way too Indiana Jones."

She smiled. "What would you call a quest for a lost city?"

He laughed but shook his head again. "The real world doesn't work like that."

"Doesn't it? I thought terrorizing people to get results was thoroughly modern. Doing it long-distance, even."

"Touché," Dan said without mirth. "It just struck me as far-fetched."

It would have me, not so long ago, Annja thought but did not say.

The café stood near a set of docks servicing river-boats somewhat larger, if not markedly more reputable looking, than the small craft Annja and Dan had seen crowding the river the day before. Dockworkers were swaying cargo off a barge with an old and rickety-looking crane. The stevedores were big men, mostly exceedingly dark and well muscled.

Although it was relatively early in the day and they were both lightly dressed and sat in the shade of an awning, Annja could feel sweat trickling down her back.

"It's not, really," she said, sipping her coffee. "Far-fetched, I mean. If you think about them just like any other…interest group or faction. A lot of governments go to extremes to protect their secrets."

"Corporations, too."

"Sure. Other groups, as well. These people's ancestors fled to escape slavery and then persecution—attempts to recapture them, reenslave them. That could account for their being a little paranoid."

"But didn't Brazil abolish slavery—what? Over a hundred years ago," Dan said.

"In 1880," Annja said. "It may be," she continued, setting the cup down and leaning forward over the table, "that Mafalda gave us more information than she intended."

"What do you mean?"

"I thought a lot about what she told us last night. She was worried, basically, that the Maroons—the Promessans, we might as well call them—might think she talked too much about them."

"So you're thinking they've got some kind of surveillance on her," Dan said. "Bugs? Or maybe something astral?" He said the last with a laugh.

"Hey, I'm as hardheaded skeptical about that stuff as you are." Although I bet I have to work a whole lot harder at it, she thought. "I'm not even sure I go so far as buying electronic eavesdropping, although with snooping gear so incredibly cheap and tiny these days, I guess I shouldn't dismiss it out of hand."

"What are you thinking?" He was all business now. In a sense she was pleasantly surprised. While he had been polite and correct the whole time they had been together, she had picked up pretty unequivocal signals he found her attractive. But he also conveyed a certain sense of superciliousness. Not quite disdain. But as if he were the professional here, not she.

Given his background, and current mission brief, she could even understand that, however it irked her. *If only he knew how wrong he was.* And yet, of course, she couldn't tell him that the last thing she needed was his protection.

Not that he'd believe her if she tried.

But now he was acting like one pro talking business with another, and that was good. "While it's not even impossible they could bug Mafalda's shop long-distance—I mean, all the way from Upper Amazonia—I don't think that's the likeliest thing. At least, it's unlikely to be their only measure," Annja said.

"Back up a step. You think they could bug the shop all the way from their hidden fortress?" Dan asked.

She shrugged. "Why not? It could be something as prosaic as a satellite phone relay."

"So you're not envisioning these people as, like, some kind of lost culture still living in the eighteenth century or whenever?"

"I think that's King Solomon's Mines," she said with a smile. "Not necessarily. Were you? For that matter, is Sir Iain? I thought his whole thing was the possibility they might possess technology far in advance of ours."

"Well—maybe. But they could possess, say, herbal techniques developed beyond the scope of modern medical science and still have an archaic culture. Or an essentially indigenous one."

"Maybe. But from what Sir Iain told me, and some research I did afterward, one of the first things the escaped slaves did was start trading with the English and the Dutch for modern weapons."

"I don't mean to be racist, but that seems pretty sophisticated for slaves," Dan said.

"I found out something pretty startling. Not all the slaves were preliterate tribal warriors from the bush. It turns out the Portuguese colonists were so lazy they got tired of administering their plantations and mines and other businesses themselves. So they started kidnapping and enslaving people from places like the ancient Af-

rican city of Tombouctou. They may even have en-
slaved their own people from their colonial city of Lu-
anda."

"Meaning—"

"Meaning they were deliberately capturing and enslaving clerical and middle-management types," Annja
said.

He laughed vigorously. "That's great," he said. "Just
great. They really *were* lazy. And so these well-edu-
cated urban slaves teamed up with their warrior cousins taken from the tribal lands and created their own
high-power civilization."

"Pretty much. That's why they were able to stand off
their former masters for so long. They were every bit
as sophisticated as the Europeans. More, in a way, because of their allying with the Indians early on. They
knew the terrain better."

"A guerrilla resistance," he said. "I like it."

"My sense is," she said, leaning forward onto her elbows with her hands propping her chin, "if this city Sir
Iain thinks exists really does, its occupants would be
pretty current with modern technology."

"Or even advanced beyond it." He arched a brow.

She shrugged. "Your boss seems to think so."

Dan frowned. "He's a great man. He's my friend.
You can call him our employer," he said, emphasizing
the *our* subtly, "but I don't like the word *boss*."

"Understood," Annja said.

"So, all right, conceivably these descendants of the
long-ago escaped slaves, the Maroons or Promessans,

might be able to bug a shop in Belém long-distance. I see that. But you seem to think that's not what they're doing."

"If they really exist," Annja added.

"Sure."

She thought a moment, then sighed. "No. I don't. A key aspect of their early survival was trade. I'd bet they've stuck with that as a mainstay of their economy. If for no other reason they'd have agents—factors—in the outside world. Belém is pretty much the gateway to the entire Amazon in one direction and the entire world in the other. And that seems to have been the connection with the German businessman your…Publico told me about. He must have had some kind of commercial relationship with Promessa. What business was he in, do you know?"

"Electronic components of some sort. Controls for computerized machine tools, possibly."

"Hmm." She regretted not pressing Moran for further details. The fact was, he had so swept her off her feet during their one and only interview, with the sheer hurricane force of his personality and passion, that she never even thought of it. "Perhaps we can call him or e-mail him. That might be a lead to follow up, too."

"Maybe," Dan said. "Publico kind of likes his people to use their own initiative."

"Well." Annja wrinkled a corner of her mouth in brief irritation. "Maybe it isn't necessary. If the Promessans keep agents here for trade, they can just as easily keep them here for other purposes."

"So their traders are spies."

She shrugged again. "There's precedent for that. They may or may not be the same people. We don't have enough data even to guess."

"So if we can spot one of these agents we might not need Mafalda's cooperation."

"That's what I'm hoping, anyway," Annja said.

For a moment they sat, thinking separate thoughts. A young woman came into the open-air café. She was tall, willowy, and—as Annja found distressingly common in Brazil—quite beautiful. She squeezed the water from a nearby beach from her great mane of kinky russet hair. Water stood beaded in droplets on her dark-honey skin, which was amply displayed by the minuscule black thong bikini she wore.

The rest of the café patrons were locals. No one else seemed to take notice of the woman as she strode to an open-air shower to one side of the café, shielded by a sort of glass half booth from splashing any nearby patrons.

Nor did they show any sign of reaction when the young woman dropped a white beach bag with white-and-purple flowers on it to the floor, turned on the water and skinned right out of her bikini.

Annja looked around, trying to keep her cool. *Am I really seeing this?* The customers continued their conversations or their perusals of the soccer news in the local paper. She glanced back. Yes, there was a stark naked woman showering not twenty feet away from her.

She looked toward Dan. He was looking at her with a studiedly bland expression. "You might as well watch," she said. "Just don't stare."

"Never," he murmured, and his eyes fairly clicked toward the showering woman.

The young woman finished, toweled herself briskly, then dressed in shorts and a loose white top. She looked up as a small group of young women came into the café, chattering like the tropical birds that clustered in the trees all over town. She greeted them cheerfully and joined them at a table as if nothing unusual had happened.

Dan let the breath slide out of him in a protracted sigh. "Whoo," he said.

"Whoo indeed," Annja said. "It's like a whole different country, huh?"

"Excuse me," a voice interrupted.

At the quiet, polite feminine query in English both looked up. Two young people stood there, a very petite woman and a very tall man. Both were striking in their beauty and in their exotic appearance. Both wore light-colored, lightweight suits.

"Are you Americans?" the woman asked.

"Are we that obvious?" Dan asked.

The young man shrugged wide shoulders. He exuded immediate and immense likeability. "There are details," he said in an easy baritone voice. "The way you dress. The way you hold yourselves. Your mannerisms—they're quicker than ours tend to be, but not so broad, you know?"

"And then," Annja said with a shrug, "there's our tendency to gawk at naked women in the café."

The man laughed aloud. "You were most polite," he said.

"She probably would have appreciated the attention," the woman said. "We Brazilians tend to take a lot of trouble over our appearance. Clearly you know that beauty takes hard work."

"You've probably noticed, we don't have much body modesty hereabouts," the man said. "But you were wise to be discreet. Brazilians also tend to think that Americans confuse that lack of modesty with promiscuity."

"They're probably right," Dan said, "way too often."

"Please, sit down," Annja told the pair. She was not getting threatening vibes from them. And she and Dan were drawing blanks so far. Any kind of friendly local contact was liable to be of some help. At least a straw to clutch at. "I'm Annja Creed. This is Dan Seddon. He's my business associate."

Dan cast her a hooded look as the woman pulled out a chair and sat. The man pulled one over from a neighboring table. Annja saw that they both had long hair. The woman's hung well down the back of her lightweight cream-colored jacket, clear to her rump. The man's was a comet-tail of milk-chocolate dreadlocks held back by a band at the back of his head, to droop back down past his shoulders.

"I'm Xia," the woman said. "And this is Patrizinho." The pair looked to be in their late twenties, perhaps a year or two older than Annja.

"Pleased to meet you," said Annja, who was accustomed to the Brazilian habit of going by first names alone. "What do you do?"

"We work for an import-export firm," Xia said. "Mostly we are consultants. We help foreign merchants negotiate the labyrinth of our trade laws and regulations."

"They're quite bizarre," Patrizinho said. "Some of our people take perverse pride in having them that way."

"And you?" Xia asked. "Are you here on vacation?"

Annja glanced at Dan. To her surprise he sat more tightly angled back in his chair than slouched, with his legs straight under the table, arms folded, chin on clavicle. He frowned slightly at her but gave no indication she shouldn't discuss their real purpose.

"We're here doing research for an institution in the United States," she said, parrying an internal stab of annoyance at Dan. "I'm an archaeologist and historian by trade. My partner is a representative of the institute."

"It's a humanitarian institution," he said. "We're here doing research on *quilombos.*"

Patrizinho raised his brows. "Not many Americans I've met know anything about them."

A male server appeared. Patrizinho ordered fruit juice, Xia some bottled water.

"What's your interest in the *quilombos,* then?" Xia asked.

"We understand that some of them actually managed to survive as independent entities until Brazil became a republic," Annja said.

"True enough," Patrizinho said. "Some of them still exist as recognized townships today."

Annja glanced at Dan, who seemed to be sulking. "We're trying to track down reports that there might be a settlement derived from a *quilombo* far up the Amazon, which has declined to join Brazil or, perhaps, the modern world."

Patrizinho grinned and tapped the table with his fingertips. "Hiding like Ogum in the forest!"

"What's that?" Dan asked sharply.

"An old expression."

"A lost civilization," Xia said. "Do you really think that's possible in today's world? With airplanes and satellites everywhere. Wouldn't it turn up on Google Earth?"

Annja shrugged. "We aim to find out."

For a moment they sat without exchanging words. A breeze idly flapped the red, green and yellow awning over their heads. From somewhere came strains of Brazilian popular music, faint and lively.

Since their newfound acquaintances weren't jumping in to offer clues to the location of the lost City of Promise, or even expand on local legends to the effect, Annja said, "Patrizinho, your mention of Ogum puts me in mind of a question both Dan and I had."

"What's that?" he said.

"We keep seeing people wearing these T-shirts. They'll say something like *Cavalo Do Xango* or *Cavala Da Iansã,* around images of colorful-looking persons. I know those phrases mean, basically, horse of

Xango or Iansã. We've seen them for Ogum, too. But who are they, and why do other people wear shirts saying they're their horses?"

"Those people are *orixás*," Patrizinho said. "You know what that means?"

"We've heard the word," Dan said.

"Xango is the thunder and war god. Iansã is his wild-woman wife, also known as Oyá, goddess of winds and storms—and the gates of the underworld. If somebody is a horse for one of them, that means they regularly serve as host or vessel for that spirit."

"You mean like in voodoo," Dan said, perking up a bit, "where ritual participants are ridden by the *loa?*"

"Pretty much the same," Xia said. "In fact many people here worship the very same *loa*. Sometimes they're even taken over by Catholic saints, they say, although the saints are usually identified with specific *orixás*."

"People advertise the fact that they regularly get…possessed?" Annja asked. For all that she liked to think of herself as a tolerant person—and she'd spent enough time among enough people in strange and remote places to have what she thought pretty good credibility for the claim—the notion creeped her out considerably.

"They believe it's an honor, to be chosen by the god or goddess," Patrizinho said.

Xia checked an expensive-looking designer watch strapped to her thin wrist. "We'd better get on our way, Patrizinho," she said, rising. "It's been lovely meeting you, Annja, Dan. Perhaps we'll get a chance to see each other again."

Patrizinho stood, too. With a serious expression he said, "We should warn you to be wary of people who proclaim themselves horses for Ogum, or of Babalu. They are the gods of war and disease, respectively. They are dangerous, cranky spirits. Not to be trifled with, you understand."

Dan smiled a tight smile that didn't reach his eyes. "I've never been real afraid of gods and spirits."

"Horses," Xia said dryly, "tend to mirror their masters' personalities. So perhaps you should keep an eye on *them*."

7

Annja opened her eyes to darkness—and the cold conviction she was not alone.

The night throbbed with a samba beat from the small hotel's nightclub a couple of floors below, audible as a bass thrum beneath the white noise of the overburdened air conditioner in the window. For a moment she lay frozen, wondering if she was having a sleep-paralysis experience.

She smelled a waft of greens and warm, moist, dark earth—

She and Dan had spent a hot, tiring and unproductive day trolling the museums, the dark shops and bustling outdoor markets for clues to the fabled lost city of Promessa. As far as Annja was concerned it was anything but promising. For all the apparent conviction of Mafalda's warning to them the day before, Annja was beginning to suspect they were on a wild-goose chase. And Annja knew enough about folk beliefs and culture to understand too well that Mafalda's role in the community practically demanded she be a skilled actress.

But now—

With a sense of foreboding rising up her neck and tingling at the hinges of her jaw, Annja turned her head.

A figure stood at the foot of her bed. It was a shadow molded in the shape of a human. As she stared, the light of a streetlight and the half-moon glowed through inadequate curtains and enabled her wide eyes to resolve the form into what seemed to be an Amazonian man, short, wide shouldered, with a braided band holding long heavy hair away from what the shadows suggested was his darkly handsome face. His lean-muscled torso was bare; he appeared to be wearing only a loincloth of some sort.

As almost self-consciously quaint as this older part of Belém could be, the apparition had no more place in the climate-controlled room in a modern city than a pterodactyl or knight in armor. I don't believe in ghosts, she thought.

"I am real," the apparition said. Did he read my mind, she wondered, or did I speak aloud?

"You must stop asking the questions you are asking," the man said. "Please. Otherwise untold harm will result."

She struggled to sit up in bed, her heart racing.

"What about the harm you're doing by withholding your secrets from the world?" She said it more to see if she got a response than from any belief that such harm was being done, or that such secrets even existed. "Isn't that the ultimate selfishness?"

The man shook his head. "You speak of things you do not understand," he said sadly. "There are many things you do not know, and cannot be permitted to know."

"That's ridiculous." Anger at the violation of her privacy mixed with the adrenaline of fear surged within Annja.

"You have been warned," the man said sorrowfully. "We are willing to die to protect our secret. Consider what we will do to you, if we must." His apparent sadness only added mass to the soft menace of his words.

Annja whipped the sheet clear of her with a matador twirl and jumped from the bed. The sword came into her hand.

During the eyeblink that the sheet obscured her vision, her mysterious sad-voiced visitor had vanished. As if into thin air.

Scowling ferociously, she searched the room, sword almost quivering with eagerness to strike. Sometimes it seemed to have almost a life of its own.

She didn't like to think such thoughts. They smacked of madness. She pushed them firmly from her mind.

MOMENTS LATER Annja found herself standing barefoot on the threadbare green-and-maroon flower-patterned carpet in the hallway, wrapped in a white bathrobe, aware that her hair and eyes were both wild. She did not carry the sword, since she felt a grim certainty she was much more likely to encounter alarmed innocent tourists or hotel staff than any crafty cat burglars.

What she did encounter was Dan Seddon, wearing a pair of weathered jeans and a look at once furious and bewildered. His own hair stood out in random directions. Annja thought he resembled Calvin from the *Calvin and Hobbes* cartoons she'd loved growing up. She fought a semihysterical impulse to giggle.

"So I wasn't the only one who had a night visitor," Dan said. "You look like an avenging angel on a bad-hair day."

"You're a great one to talk, Calvin," she said.

He looked confused. "Never mind," she said. "What did you see?"

"A woman," he said. "Tall, thin, looked African. Had one of those headdresses on, the ones with the flared tops." He had extensive experience in sub-Saharan Africa, Annja recalled. "She warned me not to keep seeking the *quilombo* of dreams."

"And I suppose she vanished without a trace?"

"Absolutely. I rolled over to turn on the bedside lamp. When I rolled back I was all alone. Creepy."

He made a sound deep in his throat that might have been a chuckle, or passed for one. "Something like this tempts a man to believe there might actually be something to the stories about these Promessans possessing mystic powers."

It was Annja's turn to produce an inarticulate noise, this a distinctly unladylike grunt of confirmed skepticism. "It's some kind of trick. It's got to be."

"Was your window open? You find any sign the door had been jimmied?" Dan looked at her intently for a moment. "From your expression I'm taking that as a no on both counts."

"Well…still. I'm not ready to buy into astral projection or anything," Annja said.

He shrugged. "Come to that, if they have some kind of technique of holographic projection, that'd be pretty significant in and of itself, wouldn't it? Moran seems to think whatever secrets the Promessans have are primarily technological, although he doesn't say much about the mystic-powers thing one way or another."

"But I smelled him. He smelled of soil and plants. Like the rain forest."

Dan shrugged. "The Department of Defense was claiming to be able to stimulate various kinds of sensory hallucinations by beaming microwaves directly into people's skulls in the late 1990s," he said. "Maybe the Promessans are using a technology that isn't really that advanced. Just secret." He uttered a short laugh. "I'm surprised the capitalists haven't started using it for ads, though. Imagine billboards beamed directly into your brain!"

"I'd rather not, thanks." Annja compressed her lips. "Still, I had the absolute conviction he was really, physically there. That I could have hit him with my…fist…if I'd only been quick enough."

Dan laughed again, in a lighter tone. "Publico said you were a martial-arts expert with more than a little rough-and-tumble experience. I like that in a woman.

And yeah, I had the same sense about the woman in my room. Although it didn't occur to me to hit her. But which impossibility is going to upset your worldview the most? Astral projection, some kind of technological projection, or teleportation?"

"I think I'll just go back to bed," she said, "and try not to speculate in the absence of sufficient data."

"Or an overabundance of uncomfortable data."

"I thought you were the hardheaded, skeptical type, too," she said.

He shrugged. "Maybe I'm more a reflex skeptic. Sometimes being a skeptic means distrusting the official explanation. Especially when you've seen official explanations revealed as flat-out lies as often as I have."

Standing in the hallway there was a sudden sense of awkwardness between them.

Dan grinned. "Guess I'll go back to bed, too," he said. He tipped his head from side to side, stretching his neck muscles.

They stood there a moment longer, not precisely looking at each other, not precisely looking away. The dingy off-white wallpaper was starting to come away in patches on the wall, she noticed. No wonder, in this humidity.

"Well," he said, drawing it out just a little, "good night." He turned and padded on his bare feet into his room and shut the door.

"Night," she said. She stood looking at his door for a couple of breaths longer. Then she went into her own room.

She shut the door with more force than necessary.

"*OLÁ*, MAFALDA!" Annja called as the little brass bells strung on the inside of the door jingled merrily to announce their entrance. "Where are you?"

Followed closely by Dan, she pushed inside. Outside it was full noon. Their eyes, dazzled by the brightness of the equatorial sun, took time adjusting to the darkness within the shop.

"Maybe she's stepped out," Dan said dubiously.

"And left the door unlocked?" Annja said. "This may not be Rio de Janeiro, but that'd be pressing her luck even here."

"Maybe the locals are afraid of her magic," Dan said.

"You don't believe in magic."

"But they do." He stopped as the door jangled shut behind them and sniffed. "What's that smell?"

It hit Annja, too. Beneath the astringent smells of herbs and powders, of dust and the moldering bindings of old books, lay a smell of sweetness. And something foul.

"Christ—" The word came from Dan's throat as though around something choking him.

On the counter to the right of the door Mafalda lay with her head, still wrapped in its bright turban, propped on the cash register. Otherwise she was nude. She stared fixedly at the ceiling.

Feathers had been stuffed in her mouth. Mystic symbols had been scrawled on her bare belly in blood.

Her blood. Her throat had been slit.

8

Fast motion caught the corner of Annja's eye. She spun, reflexively bringing up her right forearm in a deflecting block.

A wooden pole struck her forearm. It was the haft of a spear, and its bright metal tip slid forward to graze her ear. A bundle of feathers tied behind the spear tip slapped her cheek.

Above the far end of the spear she saw the eyes of her visitor of the night before, burning in the gloom like dark stars.

Before she could react further the spear was withdrawn. With lightning speed it darted straight for her eyes. She twisted her body clockwise and leaned back, allowing the weapon to thrust past her.

She caught a flash impression that Dan was struggling with an opponent of his own. She had no attention to spare him. Her own foe was remarkably fast and determined.

His third thrust came low. Annja jumped high into the air to avoid the strike at her legs. She lashed out with her right foot, kicking a set of stout jars filled with different-colored powders and crushed leaves off the top shelf of a display toward her attacker. As one heavy jar tumbled toward his head, spilling orange powder that glittered even in the gloom, he reflexively jerked the spear back to interpose the haft.

Annja used some of the energy of her fall to add momentum to a spinning straight-legged reverse kick. The back of her heel caught the spear haft and wrenched it right out of the man's hands.

He spun and darted toward the back of the shop. Annja chased him. A pair of machetes hung crossed on the back wall. The man snatched down not one but both at once, and turned on his pursuer. He waved the heavy two-foot blades in a whistling figure-eight before him.

He advanced on her, apparently unconcerned that she was unarmed. Should I expect chivalry from someone who'd ritually murder a harmless shopkeeper? she thought. Unless she intended to flee—or die where she stood—he wasn't leaving her any choice.

Hoping Dan was too busy with his own assailant to notice anything else unusual she held her right hand as if gripping something, focused her will, reached…

The sword appeared in her hand.

The man's eyes widened to see the broadsword materialize from thin air. But the two big single-edged blades never faltered in their complex dance of death. Annja was pretty sure his moves were intended to hypnotize or intimidate her, as well as pose a daunting problem in attack or defense. She didn't doubt he could trap a longer blade between his and twitch the sword right out of her hands if she got careless.

Annja opted for the direct approach. She simply whacked at one of those dervish-whirling blades with her sword.

There was a jar of impact up her arm, a strangely musical clang. More than a foot of dark steel blade shot away to embed itself in the wall, between tattered posters for local samba clubs. The man stopped to stare in amazement at the surface where his machete had been chopped off at an angle as neatly as a bamboo stalk.

Annja's strike to sever the blade had been forehand. She flowed forward and whipped the sword around in a horizontal backhand stroke that should have separated the long-haired head from wide copper shoulders. Instead the man bent his upper body to his left, away from the stroke. The blade whizzed just over his head, slashing free a lock of hair that floated downward in the heavy air like a feather.

He thrust for Annja's flat belly with his remaining machete. The speed and fury of this strike would have impaled her had she not leaped back and left like a cat.

Unfortunately the motion slammed her hip into another counter laden with Mafalda's exotic merchandise. A choking cloud of dust and bits of ground herb and tiny wisps of feather floated up to surround Annja's head as jars jostled her arm. She sneezed, eyes filling with tears.

He rushed her, raising the machete to chop her down. In dodging, she had turned half away from him clockwise. She gripped the long hilt of her sword with both hands and thrust almost blindly toward the onrushing figure.

She felt a momentary resistance as he ran onto the blade.

His eyes blazing with determination, he drove himself onward. The sword's point came out his back with a sickening sound. He fought to bring his raised weapon down in a self-avenging death stroke.

Fading strength betrayed his will. The machete fell from fingers that could no longer grip. Blood ran from the corner of his mouth. A look of infinite sadness, almost apology, came into the blazing black eyes.

Then all light went out of them. They became dull as stones. He slumped in death.

Annja grimaced. She had killed many times. And almost every time before she had killed someone who richly deserved it—at the least a violent aggressor, and sometimes a serial predator upon human prey.

She knew somehow this man was none of those. He was a good man fighting with all his strength and will for something he truly believed was right. Deluded he may have been—must have been—but fighting for the right nonetheless.

Her head spun with confusion. *Doesn't that make*

him innocent? Her mission in life—as much as she could understand it—was to protect the innocent, to preserve *innocence,* at all costs. Even the cost of her life. Yet she had just killed a man acting for reasons she could not reproach.

He *attacked* you, a voice inside her head reminded her. And that fact seems to establish pretty definitively that he either killed Mafalda or had guilty knowledge of the deed. Virtuous he might have been. Innocent, no.

All this passed through her mind in a flash, a wheel of spiritual and stomach sickness, as she released her grip on the sword. It returned to its otherwhere, infinitely far yet no farther than the palm of her hand. The dead Amazonian warrior slumped to the plank floor.

Loud crashes snapped Annja back to the moment. She spun in time to see Dan flying upside down into a tall bookcase against one wall, having evidently crashed through a long table and a crowded set of shelves. The broken remnants of these and their contents were still falling toward and clattering off the floor in an immense swirl of dust and magic powders.

Standing at the apparent launch point of his flight was a tall, wiry, African-looking woman in a headdress like a flare-topped white can. She seemed to be in the follow-through stages of having executed some kind of throw. But Annja had never seen any woman throw a grown man like that. Nor any man.

The woman straightened. For a moment she stood facing Annja. Annja felt her gaze slide past, take in the dead man sprawled on his face on the floor right behind her. The woman's handsome features twisted in a grimace of grief that tore at Annja's heart.

The woman's right hand whipped up with striking-viper speed. The very nature of the movement triggered Annja's reflexes, already set on hair trigger. She was in motion, diving over the counter she had slammed against mere seconds before, before the woman's hand came level with her dark eyes.

Annja had learned that she could dodge gunshots. Not because she could move faster than bullets, but because she'd found herself adept at reading the body motions of an opponent. She could see the motion of muscle and tendons in a gun hand, the paling of a trigger-finger knuckle as pressure was applied. When she had such warning she simply got out from in front of the muzzle before the shot was fired. It was a foolproof way of being missed.

And now it was fortunate that she acted before the shot was fired.

A green flash suddenly filled the shop. It filled Annja's head with what seemed like emerald needles, stabbing and ricocheting inside her skull. The backs of her eyes hurt. A crack like thunder seemed almost incidental.

Impossible as it seemed, she knew what had happened. In college a careless classmate had flashed a laser pointer in her eyes from across the quadrangle. Although it was a low-power device and rated safe, the headache and vision disruption had persisted for hours. The aftereffects hadn't completely gone away for two days.

This was no mere pointer. She had gotten only side-scatters of coherent light and it had severe effects. Dazzled, she hit the far side of the counter. She smelled smoke and heard the crackling of flames.

She came up onto all fours, moved cautiously forward. Another green flare lit the shop with an accompanying crack of ionized air. The counter's bulk had absorbed a shot meant for her.

She called back the sword. Her mind raced. She realized the energy weapon had some limitations, probably including a recharge time. Otherwise the woman would simply hold down the trigger and slash through Annja's concealing counter until she found flesh.

The thought chilled Annja with a dread that threatened to sap her strength. She remembered the oft-spoken words of her teachers—it was not the weapon but the wielder!

Crouching with one hand on the floor, gritty with spilled powders, she stuck her head around the counter's end. A green flash blew a corner from the counter and set the wood to smoldering. But Annja had plotted her moves in her mind. She had withdrawn her head before the other woman could fire. Now Annja launched herself in a low dive, turning it into a forward roll that carried her past the foot of the main counter, where Mafalda lay. Fortunately her blood had pooled at the other end.

A second shot shattered the middle of that counter into flaming splinters, so close that spinning fragments seared Annja's bare leg. She gathered her limbs under her and, with all the strength that fear and fury could lend her, leaped over the counter and Mafalda's body.

The energy hand weapon apparently cycled quicker than Annja had estimated. She was met by a dazzling flash that sent more emerald needles stabbing through her brain to the back of her skull.

9

Dazzling though it was, the beam itself missed Annja. Screaming, she slashed blindly with the sword. She felt it bite and pass through the scarcely yielding solidity of wood, not flesh. Blinking wildly at tears of agony, she pressed forward.

When she could see again, it was to glimpse her opponent's sandaled heel vanishing into an oblong of brilliance that must have been a back door.

A quick glance revealed Dan sitting up amid a jagged jumble of broken wood and glass, hair and shoulders dusted with bits of iridescent feather. He was holding his head in his hands and moaning.

Without further thought she followed her instinct— which was to pursue. She sprinted toward the light. She burst out into the heat and glare at full speed and shot across the narrow alley, slamming into a wall.

A green flash, blindingly bright even in the sun's full glare, blasted a gouge in the wall. Annja saw her opponent running just before she disappeared around a right turn in the narrow way. The woman had snapped a shot toward where she judged her opponent would appear, not calculating that Annja would blow right through the doorway kill zone to the alley's far side. Annja felt a cold twinge in her belly at the realization the woman could just as easily have foreseen Annja's move had she been experienced in fighting instead of merely skilled.

But every choice, she knew, could go either way. You had to take your pick—and pray.

Annja ran after the vanished woman. She put the sword away as she raced along the alley. A tall white woman chasing a black one was likely to attract enough unwelcome attention. If she was waving a sword, things would spiral a lot further out of control.

She pounded around the corner. As she did she dimly remembered something she'd read somewhere, or maybe been told—that police departments trained their officers not to pursue a firearm-wielding suspect on foot. The reason was the officer might race around a corner to find herself confronted with a felon already braced and aiming, waiting for her to show in the gun's sights.

Instead, Annja found herself confronting a broad street full of people in bright clothes staring in some consternation after the tall woman who had just plowed through them.

"Thief!" Annja shouted. It wasn't true, so far as she knew. But to call her what she apparently was, a murderer, would only bring official scrutiny she definitely did not want. At least the baseless call of thief would give some context to her pursuit in the minds of the crowd.

The fleeing woman glanced back over her shoulder. She saw Annja through the crowd. Her handsome face twisted in dismay. Already slowed by looking backward, she stopped, turned and brought up her hand. The muscles of Annja's face contracted in anticipation of a green death bolt. But she kept doggedly moving forward, slowed to a jog by the desire not to jostle the passersby.

The woman in the flared turban pointed her hand at Annja. Annja couldn't see what she held. Her brain screamed for her to duck, dodge, dive to the sidewalk. Instead she made herself forge on, slowly closing the gap, already less than thirty yards—a long shot for a handgun.

She made her eyes hold the other woman's gaze. She could see indecision ripple across the beautifully chiseled dark features like wavelets across a pond, followed by frustration.

The woman dropped her arm and stepped sideways into a door.

Murderer or not, she has scruples about shooting into a crowd, and the self-control to heed them, Annja thought. The Promessan had some conscience, at least.

The doorway had a warped wooden jamb covered

in peeling blue paint. The door had not closed all the way. Annja plunged inside.

It was dark. A bit of light fell on the floor from a fly-specked, yellow-stained window at the far end of the corridor she found herself in. Annja smelled strange spices, things boiling, some eye-searing kind of chemical cleanser. She was in an obvious tenement. Infants cried, voices sounded, music jangled and sang to her in a dozen melodies from behind doors with tarnished brass numbers nailed to them. She found the effect strangely pleasing.

But she wasn't there to savor the atmosphere. From the look and feel of the hallway the fleeing woman had not ducked into any of the apartments. Annja raced up a narrow wood stairway to her left.

She heard footsteps drumming above. A shadow fell as someone leaned into the light spilling from above. Annja ducked to the wall as a brilliant green lance stabbed down, blasting the railing to splinters a few feet from her and sending up a curl of stinking blue smoke.

She summoned the sword. She wasn't sure what good it would do her against a laser. But it made her feel better. She heard the footsteps dwindle above. Apparently her quarry had taken off down the third-floor hallway.

Annja raced after her. The sweat streamed down her face and body, and her breath burned in her lungs. She was in excellent shape but combat drained a body like nothing else. Especially the strain of mortal combat— and against some kind of superweapon to boot.

She reached the top of the stairs. The woman was almost at the corridor's end. Sensing Annja, she spun. She shouted something Annja could not understand. It sounded like an African dialect. She fired. Annja leaned over the wooden railing, almost toppling back down the stairs to avoid the shot.

The woman burst through a door to her right, into an apartment. Annja banished the sword and followed.

The people in the little flat were frightened. A short, wiry woman stood with a disregarded cigarette endangering her ebony fingers. Her companion, a younger, taller woman, had just turned away from a pot on the stove. A wooden spoon was raised and dripping. Both stared out the open window.

The two women turned to stare at Annja. They didn't seem outraged at her intrusion, or even surprised.

"What happened?" she asked in Portuguese.

"She disappeared," the wiry older woman said. She added a curse and wagged her hand as her cigarette stub finally scorched the sensitive skin between her fingers.

"Disappeared?" Annja echoed lamely.

The other woman nodded. "Out the window."

"Fell? Flew like a bird?"

"Just disappeared," the older woman said.

Annja ran to the window and looked down. There was a small yard below, mostly a tangle of weeds and shrubs. But she saw no sign of a fallen body, nor any readily visible way to get down shy of jumping. At something over twenty feet from the ground, Annja would have expected to see her quarry limping off down the alley on a broken ankle at best, if not lying totally crippled in the greenery.

She looked up. The roof came to a peak just above her head. Without pausing to think how ridiculously dangerous it was, she swarmed out, using minute fingerholds in some kind of wood-slatted air vent over the window to scramble onto the roof in defiance of sense, if not gravity.

She found herself all alone on a pitched roof of warped green-painted shakes.

The woman in the headdress had disappeared.

DAN MET HER on the street two blocks from Mafalda's shop. "Don't go there," he said, shaking his head. He was bruised, disheveled and limping.

"What do you mean?" she asked. Then she saw dirty white smoke tumbling up past the rooftops into the sky behind him.

"No," she said. "The laser did that?"

"Not exactly. It did set a couple of fires. But then when I was searching the shop the dead guy was suddenly enveloped in these roaring blue flames. It was like a blast furnace or something. Everything just boomed into flame for five or six feet around. I barely got out before the whole damn place went up."

"Are you all right?"

"Except for my pride? Sure. As well as can be expected after being thrown through various pieces of furniture by a woman. I mean, no sexism intended or anything."

"I was almost as surprised as you were."

"What about you?"

She shook her head. "Vanished. I hate to use a cliché, but in this case 'into thin air' isn't a metaphor."

She sighed and slumped. "So we got Mafalda murdered and came up dry. Not to mention set the building on fire. This is not shaping up as a successful day."

"Not as bad as it could be, though," Dan said. "For one thing, they get a hundred inches of rain a year here, and we seemed to get about a quarter of it this morning before we left the hotel. I don't think fires spread real easily here. For another—" he held up a hand to show a scrap of paper with an ugly rust-colored smear across it "—I searched her body and turned up this."

"Searched her body?" Annja echoed belatedly. "She seemed pretty naked. Where'd you find that? Or do I want to know?"

"She had it clutched in her right fist."

He handed her the scrap of paper.

"It's a shipping invoice," she said, reading it. "From what translates as River of Dreams Trading Company, way upriver in Manaus. That used to be the rubber capital pretty much of the whole world."

"A clue?" Dan asked.

She shrugged. "The name's suggestive, I have to admit. This also strikes me as just a bit convenient."

He showed her a lopsided grin. "Maybe we're just due a break." Sirens began to warble from what seemed like several directions. "The old street-protest instincts tell me that when you hear that sound, it's time to go," he said.

She glanced around. The street was crowded. People were pointing to the smoke and talking excitedly.

"What about witnesses?" she asked.

"I don't know much about this place," he said, "and you've told me the slums are a whole lot heavier down in Rio. But I still don't think these people are the sort to talk to police about anything at all."

"Maybe we shouldn't hang around to be found here by the authorities," Annja said.

His grin got wide and feral. "Now you're learning street wisdom, Grasshopper," he said. "We'll make an activist out of you yet!"

10

"Look up there," Annja said. "They're doing *capoeira* out in the street."

The sun had set low over the inland forest that grew hard up against the edges of the city. Lively music filled the lavender twilight. Two men sparred before colorfully dressed ranks of worshipers laughing and clapping their hands. A small band enthusiastically played a curious assortment of instruments, including a tambourine, a drum like a bongo, two dissimilar bells joined by a horseshoe-shaped handle, a rasp played against a stick and three different-sized contrivances like bows and arrows mated to dry gourds. The man playing the largest of these sang in a high-pitched chant.

The combatants—or dancers—seemed to time their moves to the rhythm of the music.

"Let's watch," Annja said, striding quickly forward.

Dan hung back. "I don't want to intrude on anybody's religious rituals," he said. "It can be bad for your health."

She turned to face him. "That's true," she said. "It can be rude, too. But why would these people be doing their ritual in public if they didn't want people to watch? It's part of the observance. They have private and secret rituals—trust me on that. The key being, we don't know about them. They don't hold those out on the street."

His forehead rumpled and his fists stuck deep in the pockets of his shorts, Dan shrugged. He seemed to be genuinely uncomfortable.

"Come on," she urged.

They had spent an exhausting and dispiriting day hunting for further clues to the mystery of the hidden *quilombo*. An Internet search had turned up frustratingly little on the River of Dreams Trading Company. A good dinner of seafood and the superabundant tropical fruits available in the area had mellowed them somewhat after the jagged events of the day.

Now Dan turned sullen, reminding Annja of the way he'd acted when Xia and Patrizinho had joined them at breakfast—had it only been the previous morning? It seemed a lifetime ago.

Of course it was, Annja thought, for Mafalda.

"We need to get back to the hotel," he said, "set up a teleconference with Publico."

"What's the hurry? We've hit a dead end." As soon

as the words left her mouth Annja winced at their choice. "Unless our employer has some information he's been holding back and cares to share it with us, we might as well fly back to Miami."

"Don't forget we've got that invoice scrap," Dan said, "not to mention a dead woman."

"Jesus," Annja hissed. "Be careful saying that out loud."

He gestured at the clapping, singing circle. "Nobody can hear us. Nobody's listening. Nobody'll say anything to the police, anyway."

"You don't know that," she said. "The Brazilian authorities pay snitches the same way police back in the States do. And we're foreigners, not family or friends to any of these people. One wouldn't have too much trouble giving us up to save his own hide, say."

Dan's scowl etched itself deeper on his lean, handsome face. She liked him but he had a tendency to petulance and flashes of anger that bothered her a bit.

"You've got a point," he mumbled.

She smiled and nodded. It reassured her that he was fundamentally sound.

She turned and walked toward the crowd, leaving Dan to follow or not as he chose. Several bystanders nodded and smiled as the two Americans approached. Some of them were casually dressed. Many of the obvious participants were dressed in white. Some of the women wore lacy dresses that suggested bridal gowns to Annja. She wondered at the symbolism.

"I wonder how you tell the onlookers from the worshipers?" she said to Dan.

He shrugged. He still seemed grumpy and uncommunicative. She looked at him a moment. *What's bothering him? This isn't just some weird petulance at my dragging him to do something he doesn't want to do.*

The combatants continued their acrobatic match, stepping forward, stepping back, launching kicks and strikes that the other blocked or dodged just in the nick of time. They played with smiling abandon that made it impossible for Annja to tell whether this was actually a competition or some choreographed ritual.

The twang and thump and insistent rumbling rhythm of the music seemed to get inside her bones and resonate. She felt a rising sensation of heat. Somehow she didn't find it oppressive. Oddly it seemed to well within her, owing little to the heavy, humid, tropical evening air.

The crowd cried out together. One of the combatants did a back flip away from his opponent, then both bowed. They backed into the crowd to great applause.

Then the crowd stilled except for the continued thumping of the drum. A man stepped forward. He was short and wiry, with a blue-and-green headband wound around his forehead and brown, tightly coiled hair. His clothes were shades of blue and green. His feet were bare. He walked crouching, wide kneed, holding a hand flattened above his eyes and peering this way and that.

"Are you Americans?" a woman who stood near Annja asked in English. She was small and compact, dressed in slacks and a tropical-flower blouse. Annja realized from the lines around dark eyes and smiling mouth that the woman must be older.

"Yes," Annja said.

"Do you know what's happening here?" the woman asked.

The man dropped a hand to the pavement before him. He peered left and right. Although she felt no breeze some must have come up briefly, because Annja grew aware of a smell of the dense tropical vegetation that crowded closely on Belém from inland.

"No," Annja said. "Not really."

"Welcome to the *roda,* the sacred circle," the woman said. "Now, watch."

Still crouching, the man moved to the band and snatched one of the bowlike instruments from a musician's hand. The musician showed no resentment. He merely smiled and stepped back.

The instrument was held by one end to play. Instead the man in green and blue held it in the middle as if it were a bow. He began acting out the motions of hunting through the rain forest.

"He is Oxóssi," the Brazilian woman said to Annja, seeing her perplexed expression. "He has momentarily claimed the *berimbau* for his use. That is the bow with the gourd."

"Oxóssi is an *orixá?*" Annja asked.

The woman nodded. "The *orixá* of the hunt. That man is his horse, you see."

"Great," Dan growled on Annja's other side. "A mime. I *hate* mimes."

"Everybody hates mimes," she told him. "But he's not a mime. He's a horse for a spirit named Oxóssi."

The brief wave of jungle smell had gone. Possibly it had been swamped by the smell of the cigars some of the celebrants, men and women alike, were smoking. It was a harsh tobacco, very strong. Annja realized it was making her head swim, and her stomach began to roll like a sea in a rising wind. Oddly, the feeling wasn't entirely unpleasant.

She glanced over at her companion, intended to remark on the smoke, her light-headedness, her slight but ominously growing nausea. She froze.

Dan was wound tight like a tugboat cable. His handsome face had become a purple mask; tendons stood out in his neck. His fists clenched and unclenched as if crushing walnuts.

Suddenly he thrust forward. Oxóssi's horse looked at him. Recognition came into his pale brown eyes. He nodded to the young American, then backed carefully away. His attitude suggested a hunter who had encountered one of Brazil's many venomous serpents in the bush—not fear, but rather respectful caution, wariness.

Puffing out his chest, Dan swaggered around the circle in an exaggerated display of alpha-male machismo. It looks like a bad Popeye imitation! Annja thought.

"Dan," she called to him. He didn't react. She started forward.

The diminutive woman at her side laid a gentle but surprisingly strong hand on her forearm. "No," she said. "You can do nothing. You must do nothing."

To her astonishment Annja saw that none of the worshipers seemed to be taking affront at Dan's thrusting himself into the midst of the festivities. Rather they had begun cheering and clapping in rhythm to his swagger. The drummer beat time. The other two *berimbau* began to play along.

Suddenly Dan strutted to the circle of onlookers, seizing a half-full bottle of rum from a man dressed in white with frilly sleeves. If I'm optimistic, it's half-empty, Annja thought.

"What's going on?" she said plaintively.

"Can't you see? He is taken. He is ridden now by Ogum. A great honor. But worse luck. He must be a very angry young man," the woman said.

That's true, part of Annja's mind said, rather louder than the skeptic trying somewhat desperately to scoff this all away.

Dan raised the rum bottle to his lips, tipped his head back and drank until his cheeks puffed like a blowfish and rum ran down his chin and neck and down the front of his shirt. The crowd's clapping crescendoed. None clapped more enthusiastically than the man whose rum bottle he had grabbed. The band played with redoubled vigor. The rasp and the bell joined in.

Suddenly Dan spit the rum into the street in a great alcoholic spray. He seized a torch from another participant, tossed it into the pool of liquid. Red flames flared up. Laughing, he poured on more rum. The stream caught—an arc of fire. Before the bottle could go off in his hand he smashed it in the midst of the flames, which soared up as high as his chest, garish in the near darkness. It underlit his face, turning it into a bizarre mask of joyous rage.

Again he moved with surprising swiftness and yet no apparent haste, snatching a machete from a rickety wooden platform at one side of the cleared circle. He brandished it above his head in a serious of whistling swoops. Then he pressed its point against the middle of his sternum, grasped the hilt with both hands and pushed.

"No!" Annja screamed. She could see the effort, see the muscles stand out like cords on his wiry forearms.

Yet nothing happened. The machete was not pointed like a spear, but it possessed a sharp edge. And she knew Dan was surprisingly strong for his lean build. That much effort should have punched the tip right through his flesh.

It did not. Dan tore his shirt open to reveal his pale skin remained unbroken. Then he punched both hands at the stars in an age-old gesture of triumph. The crowd gasped and then cheered wildly.

Annja's informant nodded with a certain brisk if gloomy satisfaction. "That's Ogum. Two things he can't resist—rum and showing off."

Dan began a wild swirling dance, swinging the machete. He reeled this way and that, heedless of the onlookers, some of whom began to stumble over each other in their eagerness to get out of his way. He only laughed and danced faster.

Now that he posed a clear danger to the crowd a man

in white trousers and white-and-purple headband leaped forward to confront him. Annja gasped as Dan, rage twisting his features, swung the machete at him. The man flung himself into a sideways dive. The blade hissed harmlessly above him as he did a headstand and flipped back to his feet.

"Uh-oh," the Brazilian woman said.

Dan was all over him. Closing in a flash, he grabbed the man by the throat and lifted him into the air. Annja gasped. There was no way the young activist, fit though he was, should have been able to do that.

And nobody should have been able to throw the hapless man through the air to smash a wooden cart filled with various paraphernalia at least a dozen feet away.

Annja's head spun. Heat rose within her like flames, seemingly rising up through the soles of her feet, her legs, her loins, her belly. A wind seemed to rise. Bits of paper and fallen flowers began to skitter along the cracked blacktop.

Without conscious decision her will exerted itself. The sword sprang into her hand.

She ran forward into the circle to confront Ogum, in defiance of all sense and judgment.

11

"Ahh," the crowd gasped. "Iansã is come."

Things were totally out of control as Annja entered the middle of the circle and took up a stance with the sword tipped back over her shoulder. She felt totally irresponsible. What was happening made no sense.

But it seemed Annja was thinking with a larger mind, one not altogether familiar—yet somehow not totally alien. Her mind saw wind bending palm trees and storms building waves. Lightning filled her thoughts, ripping asunder a black-clouded sky above the gates of an ancient graveyard. Troubling images, yet stirring. For all their fury, violence and darkness, they were untainted by evil. Rather they were thoughts of a warrior who relentlessly battled evil.

Dan spun to confront her. His eyes were bloodshot.

Or did they glow red? Was that a trick of the torchlight and—whatever had overcome her?

With a mighty scream of rage he launched himself at her. He cocked his machete over his left shoulder and swung a ferocious overhand cut at the top of Annja's head.

What is he doing? Annja thought in desperation as she flung up the sword to parry. What are *we* doing?

The blades clanged together with a noise like a church bell. The impact sent vibrations rippling down Annja's arm.

With a ringing, singing slide and spray of shockingly bright yellow sparks, Dan ripped his machete away and swung again at her. This time it was a two-handed horizontal strike, aimed to take her head off at the neck.

She wove her body sideways. The black blade swished by overhead.

The rushing wind seemed to fill her head, her body, her soul, subsume her. It was as if something—*someone*—else had command of her movements as she wove through a crashing, clashing, whirling battle with the man.

They spun and leaped and stabbed and slashed in a dance as wild and abandoned as any *capoeira* fight. The circle had closed around them. Faces shone orange in flickering torchlight. Many hands clapped in rhythm. The band played their strange moaning, tinkling song.

The thinking part of Annja was freewheeling almost as completely as the rest of her. Not with the passions that raged like a tornado within her—anger and joy and the fierce desire for justice—but with confusion. *Why is he doing this?*

Why am I doing this?

The sweat poured down her whirling limbs so profusely she felt as if her skin would slough. Dan's face streamed with sweat as if the tropical rains had moved in again. His features were purple, suffused with inhuman fury that seemed to mount with each attack she parried, each slash she leaped nimbly over or ducked beneath. Her own mad, self-righteous drive to withstand him likewise grew.

The end came quickly. His fury at last overpowered all traces of skill—skill Annja couldn't imagine the young political activist could ever have acquired in the first place. Screaming so ferociously that his voice failed, he ran at her, slashing two-handed with fantastic strength.

But his blows, though powerful enough to cut her in half at the waist should one connect, came looping in like predictable haymakers. Overriding the urgency and sense of presence within, the sheer muscle memory from long, exacting practice at half a dozen styles of swordplay took over. As he swung, she spun away to catch his blade from behind as she completed her circle. She sent it spinning from his hand, end over end above the heads of the crowd and away in the night.

Unbalanced, he staggered away several steps. Then he turned and hurled himself through the air at her, hands bent to claws.

She drew back the sword. A single thrust through the sternum would end this madness.

But Annja took control again. The sword went away. With the strange and terrifying strength that had filled her, she met him instead with a palm-heel strike to the center of his chest that threw him into a backward somersault to smash upside down into the weapons rack, knocking it to splinters and sending spears and machetes flying through the air and clattering on the pavement.

She stood a moment, swaying. Her head spun. Her stomach seemed to rotate in the opposite direction. The roaring wind moved up through her until it seemed centered in her head. Then it seemed to sweep upward and away.

Silence.

Swaying.

Blackness.

SHE BECAME AWARE of the taste of raw alcohol filling her mouth and scalding her tongue like boiling water. She sat up choking and spitting.

"Easy, child, easy," a husky female voice said in Portuguese. "Do you understand me?"

"Yes," Annja said weakly.

"Good, good." Strong hands grasped her shoulders and drew her back down to cradle her head on the skirted thighs of a kneeling woman. Her benefactor smiled down from a round face. She was not the woman Annja had spoken to, but a big, ample-breasted woman with mahogany skin. Other faces looked down on her, a rough oval against the sky. Their expressions seemed to combine solicitude with a certain awe.

"What happened?" she asked.

"Drink, child," a man said. He knelt by her side, proffering a bowl of water. It was cool. She sat up again, took it and drank greedily.

At once she vomited violently. The onlookers, possibly realizing such a reaction was likely, leaped nimbly out of the way.

The woman who cradled her pulled her head down to her lap again. Someone soothed her brows, then her cheeks, with a cloth soaked in cool water.

"I'm sorry," Annja croaked. "So sorry. I don't know what came over me. Over us. How's Dan?"

She tried to sit up again. She was held firmly down. "My friend. Is my friend all right?"

"He's fine," said the man who had taken back the bowl of water before Annja's explosion. "He's right over there."

He nodded to his right. Ten feet away Dan sat with his knees up and his face buried against his legs. Celebrants, most in white, knelt around him, speaking in soothing voices, touching him gently but almost furtively. It was as if they were trying to calm some kind of ferocious wild animal.

"Is he badly hurt?"

"Not at all. The power of his rider, Ogum, kept him from harm."

"But I—" Annja said. "I knocked him through that rack. Unless it was a dream."

"Oh, no. We all saw. You were ridden by Iansã of the winds," a woman said. "You and your friend are both very holy people. Very fortunate."

Some of the bystanders didn't look so sure. "Maybe your man is not so lucky to have been picked out by Ogum," another woman said. "He is very terrible."

"I am so sorry," Annja said again. "We did not mean to intrude."

It came to her to wonder if harsh tobacco was all that was being smoked, or if perhaps the incense had an extra kicker. Half the world's ethnobotanists, it seemed to her, were in the depths of the Amazon at any given moment. And while they were legitimately looking for the next medical miracle in the largely untapped natural pharmacopoeia of the rain forest, the fact was many of them were most interested in loading up on the local hallucinogens. Could she and Dan have been dosed by some kind of aerosol form of drug, she wondered.

But Annja's helpers were trading knowing glances and big grins. "Intrude?" the woman cradling Annja said. "We told you—Iansã happened. She took you over good."

"Good thing she did, too," said another woman standing nearby. "Ogum got your friend pretty hard. And he seemed pretty pissed." Whether she meant Dan or the *orixá*, Annja couldn't tell. Possibly the speaker drew no distinction between them.

"That's not possible. We don't practice *candomblé*. We're American."

"Anyone can see that, child," the man said, holding out the water bowl again. Annja took a mouthful of water, sloshed it around, turned her head to spit without endangering anybody's skirts or feet. Then she drank again, more cautiously than before. Her stomach seemed to wallow a few times like a tugboat in a high sea, but the water stayed down.

"It's a sign." The words were English. Annja recognized the voice of the trim middle-aged woman who had spoken to her before. "The *orixás* have marked you as their own. They don't do that much to foreigners. Obviously, you are acting out some great and powerful destiny."

She opened her mouth to say, "Nonsense." The syllables turned to ash on her tongue.

"Who's Iansã?" she found herself asking instead. "What's she like? And—did you see me with a sword?"

"Of course," the large, cheerful woman whose lap cradled her said. She held out the front of her T-shirt. "Iansã always has a sword. See?"

Annja half turned to look. The woman wore a shirt labeled *Cavala Da Iansã,* Iansã's Horse. It showed an African woman dressed in swirling skirts of red and pink and yellow. In one hand she carried a horsetail fly whisk.

In the other she carried a cutlass.

"Iansã," the woman said. "She is the wind, the tornado and the lightning. She fights like a man for justice alongside her husband, Xangô, the sky father, lord of thunder."

"I don't know how I'd feel about being married to the god of thunder," Annja said shakily.

The onlookers laughed. "Don't worry," the woman in the Iansã shirt said. "There are some things an *orixá* won't ask her horse to do."

"She prefers to do those things herself," said another woman, to even louder laughter.

THEY MADE THEIR WAY back to the hotel through streets filled with music and cheerful people. Walking through the humid air was draining. The night seemed full of chattering voices that pierced the ear like needles and jagged colors that bruised the eye.

Annja and Dan walked with arms around each other for support. Dan had a black eye and half his face was covered by a bruise that had already begun to go green and yellow. Annja's right hip hurt, as did her ribs every time she breathed. She didn't remember being hit during their battle. But she felt as if she'd been used to hammer nails.

The doorman on duty in his natty white cap, shirt and shorts—a pretentious touch for such a modest hotel—didn't blink when the two staggered by, undoubtedly looking overly amorous, drunk or both.

They said nothing to each other as they crossed the threadbare carpet between the potted palms in the comfortably shabby lobby, nor as they rode the elevator. In silence they walked the short distance to the adjoining doors of their rooms.

Fumbling slightly, Annja got out her key card and unlocked her door. Dan followed her inside. She did not

question it, internally or aloud. It was somehow un-
thinkable that he not do so. After what they'd been
through, they needed to be together.

12

The lobby door blew open in a swirl of air so humid and thick with smells of exhaust and the omnipresent water and jungle that it seemed to Annja you ought to be able to see it.

She looked up from noodling at her journal in a vague way on the notebook computer she had open on her lap. She wore cargo shorts, a lightweight buff-colored shirt and an expression, or so she suspected, of weary befuddlement.

She watched as a couple of black men in white linen suits swept in. They were very, very big. From the way they moved they were muscled like the workers on the Belém waterfront, though better dressed.

She made herself look away as they swept the lobby with the bug eyes of their sunglasses. She didn't want them noticing the hardening of her expression. She suspected they were gangsters. The only reason alarm bells weren't shrilling in her soul was that their body language suggested they were looking for potential trouble*makers,* not trouble themselves.

She was aware of operating at lower than usual. She felt numerous aches and pains. She still hadn't been able to process the events of the previous evening. She and Dan had clung tightly to each other until they fell into restless sleep.

Annja suspected she and Dan had inadvertently been dosed with some kind of strong psychoactive smoke. In the cold light of day that seemed more and more conclusively the case.

"So," a familiar voice said from behind her. "You survived."

She looked around as the two big men moved slowly to different sides of the lobby. Dan stood there. He was dressed in a loose shirt over cotton trousers. He looked even more tousled and unshaved than usual. His eyes were sunk in dark, saggy pits.

"More or less," she said. "Much as I hate to say it, you look like I feel."

"Yeah," he grunted.

Sometime in the dark hours of the long tropical night he had risen from her bed and left without a word. Insofar as she could remember, they had not exchanged a word since their confrontation in the midst of the crowd. She had been somewhat dreading their inevitable meeting.

A second pair of men entered the lobby. They were

white and bulky. They wore white linen jackets over what looked like T-shirts and white duck trousers. The jackets were tailored loosely enough about their wide upper torsos they might well have concealed shoulder holsters.

Even more than the two hard black men, one of whom had now taken up position near the elevators, the other by the brief corridor to the restaurant, the newcomers *looked* like the kind of men who'd be wearing shoulder holsters. Annja had recently acquired way more experience of hired muscle than she'd ever really cared to have. If these guys weren't that, with their shaved heads, their dark sunglasses, their square jaws jutting from necks wider than their heads, then it was time to look around for the rest of the film crew, because central casting had hit all the cherries.

"Ahh," Dan murmured as the newcomers took up positions flanking the hotel's entrance. "Our esteemed employer arrives."

"You know these thugs?" They weren't the pair with Publico on Annja's landing on his penthouse roof.

"Goran and Mladko," he said. "Croatian war criminals. His bodyguards."

"He uses war criminals as bodyguards?"

Dan shrugged. "It's supposed to be rehabilitation. He's all about forgiveness, you know. Besides, nobody's looking for them too hard."

Through the big glass doors Annja saw a commotion outside as hotel porters swarmed to a long, low, white limousine with dark-tinted windows. Another huge black man popped out the front passenger door and waved them off. They obeyed with alacrity. Maybe it was his size. Maybe it was his air of undeniable authority. Maybe it was the stubby little machine pistol with the magazine in the butt and the separate broom-handle foregrip he was brandishing none too discreetly.

The gunman opened the limo's rear door. At last, out came Sir Iain Moran, Publico himself, looking neat in a lightweight gray suit. He stood, stretched slightly, smiled and nodded at his bodyguards. Then he tipped his sunglasses down his nose and looked through the windows into the lobby.

Dan raised two fingers in a halfway salute. Publico beamed, nodded, swept inside.

"What's he doing here?" Annja asked. Last night's intended conference call had never come to pass.

"I e-mailed him from my cell phone after that stuff went down at Mafalda's."

Sir Iain paused between his two human pillars and swept the room with his gaze. His fine leonine head was held high, the long hair streaming down to his shoulders.

He approached Annja and Dan, beaming, a powerful hand held out.

"Annja, Dan," he said in his deep, gravelly Irish voice. "So good to see you."

"And you," said Annja a little feebly as she rose. She was trying hard to bottle up the flash of anger and resentment at her so-called partner for communicating with their boss without letting her know.

She took his hand. He shook firmly, covering her hand with his, then moved on to embrace Dan.

"Welcome to Belém," Annja said.

He smiled and nodded. "Sure, sure."

He looked to the two black men who had preceded Goran and Mladko. Annja saw no signal from them, but what Publico saw seemed to lead to a sudden decision.

"Let's walk," he said with a brisk nod of his head. "It's a beautiful day."

They walked down toward the river esplanade. The two black bodyguards preceded them. Mladko and Goran winged out from them, a step or two behind. The big man with the machine pistol followed a few steps behind. It wasn't exactly subtle. Annja gathered it wasn't intended to be. In any event, few people spared them more than a glance.

She was surprised no one seemed to recognize Sir Iain. It struck her that perhaps nobody associated Publico—dressed in a T-shirt and torn blue jeans and grimacing into a microphone with his sweat-lank hair hanging down his back—with this dapper, obviously wealthy white guy from elsewhere.

"We had just about run out of leads here," Annja said. She wasn't able to keep a note of accusation from creeping into her voice. "You didn't give us much to work with. Especially after our one major contact was murdered."

"Sorry, Annja dear," he said with a contrite smile. "But you were fully the skeptic, weren't you? I already told you more than you were willing to believe—that much was plain as the nose on your face."

"I'm still a skeptic," she said. "And I'm not sure what to believe right now." She hoped Dan hadn't felt duty-bound to e-mail him about their experience the evening before.

"What happened to Mafalda did kind of put a damper on our investigation," Dan said. "There's nothing written down about Promessa, at least that we could track down. I get the impression plenty of people know about this hidden *quilombo*, but nobody wants to talk to strangers about it."

"Do you blame them, after what happened to Mafalda?" Annja asked.

"Ah, but there we have the key bit of evidence, don't we?" Publico said almost impishly. He seemed to be taking a childlike delight in the intrigue. "The fact that she was done in is itself as strong a lead as we could ask, don't you see?"

"It means we're on the right trail," Dan agreed somewhat reluctantly.

"It may or may not," Annja said quickly. "Although it's not as in-your-face here as it is in the megacities down south, crime is a real problem in Brazil. It can hit anybody any time—or why are we walking around surrounded by men bristling with guns?"

"Point taken," Publico said with a grin.

"Dealing in *candomblé* items is a pretty well respected trade around here, but it certainly doesn't rule out contacts with a pretty bad element. Mafalda might've crossed a business associate. Or turned the wrong crime boss down on a sexual proposition," Annja said.

He raised a brow. "You really think so? I thought you found the same people in her shop who visited you in your bedrooms the night before. And who vanished mysteriously."

"Maybe," Annja said. Dan looked at her sharply; she paid him no mind. "The vanishing isn't necessarily all that mysterious. We're not from around here, and they are. They know the city much better than we do. And while I never saw Dan's nocturnal guest, mine and the guy in the shop—well, it's not as if wiry little guys who look like Amazonian Indians are rare in these parts."

"It was the same woman," Dan said flatly. "She threw me like I was a child."

"You think she displayed superhuman strength?" Publico asked. His voice seemed to hold an edge of eagerness.

"I don't know. She could have just been real good at martial arts. But it was the same woman, and she shot some kind of energy weapon at Annja."

Annja frowned. "Maybe."

Dan glared at her. "You told me—"

She held up a hand. "I know. But I've thought about it. It might have been conventional firearm using a special laser sight. Maybe it was a special effect designed to make it *look* like some kind of high-tech ray gun."

"But she vanished again on you," Dan said, "when you chased her into that tenement room."

"Well," Annja said, "again, she might just have known more about the area than I do...."

She let her words trail off when she noticed the other two looking at her closely. Dan looked outraged. Publico was openly amused.

"Ah, Annja, for a world traveler, you'd think you'd realize denial is more than just a river in Egypt," the rock star said. Publico held up a finger. "You're both forgetting we do have a solid lead—that slip of paper Dan found in that unfortunate woman's hand."

Annja looked at Dan and sighed. "It could just be coincidental, too."

"As may be," Publico said. "But you two are going to Manaus to find out for certain. And I shall come with you."

13

"He was holding out on us," Annja said. "Of course I'm pissed off."

The waiting room in the offices of the River of Dreams Trading Company in Manaus was fluorescent bright, with dark-stained hardwood wainscoting, whitewashed walls and a white dropped-tile ceiling. An array of fern or palmlike plants in terra-cotta pots, exotic to Annja's eyes but native to the surrounding forest, softened the starkness of an otherwise generically modern design, with a curved desk and chairs of curved chromed tubing with black leather seats and backs. Big modernistic murals of the rain forest splashed the walls with bright greens and reds and yellows. Pied tamarins, a famous local endangered species of primate, featured prominently, peering like troll dolls with black raisins for faces and cotton-ball wigs.

"He has his reasons," Dan said.

Publico's private jet had delivered them to Manaus shortly after noon, a few hours earlier. It had been one of the richest cities in the Western Hemisphere and possibly the richest in the Southern Hemisphere during its heyday as queen of the rubber trade. Unfortunately the invention of synthetic substitutes, and the rise of rubber cultivation in Southeast Asia, ended the frenzy in 1920.

The city had recently returned to somewhat provisional status as financial center for Amazonia and much of South America, courtesy of the global economic boom. The place had a seedy, superficial quality, as if all the glossy steel and glass high rises downtown were fancy paint over cheap plastic.

The River of Dreams Trading Company waiting room did little to dispel the impression of tackiness from Annja's mind. It was spotless, but the colors struck her as a bit too gaudy, the smell of disinfectant too strong, the Brazilian jazz playing from concealed speakers a little too strident. It was all as if they were trying to hide something.

"But to wait until now to tell us that this German friend of his had dealings with River of Dreams?" Annja said.

"Was there something that suggested to you they don't have their waiting room bugged?" Dan asked casually, hands in his pockets, studying a mural close up. "Just asking, you know."

"Oh," Annja said.

"Mr. Toby will see you now," the receptionist said, preceding them down the hallway that led into the offices.

"Toby?" Dan whispered. "Is that a first name or a last name."

"It's probably his real first name. A lot of Brazilians just use one name. And they tend to like a lot of variety in their given names."

Toby was a pretty boy. Brazil had lots of those, Annja had noticed.

"It's such a pleasure to meet visitors from North America," he effused in English, seating himself behind his desk. He had dark, slick hair, a cream-colored suit over a mauve shirt and dusty-rose tie, and a ring in his right ear. "They don't often come to Manaus."

"I'd think you'd get a lot of ecotourists," Dan said dryly.

Toby laughed. "They don't seem to visit our offices. What may River of Dreams Trading Company do for you, Ms. Callendar, Mr. Stone?" On the spur of the moment they had given the receptionist fake names. Annja hoped she could keep them straight.

Dan's expression hardened ever so slightly.

"We're here primarily for pleasure," Annja said. "We couldn't resist visiting the famous Manaus Opera House."

"It's definitely a jewel in our crown," Toby said enthusiastically.

"But we have to admit to having an interest in certain Brazilian exports," Annja continued.

"Which ones would those be?"

"Brazil nuts."

Dan stared at her as if she'd just beamed down from the starship *Enterprise*. "As you probably know, we Americans—North Americans, sorry—are growing ever more conscious of our health. *Obsessed* might not be too strong a word."

"We Brazilians are the same," Toby said, smiling toothily. "It reflects our general vanity." He made a discreet gesture as if brushing perfectly manicured fingertips down his breastbone to acknowledge his own guilt.

"Nuts are growing in popularity back home, since they've acquired a reputation as a superfood, containing numerous valuable micronutrients. Brazil nuts are in considerable demand."

"Is that so?" Toby said.

"I know the nuts will only grow in certain areas, including the Amazon Basin," Annja said cheerfully. "I also know getting them out of their husks is very labor-intensive. If I understand correctly, in the wild, agoutis often chew through the tough outer shell, then bury the nuts they don't eat. Which serves to plant new trees."

"You seem most knowledgeable."

Annja made a self-deprecating gesture. "I've done a certain amount of homework."

"And what do you wish of us in this connection?"

"Well, I understand that Manaus is a major transshipment point for Brazil nuts. And it's my understanding that River of Dreams, as an import-export concern, is highly experienced in navigating the sometimes tangled Brazilian export regulations. Now, this is all still somewhat speculative, I have to admit, but my associate and I were hoping to discuss the prospects of going into business with your company."

She looked expectantly at Dan. He was sitting back in his chair with one leg crossed over the other, looking stunned. "Huh? Oh. Absolutely," he stammered.

"That sounds fantastic," Toby said. "At the moment, River of Dreams handles no cargoes of Brazil nuts. However, your suggestion certainly has merit. I will certainly have to consult with my superiors before we can possibly discuss details. I hope that's all right with you both?"

"Of course," Annja said.

"Oh, sure, sure," Dan said, catching a sidelong look from her.

"If you have business cards—" Toby said.

"Unfortunately we were both robbed in Belém," Annja said. "Among other things, we lost all our business cards."

Toby clucked in sympathy. "Oh, dear, that's terrible," he said. "There's so much crime in Brazil these days. It's a wonder anyone comes here."

"We did manage to keep our cell phones," Annja said. She tore a page from a notebook from a pocket of her shorts and scribbled, "Anne Callendar" with her actual number. She handed that to Toby.

They all rose. "I'm curious as to how you happened

to hear about River of Dreams Trading Company," Toby said.

"Oh, I overheard my father telling some of his cronies about a business associate who'd had dealings with you. A German, a dealer in medical electronics."

Toby raised his eyebrows. "Oh, that would be Herr Lindmüller. Reinhard Lindmüller."

"I'm terrible with names," Annja said.

Toby's expression turned sad. "I am afraid I have terrible news regarding Herr Lindmüller. He was killed this spring in a climbing accident in the United States. The horrible irony is, he had an overwhelming fear of heights."

Toby shook his sleek head. "Perhaps he was trying to learn to overcome his fears by confronting them directly. Irony, as I say."

"Agoutis?" Dan said as they walked down the corridor from the trading company offices.

"They're a kind of rodent," Annja said. "I read it on Wikipedia."

He shook his head and expelled an exasperated breath. "That was a waste of time."

"Remember what happened to the last person we asked flat out about Promessa," Annja said. "What would you have done? Just asked why a murdered woman in Belém had an invoice from here clutched in her hand?"

"Well, yeah," Dan said.

"What would you expect them to say? And what

would you say if they started asking us how we knew about that? Who would we be placing at the scene of the crime—an actual River of Dreams employee, or just ourselves?"

"You think they'd dare go to the cops?"

"Why not? First off, we're the ones who fled the scene of an apparent double murder and arson. Remember, the Brazilian authorities like to toss the occasional tourist into one of their horrible prisons just to show what's what. And you don't think in a country with such Byzantine regulations, a company like this one does business without having some friends in high places."

He walked a few steps with hands crammed in pockets and head thrust forward. Then he shook his head.

"Okay. You make good points. But what was the point to coming here, then?"

She shrugged. "This is our only lead. Or at least the only one Publico's seen fit to share with us—after we turned it up ourselves. At least we've—what?—done reconnaissance."

"And what have we learned?"

"If they know anything, they're going to be a tough nut to crack. What do you think?"

He shrugged. "Mr. Toby seemed pretty smooth. I have to admit he didn't strike me as the type to blurt out deep, dark secrets just because we happened to ask probing questions."

"At least we have a pretext for continuing communication with them," Annja said. "Much as I hate to admit I'm stumped, I'm about ready to ask Publico what exactly he has in mind."

They pushed through the tinted-glass doors onto the broad front steps descending to the street. As usual, the air seemed to push back. Even though the sun was setting, the temperature hadn't dropped since they'd entered the building. Nine hundred miles up the Amazon Basin from the sea, Manaus was even hotter and more humid than Belém. It also struck Annja as a lot harder edged.

Dan turned and looked appraisingly back at the four-story steel-and-glass office building that fronted the River of Dreams warehouses.

"We might not have to go so far as that just yet," he said. "Even though it looks pretty glossy up front here, security isn't too tight. I think we might just want to pay them a visit after hours."

"You are *not* talking about breaking in," Annja said.

He looked at her from under an impishly raised eyebrow. "What else?"

14

Sir Iain Moran nodded gravely. "The notion has its merits," he said in his rumbling baritone.

Standing by the rail before the entryway to the Manaus Opera House, Dan smirked. Annja frowned. "We're talking about breaking and entering here."

"You can't make an omelet without breaking eggs," Dan said.

"Dan has a pretty rough-and-ready approach," the billionaire singer and philanthropist said. Goran and Mladko stood discreetly apart from their boss and his conversation, but close. "It's what you might expect from a hardened activist. I do have to point out that the stakes are pretty high in this game, Annja."

"You don't have to tell me," she said. "People have been killed."

I've killed one, she thought. She hadn't mentioned

it in her own reports to Publico, by voice or e-mail—among other things, the last thing she wanted to do was leave an evidence trail for something like that. But she suspected Dan had informed his boss. She hoped he'd used strong encryption.

"Ah, and isn't that an indication that we're on the right track, then?"

Annja frowned and said nothing.

"You know," Publico said, "there's even a district of the city named Zumbi dos Palmares."

"After the legendary last leader of the Quilombo dos Palmares, I'm guessing," Annja said. "You think that's a clue?"

Publico shrugged his broad shoulders. "Why not?"

He was dressed in immaculate white-tie evening dress. His graying blond hair swept down to his shoulders. The hair, the black tailcoat and stiff white shirt combined with Publico's own physical presence to produce an almost overwhelming effect.

To reduce the risk of falling under his spell, Annja turned away to lean on the railing.

"He's a popular historic figure in Brazil," she said. "There are places and things named for Almirante Cochrane all over South America, too. That doesn't seem to indicate there's a secret conclave of unfairly pilloried Napoleonic-era British admirals dwelling away up in the wilds of the Amazon Basin."

Publico laughed loudly, attracting glances from the rest of the glittering crowd drifting toward the high, white-columned entrance with its arched top. Large banners announced an international film festival for the evening.

"A hit! A palpable hit, dear lady. Maybe I feel so strongly about this quest of ours that I tend to see things that aren't there. Still, there's the little fact that my poor friend Reinhard dealt with River of Dreams."

"I still don't know why you didn't see fit to share that little nugget of information with us," Annja said. She and Dan still wore the clothes they'd worn to the frustrating interview with Toby a couple of hours earlier. She was feeling increasingly dowdy as the night's audience filed into the extravagant, domed belle epoque theater. The attendees possessed not just beauty but the ease and grace of being raised to wealth, which would forever be denied an orphan girl such as her. Or maybe that was just her insecurities speaking.

"I didn't want to prejudice you," Publico said. "I thought it important for you to develop leads on your own."

"What are you holding back now so you won't prejudice us?" she asked.

"She's got a good point," Dan said.

Publico nodded. "To be sure. Believe me, I hold back nothing vital, either to our quest or to your own survival. I will tell you that you're on the right track—and that we need to know what can be learned from River of Dreams."

Annja clouded up. It was a totally unsatisfactory answer.

"Ahh," Publico said, his craggy face lighting. "My

lovely companions arrive. Annja, Dan—if you'll forgive me, it would be uncivilized of me to keep these ladies waiting."

He left embraced by two beautiful women, one blond and Nordic looking, one exotically African. Their own evening gowns put Annja in mind of the old phrase, "a lick and a promise." It was about what they seemed to consist of.

She turned a ferocious scowl on Dan. He shrugged. Then he waggled his eyebrows at her.

She laughed. "Come on," she said. "Let's go get something to eat. I'm starving."

"LOOK," DAN SAID on the walk back to the hotel. "I know you're reluctant about breaking into the River of Dreams warehouse. I won't lecture you about bourgeois sensibilities—"

"Good."

The traffic flowed around them like a river full of luminous fish. Annja walked along hugging herself as if chilled, although she could barely stand the heat. The smell of exhaust, ubiquitous at the center of any modern city, couldn't overpower the omnipresent scent of the rain forest, stronger here than in Belém. Maybe that was why Manaus felt off somehow to Annja. She had a sense that this was temporary, an aberration, like a vacuum fluctuation in physics. The city, and all those within it, seemed to exist in a bubble that could simply collapse at any minute.

Dan showed her a wolf grin as he continued. "I will

point out that Publico has reason to believe these people—the people of this lost city—are hoarding secrets
that could ease much misery and suffering on earth. Secrets that should be shared with all humankind. *Need*
to be shared with all humankind. Are you with me on
this?"

She frowned. Then she nodded. Face it, she said
told herself, this will not be the first time you've
stretched the letter of the law out of all recognizable
shape. It won't be the last. I've killed people, for God's
sake. Why balk at a little B&E?

"I guess so." She brushed a stray lock of hair from
her forehead and offered up a faint smile.

"Good woman," Dan said. "We'll make an activist
out of you yet."

"Maybe."

He crooked an arm. After another moment of hesitation, she wound her own through his.

DESPITE ENJOYING the arm-in-arm walk, she said a firm
goodbye once they reached their floor. She was a big
girl. She could take care of herself.

The truth was she had no clue what had really happened last night in Belém. Neither, she was sure, did
Dan. She liked him, even respected him, though she acknowledged he had thorns and hitches in his step.

She knew they, like the powerful currents of anger
that ran not too far beneath his flip, hip surface, grew
out of caring. He cared deeply about the world's
poor, about the planet itself. She also knew he had

not just seen but experienced horrible things in the Third World.

So maybe he was tied to Ogum, she thought as she went into the bathroom to get ready to shower. Even an easy walk through Manaus's busy nighttime streets had left her soaked in sweat. Maybe he has reason to be.

She'd like to get to know him better, she thought, not for the first time, as she stripped off her clothes. He was attractive in many ways beyond the purely physical. No. This was not a good time to think about that.

She turned on the water in the shower and adjusted it. We'll work it out, she thought, or we won't. The most important thing is the job. She stepped naked into the spray.

WEARING A FLUFFY TERRY ROBE, a towel wrapped around her hair, Annja came around the stepped glass-brick wall that separated the bathroom from the rest of the room. She picked up her notebook computer from the table by the window and carried it to the bed. She intended to review her e-mail, answer anything that demanded it. Then to relax she'd browse the newsgroups, then hoped to sleep soundly and not dream too much.

The fairly hideous tropical-flower-pattern bedspread was turned down. A green-foil-wrapped mint waited on the pillow. Perhaps most importantly, the air-conditioning was strong and steady.

As she approached the bed, the spread at the foot of it seemed to be moving. Ever so slightly.

She froze. The motion ceased. Did I imagine that? She hadn't exactly been sleeping much of late.

She saw it again. The smallest hint of motion.

Deliberately she stooped and set the computer on the bedside table. Then she whipped back the spread with a flourish.

Fangs extended like spears as a big black-and-grey snake struck at her face.

By reflex she turned her body counterclockwise. Her right hand moved with her compact and rapid turn, a result of hours practicing martial arts.

To her surprise, she caught the snake about eight inches behind the head. It thrashed in her hand, trying again to strike at her face. She jerked her head away, overbalanced, fell sideways on the bed.

She knew if she let go, she would die.

The snake fought furiously to get free. She recognized it as an *urutu*, a South American pit viper, like a rattlesnake minus the rattles. Its venom was a hell brew that would surge through her bloodstream causing her red blood cells to explode like tiny bombs, while secondary toxins destroyed her nervous system, causing irreparable damage and unendurable pain.

The creature's body was surprisingly solid and alarmingly strong. It must have been a good six feet in length. It felt as if she were trying to hang on to an out-of-control fire hose.

Somehow she kept her grip. She managed to get her other hand around the snake's body below her first. It turned and struck for her forearm. Her cheeks pulled her lips back from her teeth in a grimace of horrified expectation.

But the snake struck only air. It could not double back upon its own sinuous body far enough to sink fangs in her flesh.

She sighed. The snake waved its head angrily, but she knew that, unless she got careless, she had won.

"Okay," she said aloud, "now what do I do with you?"

She didn't want to kill the creature. For all she knew they were endangered. In any event, this one was no longer a threat, and her spirit rebelled against taking the life of anything that didn't threaten her.

She remembered seeing snake collectors dump their captives in bags. That seemed her best bet. Holding the snake gingerly away from her at the extent of her right arm, she groped behind her for a pillow with her left hand. Grabbing it by the closed end, she shook out the pillow.

Annja sat up. The snake had quit struggling and now moved its fat wedge of a head hypnotically from side to side. The poison sacs to either side of its head were swollen, immense. Had it buried those big fangs in her arm, the snake would have pumped enough venom into her to kill a bull.

With the little finger and ring finger of her right hand and her whole left hand she managed to get the pillowcase open. Holding it well away from her body, she took a deep breath and poured the snake inside.

She expected it to explode into wild action on finding itself trapped. Instead it subsided into fat, fleshy coils and, as far as she could tell, went promptly to sleep.

"Well, that was anticlimactic," she said, holding up the improvised bag. She reminded herself to stay aware. The animal couldn't bite its way out of the pillowcase, but if it happened to brush against her, it might still manage to bite her.

After a brief contemplation she gingerly and gently twisted the top, swaying the pillowcase from her upheld arm so that the snake's weight would rotate the pillowcase. The snake weighed more than she expected.

When she had the pillowcase wound well shut she stood, walked to the bathroom door and very cautiously knotted a loop and hung it over the knob. When she let go she held herself poised to dive away, in case being allowed to hang against the door woke the viper and gave it leverage somehow to strike at her. But the captive did nothing.

Annja went to the bedside telephone, picked up the receiver, punched a single button.

"Hello, front desk?" she said in Portuguese when the line was picked up. "I have a little problem."

15

Outside the rain poured down as if it had always been raining and never intended to stop. Evidently they didn't call this part of the world the rain forest for nothing.

Annja sat contentedly in the lobby of the Lord Manaus, tapping away at the notebook computer. The rushing sound of the morning downpour provided a backdrop more soothing to her than the generic Brazilian jazz oozing softly from the hotel speakers.

She was still amused by the follow-up to last night's encounter with the snake. The concierge's supercilious disbelief when she claimed to have found a poisonous snake in her room had almost been funny. He had come around when she described the distinctive patterns of one of Brazil's most feared snakes. Obviously he recognized the design.

She suspected close encounters with poisonous serpents wasn't rare in this city in the jungle. But she didn't think snakes, poisonous or not, were common visitors inside the Lord Manaus.

The first hotel maintenance man to show up at her door in his green coveralls had been cheerfully nonchalant, clearly not taking the white North American woman's babble about vipers all that seriously. Even the fact that Annja did her babbling in Portuguese did little to dent his obvious skepticism. Then Annja pulled open the pillowcase to show him what she'd found—in a closet, she said. He turned ashen and spoke into his walkie-talkie so rapidly Annja couldn't follow him. Then he had to sit down.

Eventually a pair of maintenance types showed up carrying a metal-looped snake-catching pole and a more substantial bag. The transfer was accomplished efficiently and with minimal fuss. Annja tipped the two snake handlers and when they had gone, tipped the first responder double. He was so badly shaken she felt sorry for him. Even if it was his own fault for not believing her.

The hotel night manager had turned up ten minutes later, all unctuous concern, to reassure himself that Annja was intact, especially unbitten, and uninclined to bring any unfortunate lawsuits. She also knew the manager *really* dreaded an account of her terrifying adventure turning up and catching a million hits on the Web.

She had ducked out of the hotel early for breakfast solo at a nearby café, then got back without getting rained on. Well, except for a little on the last sprint to the door, but that hadn't done her any harm.

She was glad to have had time to herself without either Dan or their eccentric boss on hand. She'd needed it. Especially with events moving so quickly. Even if she still felt, frustratingly, as if she and Dan were stumbling around in the dark looking for clues to the hidden city.

I guess that's why they call it hidden, she thought ruefully.

She had decided that morning to say nothing about the snake incident to either Dan or Sir Iain. It added nothing they hadn't already known. Sharing it could only add complications.

As for warning Dan a similar attempt might be made on his life…he already acted like an old scarred alley cat, with his head on a swivel whenever he walked out on the street. He struck Annja as being as functionally alert as he could be. Winding him tighter would only feed his paranoia—and propensity for anger.

"May we join you, Ms. Creed?"

It was a familiar, mellifluous male baritone, speaking beautifully accented English. Annja looked up into the pale amber eyes of Patrizinho. At his side, compact and radiantly lovely despite her conservative gray skirt, stood Xia. They both smiled as if Annja were a long-lost cousin.

"Sure," Annja said. She had to force her own smile. Inside she felt tight and very, very cold. "Feel free."

She closed her notebook computer with a certain relief as they seated themselves side by side on the sofa facing Annja's chair across a low coffee table. After the initial shock of the encounter, the chill within her turned quickly into quivery anticipation, like a hunting dog straining at the leash. Or what she imagined one would be like.

"What a pleasant surprise to see you both," she said.

"Likewise," Xia said. "What brings you to Manaus? And where's your very handsome friend?"

"To answer the second question first, either still in his room or getting breakfast."

"Ah," Xia said. Her eyes sparkled. "Too bad."

Annja felt her mouth tighten. Patrizinho laughed. He was dressed in sort of retro style, a faintly pink beige jacket over similarly colored slacks and a dark green collarless shirt. "Please forgive us. We Brazilians are terrible romantics," he said.

"I notice you say 'we,'" Annja replied.

"I'm one of the worst."

"As for your first question," Annja said, crossing her legs and feeling annoyed with herself for how much she wanted to like these two people, "our research continues."

"Here in Manaus?" Patrizinho asked. "A long way to go afield to look for *quilombos*. Am I mistaken, or were they not mainly a coastal phenomenon?"

"I thought so, too. But our employer asked us to look into documents available here, at the library and university." That was what she had determined she would do today. With luck it might even obviate the need to engage in any nocturnal burglary. "We have come across hints there might actually have been *quilombos* established even farther upriver after the fall of Palmares. And there is a neighborhood here named for Zumbi of the Palm Nation."

"There are lots of neighborhoods named for him," Xia said, "even down in the Pampas, where surely no *quilombos* ever were."

"Still," Patrizinho said, "how fascinating would it be if there were something in it all? A lost civilization!"

"Patrizinho likes to let his imagination roam free," Xia said. "Anyway, if a city really has been lost all this time, might that not be strictly accidental? Perhaps the citizens don't want to be found."

Has she taken my hook? Annja wondered, uncrossing her legs and trying to act casual. Or have I taken hers? Whatever the truth about this amiable and cover-model-gorgeous pair, she suspected it would be a mistake to underestimate them.

"What are you doing here?"

It was a rough challenge delivered by Dan's voice. Annja looked around to see him standing there frowning.

Xia smiled dazzlingly at him. "Conversing with your delightful associate, Annja, of course," she said.

"Sit down," Annja said sharply to her partner. Dan looked at her. He raised an eyebrow in momentary rebellion. Then he grinned and sat in the chair beside hers.

"If you mean what are we doing here in this rather charmless and remote city of Manaus," Patrizinho said, "we simply have business here."

"Do you deal with the River of Dreams Trading Company at all?" Annja asked as casually as she could.

Patrizinho glanced at Xia. "Sometimes," she said. "Our business naturally brings us to Amazonas State on a regular basis. You know, of course, there are no roads from here to the coast."

"I know most of what moves through the interior goes by air. Or by river, obviously, here in the Amazon Basin," Annja said.

Patrizinho nodded, smiling as if she'd just spoken a rare insight. "Manaus is the natural hub for the deep-Amazon trade. Especially since it's the farthest deep-draught oceangoing ships can travel up the river. That naturally draws us. River of Dreams is what we might term a middle-scale company. So yes, we deal with them on occasion."

"So what do you make of our Brasilia, Dan?" Xia asked.

His pale eyes narrowed. His brow furrowed. "Mostly I see oppression and environmental rape. Despite your socialist president, wild capitalism is destroying the rain forest for profit. No offense, of course."

"Of course not," Patrizinho murmured.

"You might wish to be cautious assigning blame," Xia said. "Yes, the rain forest is being destroyed at a tragic clip. But were you to look deeply into our politics, you might see that—while it brings increased profits to certain sectors, such as the soya growers, who grow rich selling their produce to your health-conscious fellow North Americans—the motive for the destruction is not primarily economic. The government subsidizes it out of a desire to exterminate the Indians by devastating their habitat. Like most Latin American governments, ours regards the indigenous people as little better than animals, who disgrace our great and advanced civilization by their stubborn backwardness. It is the great unacknowledged shame of South and Central America, this ongoing genocide against the natives."

For the first time Annja heard something other than cheerfulness in Xia's voice. She spoke with unconcealed bitterness.

Dan shrugged. "Isn't it fashionable for capitalists to blame the government for their crimes these days?"

"But don't you find," Patrizinho said lightly, "that the capitalists who commit the greatest crimes do so with the active cooperation of government?"

Dan scowled. Then he shrugged. He was clearly uncomfortable continuing this conversation, Annja saw. Otherwise she guessed a potentially vitriolic debate would have ensued.

"I admit I wouldn't mind seeing this whole city plowed under and returned to the rain forest," Dan said.

"And the people of the city?" Xia asked. "Would not many innocents suffer?"

"I've been all around the world. I've seen a lot of suffering. I've seen a lot of damage to the planet. And one thing I've learned—there are no innocents."

"You don't mean that," Annja said. But his only response was a hard smile.

"It may be easier to see such things from your vantage point than mine, my friend," said Patrizinho.

Xia stood up. Annja envied her grace.

"But we do not wish to intrude any longer," she said as Patrizinho rose, with scarcely less fluidity. "You have important matters to attend to. For that matter, so do we."

Annja rose, making polite farewell noises. Dan sat with arms tightly crossed over his chest, glaring at the Brazilian pair as if they were capitalist fat cats with dollar signs all over their suits.

When they left, Annja sat and pinned her partner with a look. "Why go all Mr. Surly with the ingenue Brazilian couple?"

He sneered. "I don't suppose it occurred to you there might be something a little bit *suspicious* about them turning up right here in Manaus at the same time we're here—not to mention how they chanced to be passing through our very hotel?"

"Of course it did. It also occurred to me my best chance of getting anything useful out of them was to play along, instead of growl at them and chase them off. Did it ever occur to *you* to give me credit for having any brains?"

He glared at her a moment. Slowly a smile struggled across his face. He uttered a bark of a laugh. "Eventually it'll sink in," he said, "I hope. I've found that every time I underestimate you I wind up nursing bruises in places I never knew I could get bruised."

It was the first time he had referred, however obliquely, to the events of their last night in Belém.

"So you suspect they know something?" he asked.

"Coincidences just seem to keep piling up, don't they? Wasn't it Sun Tzu who said, 'Once is chance, twice is happenstance, three times is enemy action'?" Annja asked.

"Actually," a deep voice said from over her shoulder in a Northern Irish accent, "it was Goldfinger, in the Ian Fleming novel. I love those books. I read them every year."

"Isn't that like the ultimate celebration of imperialism?" asked Dan, who was clearly still grumpy.

Publico laughed. "You'd be happier if you learned to separate politics from entertainment, Dan my boy."

"Do you?"

The rock star laughed even louder. Heads turned to stare. Such was the magnetism of the man that stares turned to smiles when they saw him. Annja thought it happened whether the people recognized him as a superstar performer or not. "Well, sometimes I do. That's what I recommend. That's my story and I'm sticking to it."

Dan eyed him dubiously. "Did you spend the night at the hotel?" he asked.

"No. A private residence. Allow an old man his fleeting pleasures, son."

"We just had an interesting encounter," Annja said. Publico tipped his head curiously to the side. Quickly she filled him in on the peculiar appearance of Xia and Patrizinho, seemingly out of nowhere. She didn't see any need to mention Dan's hostility toward them.

The more she thought about it the more she understood it. If they actually had guilty knowledge of Mafalda's death—and the attempts on Dan's and Annja's lives—they were nothing but smiling murderers. Or accomplices to murder.

It's looking more and more as if Sir Iain's right in his assessment of the Promessans, Annja thought. If what we suspect is true, they might be a whole culture of narcissistic sociopaths.

Publico stood by, nodding and looking thoughtful. "Doesn't it seem to you we might be stirring things up, then? It seems to me that might just indicate we're getting closer to our goal."

"What now?" Annja asked.

"There may be documents to be found in the city's libraries that hold clues," he said. He grinned. "If you're lucky, Annja, you might just be finding one that'll let you off having to do anything you might find distasteful."

THE UNIVERSITY HELD no joy for Annja. However, a helpful student aide suggested she check with the city library.

"Promessa," said Mr. Viguerie, the special-collections librarian for the city library, walking along between shelves stuffed with books with cracked and age-blackened backs as Annja trailed behind. He was a middle-aged, middle-height man with a balding head and a frizzy fringe of white hair that came down in sideburns and up over his upper lip in a mustache that made him resemble a walrus. His protuberant eyes were light brown, moist and gentle behind round-lensed spectacles. "So you're interested in our famous lost civilization."

Annja's heart jumped like a frog from a pot of boiling water. "You've heard of it?"

"It was a popular legend among slaves from about the eighteenth century onward. Especially those laboring on the rubber plantations before the abolition of slavery. Even afterward, I daresay—even after emancipation, working conditions weren't always ideal."

The look he cast back over his shoulder was weary and sad. "Nor are they always today. Especially farther up the river."

Big fans swooped lazily overhead like circling condors, making gentle swooshing sounds. Somewhere airconditioning labored, not quite valiantly enough to keep the heat and humidity at bay. Annja actually loved the musty smell of libraries and books. Even though she knew lots of the smells were the odors of decay, of mildew and molds and dust, she loved them all. The libraries in New Orleans had smelled much that way. Without a family and other distractions, she had amused herself growing up by reading. The memories didn't bubble to the surface very often. When they did they felt good, like warm slippers and a fuzzy robe on a cool autumn morning.

Whereas the other library staff she'd encountered had been dressed in a business-conservative manner and acted very solemn, the special-collections head wore a lurid tropical-print shirt pulsating with scarlet blossoms, emerald vines and blue-and-yellow macaws. He wore shorts and sandals that looked as if they might have been made out of old tires.

"You're saying it's a legend, then," she said. They conversed in Brazilian Portuguese. Viguerie spoke excellent English but did not insist on practicing on her.

He smiled. "Ah, but that doesn't mean the stories aren't true. Or don't contain a germ of truth. Perhaps."

Annja moved her lower lip slightly up over her upper. *Perhaps.* That was the one answer she really didn't want.

"Here we go." He pulled down a heavy volume with hands encased in thin gloves. "These aren't rubber, by the way," he said, as he carried the book toward a reading table. "I have a latex sensitivity. Ironic, in this former rubber capital, don't you think? Ahh, let's see."

He opened the volume on the table and leafed carefully through the yellowed pages. A gloved finger slid what seemed a few microns above the yellowed , mottled paper, tracing crabbed lines of handwriting in ink that had faded to purple and stained out into the paper, blurring each word slightly. This, too, was familiar to Annja. Actually, she was accustomed to much older and worse. This book, she judged by its shape and appearance and the fairly modern spellings of the words she glimpsed, was not much more than a century old.

"Here we've an account written by a superintendent at a rubber plantation farther up the river in 1905," Viguerie said. He looked at her. "You can read it, yes?"

She nodded and read aloud. "'Lobo tells me that

three more workers ran away from the north field barracks last night.'"

Viguerie nodded. "Lobo was an overseer on the plantation. Well named—a beast of a man. In his spare time he used to shoot Indians for sport."

She looked at him. "Seriously?"

"All too much so."

She read more—silently, now, as if afraid what she might say.

He tells me they are talking again of this damn *quilombo* of dreams, where a man can be free and live forever. I sent him out armed with good Mausers and with dogs, but the rascals had got clean away.

A glint from the dim light overhead in round lenses made the old librarian's eyes unreadable. "Slavery *officially* had ended," he said. "It found ways to persist. In various forms."

She continued to read.

Even Lobo will only go so far. Parties who hunt escaped laborers tend to vanish as if the cursed *selva* swallows them alive. The workers say the Maroons still look out for their own.

"So what have we here?" An aide fluttered up. He had short spiked dark hair and a gold ring in one ear. "We don't get many *norteamericanas* in here."

"This is Annja Creed," Viguerie said, drawing himself up with much dignity. "She is an important archaeologist from America of the North."

The aide drummed slender fingers on the tabletop and pursed his lips as he read the open book. "An archaeologist hunting for the fountain of youth?"

Annja felt her cheeks flush hot. "What do you mean?"

"You're reading up on Promessa, aren't you? The mythical city of dreams?"

"The *quilombo* of dreams, yes. I'm fascinated by the *quilombo* phenomenon—as well as the possibility fugitive ex-slaves from the coast, over 1400 kilometers away, might have penetrated this far and farther up the Amazon Basin."

"But the City of the Promise is all about wonders—walking through walls, shape-shifters, living forever. Not that I blame you. Who wouldn't want to live forever and keep their beauty? I do."

"What about the dangers the superintendent writes about?" Annja said. "This Lobo doesn't sound like the sort of man who'd be easily scared off by mere superstitious rumors."

"Oh, the threat was real enough," the aide said with a flip of his finely manicured fingers. "It is today. It's just the Indians. Miserable savages, with no regard for human life at all."

His words struck her like a slap. *I guess I'm not in Kansas anymore.* No matter how much time she spent abroad, trying to keep her mind open to other beliefs

and ways as befit an archaeologist, it also managed to
find ways to shock her. She thought she caught a hint
of sadness in Viguerie's old hound-dog eyes.

"What about that report from a few months ago, in
the spring?" Viguerie said. "About a whole company
of loggers with bulldozers and soldiers who disappeared in the space of an afternoon, farther up the Amazon."

The aide shrugged. "The Indians are clever devils.
They know their land. They ambushed them. Nothing
supernatural about it."

Annja stared at him. "Surely men with enormous
machines and modern weapons don't just vanish?"

Viguerie tipped his head to the side. "And yet they
did. More than a hundred, many of them foreign mercenaries. A certain prominent state official vanished
with them. It was all the talk of the cafés for weeks."

Annja shook her head.

"Sweetie, that kind of thing doesn't even make it to
the Internet," the aide said. "You'll never see it on TV
or read it in the papers. But it goes on all the time."

16

"Remember," Dan told her softly. "It's for the greater good."

Darkness was easier to come by at this stretch of the Manaus riverfront than Annja had anticipated. The River of Dreams Trading Company warehouse-office complex lay a few miles up the Rio Negros from the deepwater port facility. The port was a blaze of light, the big freighters and container ships hives of activity at all hours. Looking toward them it was hard to imagine they were almost a thousand miles from the sea.

Looking straight across the river, at the unbroken green wall of the forest, it wasn't hard to imagine at all.

Dan led her into a space between the River of Dreams building and a neighboring structure that looked abandoned. They wore dark clothing, jeans and long-sleeved shirts, despite the hammering tropical heat. They had rolled down their sleeves as they entered the alleyway to reduce the visibility factor of their white skin.

"It's a bit unusual," Dan admitted. "But I've seen a lot of tourists do this against the bugs. And anyway, it's lot less conspicuous than running around in black from head to toe like movie ninjas." It made sense to Annja, despite the discomfort.

Given the desperate poverty of much of Brazil and the rampant crime, Annja was surprised the import-export company didn't take more overt security measures. In a land where people who rode in nice cars tended to pay armed guards to ride with them, chain-link fencing, cameras and floodlights would seem the least precautions a waterfront business might take.

Yet there was none of that. Just a battered green-painted metal door in a yellow fan of light from an external fixture with a conical shade. Annja looked around but saw no sign of activity in the immediate area.

"Looks as if a lot of the businesses in this area are derelict," Dan said. "Things look much nicer from the street out front. All part of the national preoccupation with appearance, I guess."

The humidity was so heavy Annja almost felt as if she were swimming through the air as she followed Dan to the metal door. The air smelled of petrocarbons and water and decaying vegetation.

And there were those bugs Dan had mentioned. Big bugs, little bugs, crawling bugs, biting bugs, stinging bugs—flies and gnats and mosquitoes and God knew what else. Annja was no entomologist. She wasn't squeamish, nor phobic. But that was one problem with the jungle—way too many bugs. Getting way too familiar.

From the moment she had seen Manaus from the air, like some deep-relief concrete scab crusting in the midst of the green skin of jungle by the wide brown river, she'd felt a sense that it didn't belong. Its builders had pushed back the rain forest, wedged the city in there where it shouldn't be. For a time it had fallen; the forest came back. But now the Amazonas State politicians had decided for reasons of prestige that Manaus should live again.

But the jungle abided. It smoldered with resentment as with a thousand small fires. And it pushed back.

Annja knew in her bones the jungle would win someday. She did not want to be here when the struggle found its horrible conclusion. She felt as if great green walls were about to fall. On *her.* She shuddered.

"You can get through the door?" Annja asked as Dan stopped in front of it and studied it.

He gave her a wicked grin. "You never know what skills will come in handy for an anticorporate activist."

She still had misgivings about the ethics of what they were doing. But that argument had been lost already. Even with herself, apparently.

It was the practical situation that made her stomach churn and her skin crawl. "Could it possibly be this easy?"

"You'd be surprised." As he spoke he was doing something to the door.

Annja kept her head swiveling up and down the alley. She also forced herself to remember to look up periodically. She'd sneaked up on people before by exploiting the human tendency to look only horizontally.

"There," Dan said with satisfaction. He stepped back, pulling the door open. "After you, my lady."

With tight lips and compressed brow Annja moved past him. She stuck her head around the frame in a three-second look. Then she slipped inside.

The warehouse was a cavern whose gloom seemed more accentuated than diminished by widely spaced yellow lights shining from the high ceiling. Annja stepped reflexively to the left of the door.

Dan slipped in, pulling the door quietly shut behind himself and stepping to the right. "Here you've been acting all innocent, where clearly you've done this kind of thing before," he said.

"Just clearing the fatal funnel," she said. "I do know anybody lingering in an open doorway makes an ideal target of herself."

He raised a brow and nodded appreciatively. "I'll look for an office. Why don't you scout around?"

"So why not just break into the front office, if that's what you were looking for?"

"They had better security on the pretty, glossy stuff out front."

She shrugged in vague concurrence. They went by separate paths.

It was hot and close in the warehouse, almost stifling, although Annja could feel as much as hear the hum of some machine attempting with indifferent success to cool and presumably dry the air. Metal catwalks ran around the edge of the warehouse, which was built of grayish brick. Others crossed overhead, to what purpose Annja couldn't tell. Wooden crates rose in tall stacks in some parts of the warehouse. In others, high metal shelves held boxes of various sizes. It all looked pretty straightforward.

She made a circuit of the perimeter. She was mostly interested in getting her bearings. She wasn't really sure what Dan—or Publico—expected to achieve. Doors opened into little side chambers off the main room—workshops, smaller storage areas where she guessed office supplies were kept, as opposed to stock awaiting shipment up or down the great river complex. She saw Dan nod with satisfaction as a door into a windowed office area gave way before his efforts. He stepped inside.

She saw no sign of any kind of security measures. No cameras were in evidence. But she knew that with modern technology a camera could be invisibly small.

But the whole feel of the place suggested a bygone era. Not the high, wide, long gone days of the rubber boom, but some time before omnipresent surveillance cameras and spy bugs. The fifties perhaps—at least the seventies. Some time before she'd lived, when things were simpler.

She frowned. *Stay sharp,* she told herself sternly.

But it was hard to focus without knowing what she was supposed to be focusing on. She wondered if her employer and partner were having a fit of male chauvinism, not trusting a mere woman with the real story. But why bring me in at all, if that were the case?

She found some wood crates with some paperwork attached. She studied the bills of lading. The crates, it appeared, contained medical supplies—equipment and drugs, consigned for someplace called Feliz Lusitânia. They came mostly through Belém, originating primarily from South America and Europe.

There seemed to be a lot of them. She wondered what Feliz Lusitânia might be. The literal translation was "happy Portugal."

A tiny scuffle of sound, such as a furtive small animal might make, was all the warning she had.

She spun. A dark figure was flying at her, down from a ten-foot stack of crates at her back. She raised her hands, grabbed. Using the power of moving from the hips, turning about the centerline while keeping arms and upper body essentially locked, she guided the person jumping at her past and into the stack of crates bound for Feliz Lusitânia.

At the last instant she shifted, pulled slightly down. She might have slammed her attacker into the crates headfirst, but an intrinsic sense of mercy and justice struck her. *I'm the intruder here.*

Upside down, the attacker still hit hard enough to explode all the air out in a whuff clearly audible above the thump of impact and rending of shattering wood.

Blue-and-white cardboard cartons labeled in some Slavic language Annja couldn't recognize, far less read, spilled around as the person came to rest.

She seemed unconscious, at the least stunned. She was a small black woman with dreadlocks, wearing a loose blouse, ragged shorts and sandals. Backing away down the aisle between stacks of crates so that the woman couldn't instantly spring on her again once she recovered, Annja looked around.

Two men approached from different directions, hemming her in. One was taller than her, rangy and looked Latino but had long dreadlocks shadowing his face. The other, she saw, turning her head swiftly left and right and then back, was blond and sturdy, a bit shorter than her. Both were dressed in rough work-man-style clothing.

I told Dan it couldn't be this easy, she thought. Somehow being right didn't make her feel much better.

"Back off," she told them in Portuguese. "I was just leaving." It sounded lame—was lame—but she wanted to try to defuse the situation short of violence.

"Yes," the Latin-looking guy said. "Yes, you were."

As he spoke the blond man rushed her from behind. It was what she had expected—standard tactical sandwich.

A pure back kick is one of the strongest blows a human body can deliver. A woman as fit and with such long strong legs as Annja Creed could crush a man's rib cage, especially if he added energy to the impact by rushing her, the way the blond man was. But she wasn't going there. Not yet.

The solid rubber heel of her walking shoes slammed his sternum like the kick of a horse. His forward progress wasn't just arrested—the blow lifted him off his feet and threw him flat on his back.

The blond guy landed with a whump on the stained concrete behind her. Annja turned her attention to her taller attacker. He swung a roundhouse blow toward her face—and then when she raised her guard, dropped lithely to one arm and swept her legs out from under her with one long leg.

Her fall was awkward. She managed to get an arm down to act as a shock absorber, then took the brunt of the landing on her left butt cheek, not her tailbone or elbow or something else breakable. The pain still shot up the side of her body and she knew she'd have a fabulous bruise. She also knew she'd be lucky if she got out of this warehouse suffering no worse.

She arched her back, pressed the backs of her shoulders into the concrete, jackknifed forward and upward. The motion snapped her back upright.

The dreadlocked man was already swinging his right leg for her head. With no time to reverse her forward momentum to try to dodge the strike, she stepped forward, forearms vertical, to block the kick where it was weak, at his thigh near the fulcrum, rather than at the end, his foot, where momentum was greatest. She used a powerful downward stroke of the bottom of her forearm at the juncture of his long legs. He gasped and doubled over, staggering backward as every bit of air voided itself from his lungs in an instant.

A heavy weight landed hard on Annja's back. Powerful legs locked around her waist. Already turning clockwise, Annja drove with her legs to slam her assailant into the stack of crates at her right.

Something about the exhalation driven out of the lungs of the person riding her back sounded feminine. Annja realized her initial assailant had quickly recovered from getting thrown through a crate and had gone straight back on the attack. The Promessans were tough, she had to admit.

Python-like the woman's arms sought to encircle her throat. Annja tucked her chin into the crook of her attacker's right arm to foil that. She kept turning until her back was directly toward the crate and the attacker still trapped between. She slammed her head back. Teeth gouged her scalp. The back of the woman's head was smashed into the crate with a brutal crack. Her whole body slackened. Annja's right hand tangled in her long hair and Annja snapped her body forward.

The Promessan woman flew over her right shoulder. As she did Annja's left hand caught her right wrist, still at Annja's own throat. She straightened the arm as she pulled up on her attacker's hair to keep her from splashing her brains out the cracked back of her skull on the concrete. She was still unwilling to kill under such morally ambiguous circumstances.

She knew at least one more of her previous attackers would soon recover and be right back on her. And who knew how many others were closing in? She felt no obligation not to hurt her attackers.

Annja knew she could snap the woman's locked-out elbow with just a few pounds of pressure. Instead she grabbed the captive arm above the elbow and, putting her shin against the woman's upper arm, dislocated the shoulder with a quick hip twist. It was a painful and incapacitating injury—but far less likely to do permanent damage than actually breaking a joint.

She felt as much as heard a charge from the same direction the woman had come from. Side skipping to throw off her new attacker's targeting solution, Annja snapped her head around. Her blond opponent was rushing with arms outstretched and face twisted in fury.

Evidently he didn't learn too fast—he was wide open for a power shot like the one that had put him down moments before. She rolled her hip over so that the kick was a straight heel shot backward. It was a trick she had learned from her tae kwon do buddies, and it made potent use of Chinese internal martial-arts principles of using joints in their most natural alignment, while violating the internal principle of connectivity by twisting her torso. Annja was into results, not theoretical purity—

And results she got in trumps. Her heel struck the angry blond man midway between belt buckle and crotch. As Annja danced aside, his legs shot backward out from under him. Meanwhile the upper half of him was slammed against the floor as if a giant hand had grabbed him around the legs and swung him into it. His chin hit the concrete with a loud crack.

His head lolled to the side. He moaned. As Annja turned back to where she suspected the *capoeirista* was about to attack her again she felt pretty sure he was down for the fight. He had almost certainly broken his lower jaw. She might have cracked his pelvis, as well. That would mean no matter how determined or adrenalized he might be, he could not stand. It would be mechanically impossible.

That was good. The dreadlocked man, clad in an olive-drab T-shirt and baggy khaki pants belted with a length of rope, was indeed back on his feet and approaching her in a sort of forward-leaning crouch. He did what she recognized as the standard *capoeira* dance, stepping forward and back, with wide swings of arms and hips. It was clearly intended to distract or even hypnotize an opponent, while keeping the *capoeirista*'s body in motion.

Her counter was to stand with weight on her back foot and arms raised, hands relaxed, not clenched into fists. When it came to fighting, anyway, the *capoeirista* was clearly a better dancer than she. She'd already had success letting him attack first, however inadvertently, and counterattacking. Now she figured on letting him commit and using her catlike reflexes to parry or evade and then slam him again before he could recover.

Because of his constant, smiling motion, side-to-side, back and forth, she forced her eyes to stay in soft focus, rather than focusing directly on her foe. It saved her life.

High and to her left, motion caught the very corner of her peripheral vision.

The distinctive motion of an arm raising a weapon to fire.

17

Annja threw herself flat on her back, legs drawn up, ready to kick with powerful leverage if her opponent leaped for her.

A green spear of light cracked through the space Annja had occupied a heartbeat before. Planks of a crate splintered explosively as moisture in the wood flashed instantly into steam. A feather of greenish smoke wisped upward. Annja's nostrils filled with the smell of charred wood. She saw no flame.

Her opponent seemed more disoriented by the blast than she was. Guessing he was seeing nothing but great big magenta shards of afterimage, she launched herself into a forward roll, body tucked in a tight ball to keep low out of the laser's field of fire—she hoped. As she rolled over the top she whipped out her right leg into an ax kick that smashed her heel into the face of the dreadlocked man.

The impact snapped his head back and drove his body down. Before he could step back—or fall—and take the weight off his feet, Annja rolled on her right side and snapped a brutal shin kick against the inside of her opponent's right knee. The leg buckled with a loud snap. The man uttered a loud groan and collapsed, grabbing for the shattered knee in agony.

A shadow fell across Annja. Some instinct made her roll to her right, to slam against the crate on that side of the narrow aisle. As she did another green beam stabbed down with a crack. Concrete exploded away, stinging her calf through the jeans she wore.

Her own eyes dazzled with pink afterimage lines, ears temporarily deafened by the noise, head full of the stink of ozone. Annja knew her assailant was standing right over her. In another second he or she would lean forward, correct aim and blast her apart with the energy gun.

She formed her right hand as if grasping a hilt. Obedient to her will, the sword appeared to fill it.

She jumped to her feet. Her enemy stood on a single crate. Taking the sword in both hands, Annja swung blindly right to left at the level of her shoulders.

The sword's blade bit deep into the wood of a crate on her left. But not before passing, with the slightest of hesitations, through the lower legs of the laser wielder.

She heard a thump as he fell backward onto the

crate. With a scream half of fear and half of fury she wrenched the sword free.

Her vision cleared. To her astonishment she saw the person whose legs she'd just slashed, a young man whose face was probably not usually this paper-pale beneath long brown hair and a backward baseball cap. He was levering himself up to a half-sitting position with one hand so he could point his matte-silver hand weapon at her with the other. Reversing her grip on the sword, she stabbed forward and down with frenzied speed. The blade punched through his sternum to split the heart beneath. He sagged. The laser fell from lifeless fingers to the top of the crate.

Rather than try to wrench her sword free from the embrace of his rib cage, she released it. It vanished. She grabbed the pistol.

Another beam ripped the top of the crate.

Two loud cracks echoed through the warehouse. These differed from the thunderclap sounds of ionized air rushing back into the temporary vacuum created by the beam's incredible heat. They were deeper, louder. Handgun shots.

Annja looked up to see the figure who had shot at her from the catwalk slump down to the perforated metal walkway.

Her first thought was amazement that Dan had risked packing a firearm. The second was that she was lucky he had. Even a magic sword was not the ideal weapon to bring to a gunfight. Especially when the guns were wonder weapons that apparently shot energy beams instead of bullets.

"Remember Mafalda!" she heard him call from somewhere away to her left. She nodded, as if he could see her. Maybe mercy was misplaced with these people, she thought.

Moving bent over down the line of crates toward the warehouse's side door, Annja reminded herself she had no way of knowing if any of these people were actually involved in the shopkeeper's death. But she could afford to hold back no longer.

Gunshots cracked, then two more of the differently pitched thunderclaps she had learned to associate with the beam weapons. She reached the aisle's end. The doorway waited invitingly, barely twenty feet away, although out of her direct field of vision.

It might as well have been a thousand feet away if an energy gunner covered it. She had no illusions of being able to move faster than light. Nor was she going to be able to read the intent of a shooter half a room away.

Still bent over, she chanced a three-second look right. She saw nothing. Lowering herself to a squat, in case she'd been spotted the first time and a shooter had sights lined up at the level her head had last appeared, she peered the other way.

Sixty feet away Dan stood by a wall. A slight woman with long black hair crouched on the catwalk above him, holding an energy pistol in both hands with the barrel pointed toward the ceiling. The woman kept leaning cautiously over the rail, evidently reluctant to expose herself to the unseen intruder's fire.

Peering intently upward as if he could see through the catwalk, Dan didn't notice Annja. Instead he leaned out and triggered his semiautomatic handgun blindly.

Annja guessed he hoped to make his unseen antagonist flinch back long enough for him to break for the cover of the crates, or even to the door. It backfired dangerously. Despite the muzzle-blasts going off almost under her feet, the Promessan woman never flinched. Instead, learning exactly where her opponent was, she vaulted lithely over the rail and dropped to the concrete floor with apparent unconcern for injury. Her hair waved above her head like a black banner. She twisted in air like a cat. With a recoil-free weapon she could shoot as soon as she saw Dan, before she even landed—

Annja leaned out with her left hand bracing her right and fired as soon as she got a sight alignment on the woman's khaki-clad back.

It was a strange experience. Other than a click of the trigger breaking—felt rather than heard and almost certainly engineered so a shooter would know when the weapon fired—there was no reaction. Then a green line of light, dazzling in the gloom, appeared between the muzzle and a point between the woman's shoulder blades.

Steam exploded from her back. She arched convulsively backward, fell hard on her back, thrashing. Dan snapped his weapon down and pumped three shots into her as she writhed. She went still.

"I'll cover you," Annja called. "Go!"

He sprinted to the door, yanked it open. Stepping out

into the spill of yellow light from the lamp above the door, he pivoted, dropped to a knee to aim back into the warehouse from the cover of the door frame.

There was no response, either shouts or shots. Annja waited a beat, then darted straight for the exit. Her cheeks went taut with anticipation of a lethal light blast between her shoulders.

But she also made the door without drawing any reaction from within the warehouse. The security response team was either all out of action or hunkered down.

She did not slow down. She turned right to run toward the waterfront. The upstream docks were dark. Seemingly derelict warehouses lay that way.

She glanced back over her shoulder. Dan was still crouched in the doorway, handgun leveled, looking at her oddly. "Come on," she shouted to him, scarcely slowing down. "Follow me!"

After a moment, during which Annja resolved to let Dan make his own escape if he failed to follow, he did. She reached the corner of the next building and ducked into the enfolding shadow of a loading bay. Suddenly winded, by the fight more than the brief flight, brisk as it had been, she bent over, braced her palms on her thighs and tried to catch her breath.

Dan caught up. "Another dry run," Annja panted. She knew trying to breathe hunched over and tensed up like this was self-defeating, but it took her a moment to tame her body's oxygen panic and force herself to stand erect. "Lives lost—for nothing."

"Not so," Dan said. He held up something small and dark. The lights of the docks downstream shone through it vaguely blue.

"Thumb drive," he said with a grin.

"FASCINATING," Sir Iain Moran said. He turned the captured energy weapon over and over in his hands. They were big hands, as Annja would expect—he sometimes played guitar or keyboard with the band, although he primarily served as vocalist. But they were more square and powerful looking than she'd expect from a billionaire musician, scarred and callused in ways that wouldn't be accounted for by hours of practicing on hard steel strings. She wondered what he'd done to earn such hands.

The three were gathered in his top-floor suite in the Lord Manaus. It had the same somewhat raffishly gaudy color scheme as Annja's more modest room. His Croat bodyguards were nowhere in evidence. Dan sat on a sofa tapping industriously on the keyboard of a notebook computer opened on a coffee table in front of him. The thumb drive full of data from the warehouse computer was stuck in a USB port.

The weapon Annja had taken from the young man she had killed was utterly unprepossessing. She expected an energy weapon to be futuristic looking. Instead it looked like a handgun, very compact and solid in its lines. Its finish looked like the brushed-stainless-steel revolvers she had seen. But instead of having a slide that reciprocated to eject an empty casing and chamber a fresh round, it seemed made all of one piece. And instead of a hole in the end it had what appeared to be a glass lens, about half an inch wide.

Publico tossed it on the bed.

Annja raised an eyebrow. "That's it? I bring you back a genuine ray gun, and you toss it on the bed?" She had initially assumed it was a laser. On reflection she decided she had no grounds to assume even that. It was an energy gun that appeared to involve a beam of emerald-colored coherent light. But the laser might be a low-powered sighting mechanism for all she knew.

"It's a pretty toy, I grant," he said. "And a lethal one, to be sure."

"But—doesn't that prove everything? The existence of some wildly technologically advanced civilization— somewhere, anyway, and most likely up the Amazon where you thought it was all the time."

"It hints. Not proves."

"But—"

"It's not that big an advance over what exists now," he said. "Indeed it may not be an advance at all. You'll have to trust me on this, Annja. I have certain contacts. Along with which goes access to certain information not precisely widely known."

"But I thought lasers still needed these huge, un- wieldy energy supplies."

He just smiled a craggy, knowing smile. Annja frowned, genuinely puzzled.

"If somebody's got handheld energy weapons

now," she said, "why haven't we seen them in action on the news?"

Publico shrugged. "What kind of advantage did they give our putative Promessans? Dan brought a person armed with one down with a common handgun. You yourself won this one away from an enemy despite being unarmed."

Annja brushed a hand back through her hair to distract the older man's attention from her face. Evidently the crates had hidden her use of the sword from her partner. Or perhaps he'd been distracted by staying alive. And what he had seen that night at the *toque*—well, he must have decided his memories of that night, if he even had any, were not to be trusted.

"Think about it," Dan said from the computer. "What good would ray guns do against enemies who use ambush tactics, like rocket-propelled grenades?"

"I just have a hard time believing the government would cover something like that up," Annja said. "It smacks of conspiracy theory."

Dan snorted. More diplomatically, Publico smiled. "What d'you think it means when they classify something top secret, then, lass? What's that but a cover-up?"

She sighed and waved a hand. "All right."

Dan slapped his thigh. "Yes!" he exclaimed. "Got it."

Publico and Annja looked at him. "Broke the encryption." He shrugged and smiled self-deprecatingly. "Don't give me too much credit—it's really all down to the software on this box."

Frowning slightly, Annja looked from him to Publico. The older man shrugged.

His mouth twisted in an ironic smile. It struck Annja she had often seen the same expression on Dan's younger, less weathered face. She wondered if the young man had copied it from the older. She knew Dan idolized his boss.

Or maybe they're just two of a kind, she thought.

"In the course of my humanitarian work," Sir Iain said, "my aims have at times coincided with those of certain—let's say, powerful entities. To help me do this work, these allies—temporary, I need hardly add— have seen fit to share with me certain tools not available to the public at large."

Her eyebrows rose. "No Such Agency is sharing its decryption tools with you?"

"Now, lass, I never said NSA," he said.

"You wouldn't," she said. "I thought you got to be a billionaire by being an antiauthoritarian rebel."

"Annja my love," he said, "nobody gets to be a billionaire by being a rebel. Never by its lonely self. Indeed, I didn't make most of my money through music at all. Rather it's the outcome of ethical, and judicious, investing."

"When you've got as much loot as Sir Iain," Dan said, "you're a powerful entity all by yourself. But don't worry. He's still a rebel. Just a rebel who fooled the straights into letting him get power."

"Now, don't go exaggerating my influence, Dan my lad," Publico said. "A billion doesn't go near as far as once she did. So—"

He walked over to the table rubbing those big, well-used hands. "Now, what have you to show us today?"

Dan turned the computer so its wide-screen monitor faced Publico and Annja. "The bad news is, it's in Portuguese. I think."

"And the good news is—" Sir Iain turned and performed a courtly mock-bow and hand flourish in Annja's direction.

"I guess this is where I earn my plane fare," she said. She knelt on the floor by the table.

"You want a chair, lass?" Sir Iain rumbled.

"I'm fine." She waved distractedly. Dan had opened what looked from its formatting like an e-mail.

"It talks about a place called Feliz Lusitânia," she said. "Somebody injured there, badly. Could be dying. They seem to think it's important to get to him before he says something dangerous."

"They're cryptic even in their encrypted communications?" Dan asked.

"Not really. Or not necessarily. It's like a lot of conversations—sometimes you get what look like gaps to an outsider, but they're really things that both parties know and so go without saying."

She looked up at her employer. "I saw crates of medical supplies consigned to Feliz Lusitânia in the warehouse."

Publico, leaning attentively forward, reared back at the words. His high cliff of forehead rumpled in concern. "I know that name," he said.

"What is it?" Dan asked. "Some kind of theme park for ecotourists?"

"Only as envisioned by Hieronymus Bosch, my lad," Publico said. "It's a gold camp. Or put another way, a blight on the face of the Earth. Or put yet a third, a wee taste of Hell on Earth."

"You know about it?" Annja asked.

The leonine head nodded heavily, as if weighted with sorrow and world-weariness. "Aye. Too well. The world as a whole does not. There are interests far more powerful than I who prefer it that way."

He put a hand each on Annja's and Dan's shoulders. "But there you must go, if you are willing. You must find this injured person, aid them if you can. But you must find out what he or she knows."

"I'm in," Dan said promptly.

"I didn't come this far to back out now," Annja said, a little more emphatically than she intended. She wondered if she herself had some kind of secret agenda—secret from herself, as well.

"What about you, Publico?" Dan asked. Annja noticed that when he called his employer "Sir Iain" it was always with a slight edge of irony. When he used the name "Publico" he sounded almost worshipful.

Moran shook his head. "I'll see travel arrangements made for you, of course," he said. "You must go by air—time presses, and a riverboat moves too slowly. As for me, my responsibilities, you know, are wide, as well as vast. I'm called overseas on business that cannot wait. Even for such as this."

BUSINESS REPLY MAIL
FIRST-CLASS MAIL   PERMIT NO. 717-003   BUFFALO, NY

POSTAGE WILL BE PAID BY ADDRESSEE

GOLD EAGLE READER SERVICE
3010 WALDEN AVE
PO BOX 1867
BUFFALO NY 14240-9952

Get FREE BOOKS and a FREE GIFT when you play the...

LAS VEGAS

GAME

Just scratch off
the gold box with a coin.
Then check below to see
the gifts you get!

YES! I have scratched off the gold box. Please send me my **2 FREE BOOKS** and **gift for which I qualify.** I understand that I am under no obligation to purchase any books as explained on the back of this card.

▼ DETACH AND MAIL CARD TODAY! ▼

366 ADL EF6L

166 ADL EF5A
(GE-LV-07)

FIRST NAME

LAST NAME

ADDRESS

APT.#

CITY

STATE/PROV.

ZIP/POSTAL CODE

7	7	7	Worth TWO FREE BOOKS plus a BONUS Mystery Gift!
🍒	🍒	🍒	Worth TWO FREE BOOKS!
🔔	🔔	♣	TRY AGAIN!

Offer limited to one per household and not valid to current Gold Eagle® subscribers. All orders subject to approval. Please allow 4 to 6 weeks for delivery.

He patted their shoulders. "But I know whatever must be done, the two of you are right to do it. None better in all the world."

18

"Look out there!" Dan shouted.

He had to yell to make himself heard over the whine of the turbines and chop of the rotor blades. The vibration of the machine made itself known both audibly and in alarmingly tactile ways. It felt as if it were in the process of shaking itself to pieces a thousand feet above the verge where river met rain forest.

Dan sat strapped in a seat at the cabin rear. Annja sat in the open port-side door of the helicopter for whatever cooling effect the humid, heavy, stinking breeze of their passage could bring.

For hours she had watched the green of the triple-canopy forest, all but unbroken for mile after mile. The airfield where the de Havilland Canada Twin Otter had deposited them had seemingly been scraped from the forest in the middle of nowhere, with nothing in evidence to justify its existence but a little stream rippling along one side, past some warped plank buildings that constituted whatever facilities the place possessed. Annja and Dan had not entered them. They had been shepherded immediately from the twin-engine passenger plane to the olive-drab helicopter waiting with rotors lazily turning on a single square of warped and melting asphalt twenty yards wide. Without ceremony, or even a word spoken, it had risen into the hot, hard sky and flown away to the west northwest, following the wide brown undulation of the river.

Inside, the chopper stank of grease, of sweat and fear, of lubricant spilled and burned, of old gunsmoke, of hot metal and mildew and dust. The air was so thick with smell and humidity that breathing it was like trying to inhale through a linen cloth. Easier breathing was worth risking sitting in the door that lay open to emptiness, as far as Annja was concerned. She didn't know a lot about helicopters, but she suspected from the start this one was a UH-1, the famed Huey. Of Vietnam War vintage.

If it was a person, it might have kids old enough to vote, she thought grimly.

The rain forest flowing below was almost hypnotic. It was all but monochromatic, the jungle, but its green had a million shades, if you stared at it long enough. It could absorb you, draw you back into nature, to your constituent raw materials....

Dan's cry had broken Annja's reverie. Maybe that was a good thing. He was leaning to his right in his seat and pointing forward. Two muscular black men in

green and tan sat like sphinxes flanking the hatchway
to the cockpit, one holding a long black M-16 muzzle
up between his knees, the other a stainless-steel-and-
black shotgun. They had nodded in polite, if grim, acknowledgment when the two North Americans came
aboard. Then they had simply refused, after the fashion of stone statues, to respond to any conversational
overtures, in English or Portuguese or Dan's halting but
serviceable Spanish.

Annja wondered if they were there to keep the pas-
sengers from rushing the cockpit and hijacking the ancient helicopter.

She rolled back toward the cabin's center. She
wasn't prone to fear of heights, but somehow moving
away from the open door and that next long step made
her stomach roll and the skin between her shoulders
creep. Trying not to bump into one of the long-gun
guards, she came to a three-point stance and peered out
the front windscreen.

It wasn't that easy. She suspected the windscreen
hadn't been all that clean to begin with. And after fifty
or a hundred miles of Amazon Basin bugs—*serious*
buggage—it was like trying to peer through green jam
smeared on the walls of a jar. Between that and the
glare of the setting sun, a little off their bow, she wondered how the pilots saw to navigate.

After a moment she made something out—a wide
yellow gouge, not just from the jungle's green hide, but
from one side of the river itself. For a moment Annja
wondered if some giant meteor had struck recently,

blasting a crater a mile or more in extent. But no, that was ridiculous; it would have knocked down trees for many more miles all around—not to mention been all over the news for weeks.

Away off on the far end of the gouge she made out big yellow machines gouging at the earth like vast metal insects. Closer by were oblongs that looked like cargo containers, ranked and stacked in thousands. Here and there were clumped wooden buildings and even corrugated Quonset-style structures inside fences. A high fence seemed to run around the entire perimeter of the gaping yellow wound, as if somehow to contain its infection.

The stink of the place rose up like an invisible wall to smack them. The jungle always stank of tepid water and tannin and green growth and whatever had walked or crawled upon the earth, flown above it, clambered through the trees or delved below and died down there and began rotting away.

But this was different—stronger, harsher and far more revolting. It was the reek of raw human sewage by the liquid ton. It was mixed with a choking smell of burning diesel fuel. Annja realized it didn't just come from the earth-scraping machines ceaselessly at work on the camp's far side. Dozens of pillars of black smoke winding into the sky from seemingly random locations suddenly brought to mind the none-too-fond reminiscences of Vietnam vets she had known, of the most odious and onerous duty of the whole misbegotten war—shit-burning detail.

The smell of filth, burned and raw, was not the most

horrific thing to assail her senses. Far from it. She thought she might have to shave off her long hair and burn her clothes and shower for an hour to rid herself of the stench.

But she might never rid herself of the nightmares brought on by what she saw.

First was the cage. A huge open box out in the sluggish river, south of the discoloration. Annja's mind at first made no sense of it. Or refused to, until she could no longer deny to herself that it was filled with a score or more people, emaciated men and women dressed in rags the color of the river mud, bent over doing something in the knee-deep water.

"What is going on here?" she asked the M-16 guard. He did not speak or meet her eyes.

She looked back through the hatch into the cockpit, out through the stained windscreen. Just outside the perimeter fence she saw a line of X's. Annja frowned, puzzled. As the helicopter got closer she realized they must be steel I-beams crossed with ends buried in the yellow earth. On each of them hung a twisted, wizened shape.

"I can't be seeing this." Annja choked, clamped her mouth on a sour surge of vomit.

"Sure, you can," Dan said in a dreamlike voice. "It's what the world's really like. Not our white-bread existence back home."

The guards took up station in the open doors.

The helicopter swept over the perimeter wire. Annja could clearly see the razor-tape spirals that topped it. As they passed one open area Annja gasped at the sight of a dozen or more raggedly dressed men kicking a figure lying on its side in a fetal curl. Others struck at the victim with long rods of wood or possibly lengths of metal pipe.

Some distance away to starboard a group of six or seven men in camouflage battle dress patrolled a winding alley between shanties and containers with long guns in their hands. Most of their faces were pale beneath boonie hats. Beyond them, as the chopper clattered heedlessly toward the center of the great compound, two groups of men in different-colored camouflage shot at each other across a patch of water. The water's surface showed a rainbow sheen of oil to the morning sun. A body lay in the midst of it, a person facedown, wearing a blue shirt and shorts and not moving. On the far side a pair of men in gray-and-black urban-looking camo dragged a prostrate comrade by the collar to the dubious shelter of stacked plastic drums, some blue, some yellow.

The guard in the door by Annja put his M-16 to his shoulder and fired down into the camp. If the noise of the helicopter's slow suicide was loud, the reports of the burst were freakish, more like being swatted in the sides of the head with metal paddles than sounds.

"Yow!" Dan yelped. He clapped hands over his ears and fell sideways out of his seat.

Wide-eyed Annja stared up at the guard. A shiny brass spent case shaped like a little bottle rolled against her left shoe.

"Aimed at us," the guard explained in Portuguese in

a bass rumble that was audible beneath rather than above the helicopter's general cacophony.

Hanging on to the seat, Dan had picked himself halfway off the floor. "What'd he say?" he screamed.

"Somebody down in the camp was aiming a gun at us," she shouted back.

"Jesus Christ! They shoot at random aircraft coming in? They *shoot* at them?"

"Apparently so."

"What if it's the mail? What if it's bringing medical supplies?"

"Evidently someone doesn't much care."

Annja looked up at the rifleman. His stone reserve seemed to have cracked, if only slightly.

"It's a bad place you go to, missy," he said. "I'm sorry."

At the heart of the camp stood the largest concentration of actual buildings. This was surrounded by another high fence topped with razor tape. Just inland of it lay a second square compound perhaps fifty yards square. Its walls were irregular and multicolored. As the chopper approached, descending and slowing at last as if reluctantly, she saw they were made of random sheets of painted metal. They might have been hammered out of old metal car bodies. Improvised or not, they were also topped with the inevitable razor tangles.

A paved square in the barren yellow yard inside had been painted with a big yellow circle. The chopper sank toward it.

Crouched behind Annja and craning to look between

her and the M-16 guard, who stood tensely with black rifle shouldered and leveled, finger on the trigger, Dan pointed to a gateway through the sheet-metal fence. It was high and wide enough to admit a single big vehicle, maybe even a semitrailer. Above it arched a sign of what looked like inexpertly welded wrought iron.

"What's that say?" he yelled. "That doesn't look like Portuguese."

Annja read. "It's Italian. It means, 'All hope abandon, ye who enter here.' Somebody's got a sense of humor."

"Isn't that from—?"

"It's from Dante's *Inferno*," she said. "The sign above the gates to Hell."

"Oh God," Dan moaned.

For all his hard-edged street-activist manner he cursed scarcely more than Annja did. She shared the sentiment, though.

A flabby middle-aged man in a white suit was running toward them bent over, clutching a white Panama hat to his head. The chopper came to a stop. Annja had felt no impact of landing, however slight. Looking down she saw the skids still hovered six inches above the black pavement.

Dan glared at the guard. "Aren't you going to at least *land?*"

"You go," the guard said.

Annja hastily shouldered the rucksack she had brought. Still holding the fore-grip of the rifle in his left hand, the guard took his big right hand off the pistol grip to grab the collar of Dan's shirt and heaved him out of the helicopter as if he were a bag of puppy chow. To his credit Dan landed on his feet and balanced, although his posture was that of an alley cat dumped in the middle of a Rottweiler run. Which, Annja thought as she leaped down as gracefully as she could in turn, was just about right.

The guard thoughtfully pitched Dan's backpack out after him. It just missed the young activist. Twin turbine engines whined. The rotor chop increased in speed and pitch. The helicopter jumped into the cloudless blue sky. Rotating around its central axis it tipped its blunt snout down and shot back the way it had come at the best acceleration its aging power plants could give it.

The plump man stopped twenty feet from the bewildered Americans. He straightened up, dusting himself off. Despite frequent rains—those went without saying hereabouts—the surface of the landing field beyond the asphalt apron managed to accrete a yellow scum of dust, which the fleeing Huey had duly kicked up into a yellow cloud. The man might have saved himself the effort. The suit, once presumably bright white, now looked like a Jackson Pollock canvas of many-colored stains.

"You are Dan Seddon and Annja Creed?" he asked in English. He had bulging dark eyes and a mouth-fringing black beard. Frizzy black hair stuck out beneath his hat brim to either side of his face, which ran with sweat in sheets.

"We are," Annja said.

"I am Gustavo Gomes," he said. "Welcome to Feliz Lusitânia."

An explosion shattered the heavy air.

19

"Forgive my laughter, my friends," Gomes said to Annja and Dan, who lay on their bellies on the packed yellow dirt just beyond the black asphalt landing apron. "You look so comical there hugging the ground."

"That explosion—" Annja said.

"It is nothing. A shot for the mining operation, nothing more. Probably they clear big fallen logs. We are not under attack here."

Gomes drew a handkerchief from his pocket and wiped sweat from his face. It struck Annja as being like taking a mop to a beach with the tide coming in. "If you will please follow me, and not dawdle," he said, "I'll see you inside the citadel."

He gestured toward the gate. Beyond it lights blazed into life against the rapidly advancing tropical twilight, up on towers inside the inner perimeter. Annja and Dan shouldered packs and followed their guide.

A fenced-in passageway fifteen yards long and maybe twenty feet wide ran from the landing pad to the citadel. A chain-link gate swung open before them. Annja realized that machine guns in a pair of towers flanking it were tracking them as they approached.

Annja's shoulders tensed and her stomach crawled as if she'd swallowed a nestful of millipedes. She found little to love about being entirely at the mercy of the men behind the weapons, and the steadiness of their nerves and their trigger fingers.

Our lives depend upon the goodwill and judgment of men who'd guard a place like this, she thought.

They passed through the inner gate. A pair of men in mottled-green-and-brown camouflage battle dress waited inside. They carried Brazilian-made IMBEL MD-2 assault rifles. They stared at the newcomers with a blend of contempt and disinterest before turning away to close and secure the gate.

A rattle of gunfire sounded from somewhere outside the wire. Annja winced and forced her mind not to envision what the sounds might mean.

"So," Dan said conversationally, "was that more stump clearing?"

Gomes frowned. "Please don't make such jokes, Mr. Seddon. Your employer, Sir Publico, understands the realities of what goes on in here."

It was as if a fire hose suddenly blasted ice water between Annja's shoulder blades. "He does?" Her voice sounded half-strangled to her own ears.

Dan looked thoughtful. "He knows about this place," he said in carefully metered tones. "I suspect he does what he can to mitigate things."

"Oh, yes," Gomes said with a wide, oily smile. "Of course he does. He tries to help. He sends us the medical supplies!"

Annja kept one eyebrow raised. "You mean those shipments I saw in Manaus might have been his all along?"

Dan shrugged. He looked honestly embarrassed— and honestly befuddled. "I don't really know. I know he knows about this place—just like he told us. But that doesn't mean he knows everything that goes on here."

The sky had gone indigo overhead, shading into black downriver. Off to the west the last of the day lay in bands of sour lemon and ochre. Their guide led them between the neat pitched-roof structures that made up most of the buildings inside the interior wire perimeter. Annja decided they were some kind of prefab housing. People moved back and forth between them rapidly, with their heads down and shoulders hunched. The place hummed with activity, but it was spiritless— more like a kind of barely controlled frenzy than enthusiasm.

Gomes ran on about showing them their quarters and then taking them to eat in the commissary. "There is little to do here in the evenings, I'm afraid, although you will have satellite television in your rooms."

"What exactly do you do here, Mr. Gomes?" Annja asked as he led them to one of the khaki-colored pre-fab buildings with the green trim.

"I am a bureaucrat," he said artlessly enough. "An administrator. I help to run things. I have no real power here, of course. No one does, except the directors."

AFTER THEY HAD DEPOSITED their packs in their adjacent rooms, which were surprisingly neat and comfortable, they joined Gomes in the nearly empty commissary.

"We use both open-pit and sluicing methods here at Feliz Lusitânia," he said over a meal of beans, sausage and rice that made Annja feel suddenly homesick for New Orleans. "There are rich alluvial deposits present, both on land and in the river sediment. We extract much gold."

The commissary walls were bare, as were those in their rooms. The obvious reason was tightfistedness, the desire to squeeze every possible penny of profit from this great yellow wound in the rain forest for minimum overhead. Annja suspected something more underlay it. Life was cheap in Feliz Lusitânia. What went on there was so raw and elemental that any kind of ornamentation would have been absurd frivolity.

"What's going on out in the river?" Dan asked.

Gomes fluttered his eyelids momentarily. The motion, like the size of his eyes, was exaggerated by the lenses of the glasses he wore. He looked everywhere but at the two young North Americans, then cleared his throat, scooped up, chewed and swallowed another mouthful of food.

"You both are to enjoy our complete cooperation in your efforts, whatever they may be," he said in a tone that suggested, if they wished to confide in him, they'd find a ready ear. "That comes from Director Oliveira himself."

Again Annja wondered what ties Publico had to this hellhole—and just what strings he'd pulled for them. "We appreciate that," Annja said. "We'll let you know what we need when we…get our bearings better."

"And what about those poor bastards crucified outside the wire?" Dan demanded.

Annja looked down at her plate, cheeks flushing in sudden shame. *I should have asked that,* she thought.

Gomes compressed his lips to a line. "We attract unwelcome attention from outside. A very great deal of wealth flows through here."

"Attention from photojournalists and the like?" Annja asked.

"No, no, nothing like that. Raiders. Bandits."

"Through all this jungle?" Dan said in a tone of obvious skepticism.

"The river is a most broad highway."

"You get that many people trying to attack such an obviously well fortified camp?" Annja asked.

"Well, and malcontents—" He stopped, blinked. "Well, of course, order must be kept. Otherwise anarchy will swallow us all. And in any event they were dead when they went up—mostly…."

Dan gave his head a sliding sideways shake, smiling an ironic, twisted smile. "So here we see jungle capitalism in all its unfettered glory," he said.

Gomes drew himself up in his chair. "Not at all! The majority owner of this great enterprise is the state of Amazonas, and its proceeds go for the welfare of our people! Although to be sure we have foreign investors. What we do here we do for the greater good."

"So the ends justify the means?" Annja asked.

Dan shrugged. "Sometimes they do, Annja."

Gomes picked up his hat from the table beside him and settled it over his bald spot. Summoning his dignity, he rose.

"I fear I must leave you to attend to other duties," he said. "If you have needs, ask a staff member and they will be attended to promptly."

"I'll bet," Dan said.

"You must understand, my North American friends," Gomes said. "That inscription over the gate from the helipad—that does not refer to the poor devils in the cage, or out in the settlement. They know their fate, and how thoroughly it is sealed. And in any event, they usually do not arrive by helicopter.

"No, those who are advised to abandon hope on entry are the lower managers and administrators, the physicians, the skilled workers, the people who actually run this place. Such as my poor self. Because otherwise, we might imagine we had more chance to escape than those poor devils panning gold in the river.

"I leave you with one final bit of advice—you have

the option of leaving Feliz Lusitânia. It is a rare and precious gift. I should contemplate that deeply, were I you. And also, the wisdom of not asking questions whose answers cannot possibly do you any good. Good night."

THE RAIN CAME not long after they returned to their rooms. Publico had instructed them to leave their computers and cell phones behind, as they were unwelcome at the camp. Annja found her mind too agitated for reading and her soul too desolated by the day's sights, sounds and smells to sleep. And the rain fell with fury that seemed unusual even for what was a rain forest. It was violently pounding, as if trying to batter down the camp and wash every trace of it away down the Amazon a thousand miles to the sea.

At last, wearing only her long shirt over her panties, she rose and left her room. Dan answered the door promptly when she knocked. He had on only jeans. His hair was tousled, as if he, too, had tried to sleep and been denied.

They didn't speak. No words were necessary. Their bodies met in a fervent embrace. Their mouths met in a kiss. They moved to the bed and made love with a fierce intensity. Then they lay and clung to each other like small animals on a natural raft of vegetation, out on the storm-stirred river, until sleep finally overcame emotion and they slipped into blessed oblivion.

20

Annja and Dan ate a subdued breakfast of somewhat crusted eggs, wilted bacon, bread and fruit from a buffet-style spread of covered hot trays that seemed left out for latecomers. Aside from the sounds of people puttering back in the kitchens, conversing in what Annja guessed was an Indian language, there was no sign of anyone at all.

The pair ate quietly, avoiding each other's eyes. The physical intimacies of the night before had led to no increase in the emotional intimacy between them. What that left between them, Annja wasn't quite sure. A shared sense of purpose, of comradeship. Respect and even affection. But anything deeper—that particular yawning gulf in Annja's life was not, it seemed, going to be filled by Annja's co-worker.

In the light of day—brutal in every sense—Dan was

a different man. It wasn't as if the sensitive and vulnerable youth of the night before was either illusion or facade, she decided. It was just that the danger and the sheer raw evil of their circumstances brought out another aspect of him, harder edged, more certain. More at home. Maybe he really is an action hero, she thought.

"I guess they know we're here," Dan said after they had mostly finished. "The camp administration, I mean. God knows what they think we're doing."

He took a sip of his coffee. "I wonder how the hell we're supposed to proceed from here?" he said. "I don't know about you, but I'm not ready to go wandering outside the citadel by myself. Call me a coward."

Annja shook her head vigorously. "No. Or I'm one, too. I know you're brave, Dan. You've got nothing to prove to me. But suicide to no purpose isn't bravery. Not in my book."

He looked at her with amusement. "You know, I think that's the first really personal thing I've heard you say."

She shrugged. "Well our conversations have run largely to business, small talk or political statements, haven't they?"

He laughed. "With me making most of those last, huh? Am I really that bad?"

She opened her mouth to protest when he looked past her and his expression shifted.

"Don't look now," he said, "but either our guide just got here or Hell's got a new work-release program."

Annja turned in her chair. His description was spot-on. The woman standing just inside the entrance to the commissary had the hunched shoulders and swiveling head of something's prey and big, gold, frightened-waif eyes. She was almost skeletally gaunt—not anorexic, but something visibly other, as if all excess had been melted out of her by an eternal flame of fear. She looked all around the commissary as if expecting to see something terrible lurking in wait, coiled to spring. Then she looked back toward them.

Annja decided standing up might look more welcoming than threatening, so she did that. "Hi," she said in Portuguese. "I'm Annja Creed."

The woman set her narrow jaw and nodded once, almost spasmodically. She came forward, with fast steps, eyes downcast, shoulders slumped, and head forward—the demeanor of a true victim. "I am Dr. Lidia do Carvalho," the woman said apologetically in clear but accented English. "I was told I am to be your guide."

Dan stood up. "Pleased to meet you," he said. "I'm Dan Seddon. Thanks for coming out to help us."

She nodded. She would not look up.

"Listen," Annja said. "We can make other arrangements. You don't have to go."

The head came up. Lidia looked as if she had cut her hair herself, possibly with pruning shears. It was as if vanity had no place in her life. Only survival.

Those huge frightened-cat eyes met Annja's. "Yes," the doctor said. "Yes, I do."

SHE LIVED OUT HERE in the citadel, she told them as they scurried from cover to cover among the ramshackle dwellings. She was part of the camp's small medical staff, recruited from the city of Cuiabá in the high-plains farm country of Mato Grosso State. It was an economically distressed area and jobs weren't easy to come by.

"Even for doctors?" Dan asked. Off in the distance they could hear shouts, shots, screams. They weren't forty yards from the gate between the citadel and the colony, still in sight of its own forbidding machine-gun towers. "Surely they have socialized medicine here in Brazil."

"With ample free injections for the poor," Lidia said grimly, "of saline solution. Medical education is cheap. Real medicines are expensive. And government jobs go to the well connected. Come, now—I think it's safe to move."

She seemed to have a knack for slipping through quiet ways, little traveled by either starveling workers or the armed patrols. The workers weren't much in evidence anyway. They labored or slept at this hour. The mines ran twenty-four hours a day. Still, Annja's stomach was a constant sour knot of tension from anticipating ambush at any moment.

"You work out in the colony?" she asked.

"Yes."

"But you said you were staff," Annja said. "Couldn't you live in the citadel?"

"Yes."

"And you choose to live in this?" asked Dan, his eyes narrowed in disgust and dismay.

They halted behind a structure cobbled together from a random assortment of warped planks. The smell of sewage and decay were stronger than most places. Annja blinked tears from her eyes.

"Oh, yes," Lidia said. "Much safer."

"You have got to be kidding," Dan said.

She shook her head—a quick, furtive gesture. "Out here I enjoy a certain status. I have protectors. People understand that I help them."

"What about drugs?" Annja asked. "Don't people try to steal them from you?"

Lidia held up a cautioning hand. A hundred yards or so ahead a ragged pack of men walked past the alley mouth. They were skinny and so sunburned Annja couldn't tell what race they belonged to. They clutched machetes or wooden clubs.

"I have antibiotics and such things only," Lidia said. The gang passed without a glance aside, as if intent on some goal. "Nothing recreational. The pain drugs are available at a special kiosk right outside the citadel fence. It is heavily guarded day and night. Sometimes, of course, there are those who won't accept that I have nothing to ease their pains of mind and spirit. My shack where I live—not so different from this one, but I try to keep it clean—is ransacked frequently. That doesn't matter. I have nothing even for the most desperate to find worth stealing. And when people try to force me to give them drugs, or to do other things, I have only to scream. Then the people from the vicinity come. They take the people who are attacking me and do things to them. Terrible things."

She looked up at Annja. For the first time she almost met her eyes. "I should try to stop them, of course. Or feel worse about it. But I am weak. I fear that I cannot."

Annja felt an urge to touch her reassuringly on the shoulder. She didn't. She feared it would be perceived as patronizing somehow. Maybe it would be patronizing.

She had ample experience with poor people, and with people in the hinterlands of developing nations. In general she and they got along fine. She wasn't hard to get along with—for people of goodwill. Simple respect and friendliness, she found, went a long way.

She had never experienced anything remotely like this.

"Then why not live in the citadel, where it's safe?" she asked.

Lidia uttered a bitter laugh. "Safe? It's far worse than out in the colony. Here I have some status. I have protectors, as I told you. Inside—"

She shook her head. "Inside they play the games of power. And no one has a friend."

"But aren't they all in this together?" Dan asked. "The bosses, I mean?"

"What?" she asked. "Do you believe in honor among thieves? You are very naive, young man, though you think yourself hard."

"But their class loyalties—"

"Do not exist outside of the air-conditioned classrooms of the universities," she said. "I, too, once believed in such things. Then I came here and saw the truth. Whatever they call themselves, socialists, capitalists—those who have power are all mad things, struggling constantly with each other for more. Inside the citadel, without a powerful patron you are waiting only to be collateral damage—or a plaything for those with the sort of mind to crucify workers who try to run away!"

"So that's what that's all about," Dan said.

"But we're in the middle of the rain forest," Annja said. "I'd think it would be easy to disappear, once you got away from the camp." Not that that guaranteed safety or survival, she knew. Spanish and Portuguese soldiers and explorers had perished of hunger in droves out there, despite its being perhaps the Earth's most nutrient-dense environment. What doomed them was what would likely doom city-dwellers who tried to trek through the woods—simple ignorance. The early explorers simply hadn't known what to eat.

"The Indians turn them back," Lidia said.

"They cooperate with their exploiters?" Dan asked.

Lidia laughed again. "Exploiters? The directors bribe the local tribes well. And the Indians get rewards for any stragglers they bring back—bonuses if they are still alive. As they get paid when they bring other Indians in as slaves."

"My God," Annja said. "Oh, my God."

"You didn't know things like that went on?" Dan asked.

She looked in his eyes. It was like looking through windows to a private hell. "No. I never imagined any such thing. I've seen bad things—terrible things. I've witnessed starvation and disease and even massacre. But—nothing to compare to this."

"All I know is we're a terrible species. And we do terrible things, and the Earth might be better off without us," Dan said.

To Annja's amazement Lidia favored him with a flat, angry glare. "I at least," she said, "know how to distinguish between the victim and the victimizer!"

She walked on, leading them farther into the reeking horror of the camp. Dan stood a moment staring after her, opening and closing his hands.

"I wish I did," he said.

ANNJA DARED a second glance. The small patrol had vanished. "Right," she said to Lidia. "Let's go."

The slight doctor led them out across the broad space through which the mercenaries had marched moments before. As soon as she turned the corner of the container hut Annja had to jump to avoid tripping over a dead body, in cutoff shorts and a torn shirt pulled up around its belly. It had begun the bloat in the heat—thankfully it lay facedown. It seemed to be a male.

They had not smelled it from less than ten feet away. It was the third corpse they had encountered that day.

"How come everybody hasn't died of cholera or some other disease?" Dan wondered in a quiet voice as they scurried across the open space and slipped down an alley with containers on one side and plank hovels on the other. Even the three of them, carrying little spare body fat among them, had to turn sideways to negotiate the passage.

"The patrol will probably report the body," Lidia said, "and another team will come out to pick it up and carry it away to dump in the river. And they give out *lots* of antibiotics."

No doubt breeding all kinds of resistant strains of bacteria in the process, Annja thought. Under the circumstances it was the least of their misdeeds.

Lidia told them how the camp drew workers from all over South America and even beyond with promises of high pay. "All lies," she said, "of course. But once here—well, you've seen what happens to those who try to run away. And they might be the lucky ones."

"How is that even possible?" Dan asked.

"You saw the cage, out in the river?" Lidia asked.

"Oh, yes," Annja said.

"Once you go in the cage you never come out—alive," the doctor said. "It is for people who really annoy the directors. Sometimes failed subordinates, or unlucky rivals. Or sometimes international campaigners who make their way here to reform the camp." She looked meaningfully at Dan.

"I'm not that kind of campaigner," he told her. "I'm more the proactive sort, you might say."

Lidia frowned and looked quickly away. She evidently disliked Dan. Annja understood. In the doctor's circumstances it would be prohibitively hard to make herself look inside the young man and see the genuine care there—and the pain.

"What do they do in the cage?" Annja asked.

"Pan for gold," Lídia said with a wild little yip of a laugh. "Like your gold rush, yes? They glean what is missed by the machines sluicing out in the river or scraping at the land."

"What if the prisoners don't work?" Annja asked.

"Then they don't feed them. Anyone. After a while the holdouts either come around or their fellow sufferers drown them in their sleep."

Annja swallowed hard.

"Of course they don't last long," Lidia said, almost clinically now. "Aside from the grinding labor and the privation and exposure, there are the heavy-metal salts."

"Heavy metals?" Dan asked.

"Oh, yes. The Amazon Basin is rich in heavy metals, didn't you know?"

"So the radioactivity gets them?"

"Not at all. That would take years, decades. Heavy-metal poisoning works much faster." She shook her head. "Then there's the mercury used in amalgamation-extraction methods in the open-pit operation. Workers get the mercury on their skin or breathe in the vapors. Eventually they become so deranged and feeble-minded they can't function anymore. Then they go in the cage—or are simply set loose in the colony to fend for themselves."

"What happens to them in here?" Annja asked.

"They kill or are killed," Lidia said.

"So that scraggly looking bunch we saw earlier—" Dan said.

"A gang of former laborers."

"They fight the guards?" Annja said.

Lidia shrugged. "Or each other. Here, life is boiled down to its essentials. Some people choose to cooperate with one another. Others live as if it's a war of all against all."

She led them onward. The colony must be larger even than it looked from the air, Annja thought. The tension had her heart racing and the sweat soaking her more than the brutal river-basin heat would account for.

Automatic fire roared ahead of them. More than one gun was firing. Then something blew up with a crack like an ax splitting the sky.

21

Crouching, Lidia led them forward to peer above a line of plastic drums. Annja's heart was in her throat and thrashing like a wounded bird. She saw nothing in their immediate vicinity. One or two streets to their right they caught glimpses of men running, shouting, shooting.

"What's going on?" she asked in a low voice.

Lidia shrugged. "Mercenaries fighting."

"Private dispute," Dan said, "or some kind of rivalry coming from the top down?"

"Who knows? Both are possible. But we must get close," Lidia said.

"Why?" Annja asked in alarm.

"Our objective lies that way," she said.

"Can't we just go around?" Dan asked.

"We must cut as close as we can. This is a very bad part of the colony we come to," Lidia said earnestly.

Annja shared a wide-eyed look with Dan. Worse things than a firefight? she wondered.

Gunfire rose and fell in surges. A grenade thumped. Someone screamed briefly.

"Some people are seriously annoyed at each other," Dan said.

"I guess we go get a closer look," Annja said in resignation.

They slipped forward as furtively as they could. That seemed to annoy Dan.

"Why creep around like mice?" he demanded. "The camp inhabitants are either heading somewhere else in a hurry or lying low, given the amount of kinetic energy and flying chunks of metal being tossed about so cavalierly by those boys up ahead. And none of them's going to be paying the least bit of attention to anybody but who they're shooting at. Or who's shooting at them."

Annja kept her head turning from side to side. "I don't want to die for an assumption. Nor get run up on by reinforcements. Not to mention some new team looking to get in the game."

Dan drew in a long unhappy breath. "Good point."

They advanced between two rows of the two-story containers-turned-dwellings, into a region of ramshackle huts. In fact this seemed the end of the scrapped containers, which, hot as they'd be in the sunlight, at least were sturdy and would keep off the storms. In front of the trio a nasty shantytown stood, or leaned, for at least a hundred yards before butting up against the twelve-foot perimeter fence. The spirals of knife wire at its top glittered in the sun. Beyond stood the green wall of the rain forest, at once inviting and forbidding.

Lidia led them into a hut. Annja hung back, perhaps even more unwilling to violate a private dwelling than she would have been in some ritzy suburb back home. Some modicum of personal space was about the only thing resembling dignity these people had. To invade that seemed wrong.

"It's all right," Lidia said, with the closest thing to a smile Annja had seen ghosting quickly across her features like a cloud across the sun. "No one lives here right now."

The place stank of death and buzzed with flies. Annja guessed an occupant had died and spent a few days decomposing in the jungle heat and humidity before being collected by the periodic sanitation sweeps. The hovel seemed to consist of planks and shreds of reeking cloth.

They seemed to have entered the no-man's-land of the battle. To their left Annja saw men in bluish-gray camos leaning out from cover and shooting with what appeared to be M16s and the shorter M-4 carbine versions. They had the beefy, well-packed look she associated with the U.S. military, and seemed to be mostly white or black. Annja guessed they were North American mercs—or security contractors, as the government liked to say. She suspected that they, too, had been attracted to Feliz Lusitânia by honeyed lies and trapped no less thoroughly than the wretches in that horrific cage in the river. There were ways to keep even men with guns in their place.

Chief among those were other men with guns. Those men wore green-and-black camouflage. They might have been Brazilians, but for some reason Annja wondered if they might hail from Cuba or even Africa. One reason was their weapons—they fired chunky assault rifles with an unmistakable broken-nosed profile.

"Kalashnikovs?" she asked. "Do the camp directors equip their forces with those? Russian-made guns?" She added the latter in case the doctor wasn't up on firearms minutiae.

"Who knows?" she murmured. "They hire killers from all over the world. Wherever they can get them."

"Why would they equip guards with RPGs?" Dan asked. "Those're antitank weapons, and there's a notable lack of armored vehicles around here."

"The guards use them sometimes," Lidia said. "So the factions smuggle the rockets and launchers in to their own fighters. Among other things."

"They smuggle in rockets to blow up their own armored cars?" Dan shook his head. "This place is totally screwed."

A beefy mercenary leaned out to fire off three quick 3-round bursts from an M-4. One of the smaller men in green and black hopped out from the dubious cover of a lean-to and sent an RPG buzzing and smoking from his shoulder launcher. The merc dived out of view. The shack he had been using for cover erupted in a white flash and white smoke, followed quickly by billowing orange-and-blue flames.

"Great," Dan said. Annja was pleased to see that, like her and Lidia, he was keeping low. She tried not to think just how little protection the shack would give them against a random burst of gunfire. "If a fire starts—"

"Not much danger of that," Lidia said. "It rains so much, the wood is constantly soaked." Even as she said it the flames were dying down. Whether the shooter or any of his buddies had been killed or injured by the blast, Annja couldn't tell. She couldn't hear anybody screaming, anyway.

"We need to move," Annja said.

"Which direction?" Dan asked.

Another merc whipped around a corner on the far side of the street from the smoldering wreck of a shack to fire a grenade launcher up the street. The RPG man had already ducked into cover. Three grenades boomed off in the street and inside one of the huts. The blasts caused little visible damage as the gaps in the walls allowed a lot of the blast pressure to escape.

"Left," Annja said. "The ones in gray seem to put out a way bigger volume of fire."

Dan grinned. "I like the way you think."

To Annja's surprise they got past the firefight without great difficulty. The worst part was crossing the relatively wide road where the shoot-out was actually taking place. Lidia insisted on crossing no more than thirty yards behind the rearmost of the mercenaries they could detect. Yet despite what the movies showed, Annja knew from firsthand experience—both dealing out gunfire and receiving it—that bullets don't evaporate harmlessly into thin air if they miss. Indeed, modern high-velocity rifle rounds don't reliably stop even when they hit their targets.

Annja doubted anyone would pay them any mind. The two groups were too intent on killing each other, and not being killed by each other. But there was a rhythm to a firefight, Annja knew from experience. Lidia and Dan both seemed equally aware, probably for the same reason, she figured.

After observing for a while they were able to anticipate the lulls. They made their move at an opportune moment. They found themselves in surroundings that managed to be even less appealing than the quarter-mile or more of hell they'd crossed to get there.

Where earlier they had seen few people except for armed gangs of one sort or another, now they caught flashes of furtive movement inside shadowed shacks, gleams of sunlight on eyeballs peering through windows or less formal gaps in rude walls. Now and again a man or even a woman, usually lean and scarred as an old wolf, stood glaring at them openly from a doorway.

"What's with this action?" Dan asked. Following Lidia's example, he and Annja walked upright down the middle of the streets and alleys. Annja felt the constant pressure of eyeballs—there was clearly no point in stealth any longer. "Don't these people have jobs to go to?"

"Not anymore," Lidia said. "They have found they cannot escape outside the walls, between the selva and the Indians. But this part of the camp they can escape to. The guards do not come farther than those we just came past."

"Why doesn't the whole slave-labor population just flood right into here, then?" Dan asked.

"Because even the slaves enjoy some measure of security. They are fed, if badly. Here there is no support, no security, but what one can grab for oneself. Or one's comrades."

"But you seem pretty familiar with this part of the camp," Annja said, "and pretty unafraid." Indeed, the gaunt doctor seemed to be walking more erect than at any time since she had crept apologetically into the commissary in what seemed like a whole earlier incarnation.

Lidia smiled again. "I live here. I told you, I provide valuable services to the community, which everyone recognizes. These people protect me precisely because they are so desperate. And here at least I am safe from rape by the guards."

Annja shuddered. No matter how horrible life in this hole seems, she thought, I just keep finding out it's actually *worse*.

"So even in the Citadel—" Dan began.

"Please," said Lidia without looking at him. Annja waved a pipe-down hand at him. He actually looked sheepish for a moment.

THE MAN THEY SOUGHT had obviously been dying for a long time. And he'd been dying hard.

Looking at him lying on a pile of rags with a skinny woman kneeling by his side and mopping his face with water from an old paint can with the label long gone, Annja guessed they had arrived just in time.

A peculiarly horrific, sweetish smell came from him. It seemed concentrated on a bandage, which must have been white at one point, and was now pretty thoroughly blackened, wound about his narrow middle.

"Gangrene?" Dan asked, sniffing and then wincing. "I thought you could only get that on an arm or a leg."

Lidia shook her head. "Anywhere in the body where blood supply is cut off," she said, "the tissue dies and becomes gangrenous. It is far advanced in his bowels. He suffered multiple gunshot wounds. It is a wonder he has hung on so long."

"Was he shot here? In the camp?" Dan asked.

"I do not know. He simply appeared here, two weeks ago, already wounded. He had bandaged himself after a fashion," the doctor replied.

"Appeared here?" Dan echoed. "You mean, in the camp?"

Lidia nodded.

"But how can somebody get into a place like this? And why?"

She shrugged. "There are ways. The walls are meant to keep men in not out—and even then, there are always ways for those willing to take risks. And there are those for whom the forest and the poisonous snakes and even the Indians are no barrier.

"As to why, the good God might know. But he has clearly turned his face away from the camp. If you ask him, I promise he will not answer. No matter how loudly you scream and plead."

Annja looked to the woman at the dying man's side. She was emaciated, as well as of slight stature. Annja could not tell how old she was—she might have been a prematurely aged teenager or a middle-aged woman.

"Please," Annja said in Portuguese.

The woman never glanced her way.

"If she understands Portuguese," Lidia said, "or English or Spanish, she never shows a sign. I believe she is Indian, but even that is a guess. She appeared two days after he did."

"What's he doing here?" Annja said. "Other than the obvious."

"You mean dying? Why do you fear to say the word? Believe me, he knows," Lidia said.

"I'm sorry," Annja whispered.

"He waits," Lidia said. "That much I know. He has said as much."

"What else has he said?" Dan asked.

Lidia frowned. She shook her head sharply. "Strange things," she said. "Impossible things. He is delirious. He cannot separate legend from fact."

Annja knelt on the other side of him from his faithful attendant. The stench of his decay was like a blow. The crouching woman shot her a hot-eyed look, but something in Annja's manner seemed to reassure her. She went back to her monotonous task of giving the man what tiny comfort was available. Annja wondered what he was to her, and she to him. Lover? Daughter? Comrade in arms? She doubted she would ever know.

Leaning close to his ear, she said, "Promessa."

With startling speed, his hand flashed out and caught her by the right wrist. She managed to quell the urge to flinch away.

"I did wrong," the man said with enormous effort. "I hope that I have paid enough. And I must have, for now you have come to take me home to the *quilombo* of dreams!"

He turned his ghastly face to her and smiled. His teeth seemed to swim in blood. Through it they looked shockingly white.

"What do you remember?" she asked, hating herself.

The tortured brow furrowed, causing the sweat to eat new runnels through the grime that caked his face despite the silent woman's constant attention. "I was not—not supposed to remember. Yet now the memories come back to me. Sweet, so sweet."

"Now is when you are supposed to remember," she said. She was improvising. It was a desperate game—if he spotted any inconsistency, any falsehood, he would shut up and no influence she could bring to bear on him would restart the flow of information she so desperately needed.

But hope betrayed him, as hope so often does. He wanted to believe. So whatever might have rung false about Annja or her words—he did not hear them. Hope of redemption, of homecoming, was all that remained to him.

"You must know the way," she said.

He smiled. "Yes. And the outside people can never find it." Again he smiled a terrible smile.

"Only by proving that you know," Annja said, "can you earn what you desire."

She felt Lidia's gaze boring between her shoulder blades like laser beams. Well, Annja thought, the cause is greater than you know. Greater than we dare tell you.

"I will try," the man said. The strength with which he clung to her wrist was astounding. Either he had been inhumanly strong in full health, or his will was simply that strong. "I see the tree."

"The tree," Annja said. She heard Dan's sharp exhalation at her side. A tree? That's what we have to go on. Among all the billions of trees in the Amazon?

The dying man nodded. His eyes gleamed. They looked past Annja, seeing the glories of the City of Promise. "The tree with nine trunks. On the right bank. That marks the border. The city lies mere leagues beyond."

He sat up and looked at her. She realized for the first time his eyes were bright blue.

"Do I pass the test? I want so much to come home. Can I—?"

The staring blue eyes rolled back in his skull. He melted onto the stained, sodden pile of rags. The

woman slowly raised her head. The look she gave
Annja was pure hate.

"You filthy beast!" a female voice cried in Portuguese from behind. "What have you done to him?"

22

The voice did not belong to Dr. Lidia do Carvalho. Annja knew at once who it must be.

The real Promessans had come to collect their own. Or to still his tongue. In either case they were too late.

For anything but vengeance.

Annja spun away from the corpse, straightening to confront the woman who had spoken. She was a tall, lean, young African-looking woman with a dark green band around bushy hair, a loose olive-drab blouse worn tails out over khaki shorts and athletic shoes. Her eyes blazed with outrage.

Annja realized it was the woman she had pursued from the murdered Mafalda's shop in Belém.

"Go," Annja said to Lidia from the corner of her mouth. Without looking up, the doctor grabbed the squatting woman by the arm. The woman resisted. With surprising strength Lidia hauled her to her feet, away from the corpse of the man she had tended so lovingly and out into the merciless sunlight. The little doctor lived in a state of pure terror and seemed all but totally beaten down by life. Yet she kept on, kept doing what she could. For that Annja admired her.

"Don't cause problems for her," Annja told the Promessan woman when the other two had gone. "She had no choice."

"There is always a choice," the woman all but spit. "Why did you kill him?"

"What, are you mad because we beat you to it?" Dan asked.

"We didn't kill him," Annja said.

"What did he say to you?" she asked.

Frantically Annja weighed their options. If the newcomer really was Promessan, Annja doubted that either she or Dan had any prospect of talking their way past her. And although she was wiry, it was the wiriness of strength, not privation, meaning she wasn't of the colony.

"Enough," Annja finally said. "You won't be able to selfishly hoard your secrets away from the world for very much longer."

"So you are just another colonialist, Annja Creed, come to steal what we have made by our own sweat and suffering. Come to enslave us again!"

Annja frowned. How does she know my name?

Dan's hand dipped under the loose tails of his shirt. It came out holding the same handgun he'd used in the warehouse in Manaus.

"They're surrounding the hootch!" he shouted as he raised the handgun to point at the tall newcomer.

With startling speed she crescent kicked the pistol. She failed to knock the weapon from his hand but did kick it aside. It went off with a noise that seemed to billow the torn cloth hangings that served as part of the shack's walls.

She spun rapidly into a back kick that caught the young activist in the stomach and knocked him crashing out into daylight. Other figures moved outside. Even in a glimpse Annja could see they lacked the scarecrow gauntness and feral furtiveness that characterized colony inhabitants, even the armed gang members.

Shots went off outside. But Annja snapped her attention back to the tall woman as the most immediate threat. Reaching behind her shoulder, the woman produced a machete and swung it at Annja's head.

Off balance and with no time to concentrate the sword into being, Annja fell over to her right. She landed hard on her right hip. The floor was packed earth topped by a layer of unidentifiable muck.

The Promessan rushed at her, raising the machete for a killing downstroke. Just as simply Annja fired out with both feet, kicking her attacker in both shins and knocking her legs right out from under her.

Annja rolled to her right as the woman sprawled across the corpse. Immediately Annja reversed, rolling back to use her right hand wrapped over her left fist to piledrive her left elbow into her opponent's kidney.

The woman screamed in pain and arched her back as if being electrocuted. The machete flew from her hand.

Annja sprang to her feet. Motion blurred in the extreme right corner of her peripheral vision. She ducked left and spun away. The motion took her farther from the doorway to outside. An interior wall, augmented like the exterior walls with random sheets of drab cloth, partitioned the shack into at least two rooms. From a dark doorway in the wall something long and mottled and as thick as Annja's thigh appeared.

It crashed against the outer wall. Annja straightened to find herself confronting a giant anaconda. She knew anacondas were contenders for largest snakes in the world. But its sheer size was almost as great a shock as the fact it had appeared from nowhere.

The snake reared up to fully her height and turned to gaze at her with large golden eyes. It sent a chill down her spine.

The serpent opened its mouth wide. It was pink and edged with an alarming array of back-curving teeth. It struck right for Annja's face.

She dived to her right, back toward the dead body and the writhing woman. She put a shoulder down and rolled as the anaconda struck the wall. Planks cracked loudly.

Annja came to her feet. The woman suddenly rolled and tried to grab her legs. Annja kicked her hard in the face, felt as much as heard her jaw break.

The sword filled Annja's hand. The anaconda coiled by the wall, preparing for another strike. It seemed to recognize the sword as a threat. With a speed that belied its bulk it turned to its right and slithered out through a low gap in the wall. Momentarily transfixed by the creature's length, Annja leaped forward to slash belatedly at its tail. She missed. Her blade bit deep into the mud-scummed earth floor.

She heard noises behind her. She ripped the sword loose and turned in time to smash a machete blade descending toward her head with a clumsy forehand stroke. She put her shoulder down and slammed it into her attacker's chest. He was so surprised that Annja virtually clotheslined him, despite hitting him so close to his center of gravity. His legs ran out from under him and he fell with a squelch in the mud.

Outside she heard shots. Several from close by she guessed were Dan's. Other guns were clearly firing, too. What's going on? she wondered.

As she was distracted a second man swung a machete diagonally at her. She barely managed to block it with the flat of her blade.

The man looked European, possibly even American. He was taller than Annja, with rippling spare muscles in arms left bare by a tan shirt with the arms torn off, a stubble of dark blond beard, glaring green eyes. Those eyes widened in surprise.

Nobody expects a broadsword, she thought. She took advantage of his lapse to get her right knee up to her chest. She pushed hard with the sole of her shoe against his sternum, throwing him back.

The sound of the thin scum of mud sucking at a shoe

brought her around fast. The first man, whose machete she had smashed, was trying to plant a combat knife between her shoulder blades. She ran him through the heart with her sword. He gasped and goggled at her as life fled him. She tore the blade free and turned to meet the attack she knew was coming.

The blond man cried out hoarsely as he saw his comrade die. Annja's blow slashed his descending forearm and connected with his chest. He fell, pumping blood into the muck.

More men crowded in through the hut's entrance. They held weapons of various sorts. She turned and hacked at the planks of the wall and snapped a way clear into the unforgiving light of day.

Not four yards away she saw Dan crouched behind a line of big red plastic drums. He was jamming a fresh magazine into his gun. Two bodies lay in the street. A wide, grooved trail with hints of red led to the mouth of an alley across the road, suggesting someone may have been hit and dragged to cover.

"Get down!" Dan whispered. As he glanced toward her she made the sword disappear. She dived toward the barrels.

A boom buffeted her ears. Something clattered above her as she tucked and rolled and came up next to Dan, trying not to be aware of the hideous stinking muck that smeared her from knees to hair. Glancing up, she saw a pattern of small holes in the planking. She knew instantly it was buckshot.

"The Promessans are using shotguns?" she asked.

Dan leaned around the side of the barrel barrier and fired twice at a target Annja couldn't see. "I don't think so."

"I thought the camp guards didn't come here."

"I don't think it's them, either. This looks more like gangs, converging to defend their turf."

Annja was looking back toward the hole she'd made in the wall. She was surprised the Promessans hadn't come boiling right out after her. Perhaps they were tending to their fallen comrades inside. Just as likely they were none too eager to blunder after somebody who'd single-handedly put three of them down, two probably for good.

"We have to go," she said.

From somewhere behind and to their right a green beam winked. A corner of a plank structure exploded into a gout of steam.

"Right," Dan said. He jumped up and ran for the far side of the street.

The shotgunner, a feral-looking man in a filthy head-band whose refugee gauntness clearly marked him as a denizen of the colony, leaned out to take a shot at them as they broke cover. A green beam speared into his right eye. There came a grenade-like bang and he fell. Annja did not look too closely as she and Dan flashed through the open, uneven doorway of the hovel across from the one in which the wounded Promessan exile had died.

From her left Annja heard a snarl. Hair rising at the nape of her neck, she turned.

A big cat stood ten feet away. It was heavy bodied, although no more than two yards from nose to tip of thick, twitching tail. Its fur seemed almost to glow with a light of its own through rosettes like sunspots; its eyes were huge and green. It was clearly what the natives called a golden *onza,* a beast the educated city folks at least affected to believe was mythical.

What it was doing in the midst of this man-made hell made Annja's brain ring with cognitive dissonance. Yet it was no more strange than the twenty-foot anaconda.

Dan snapped two shots at the cat. The creature spun away and vanished into a back room.

"What the hell was that?" Dan demanded.

Annja shook her head. For a moment she had been entranced by impossible thoughts. Can't give into fantasy, she told herself sternly. *Especially now.*

From the street came angry shouts. Annja heard gunshots and the sharper snaps of energy beams ionizing air. "Nothing," she said. "We need to keep moving."

The look he shot her was skeptical. She knew it was nothing to what he'd look like if she told him what she'd dared imagine, just for an instant. "We're right up against the jungle here," she said.

"If you say so."

"I do. Now, go. We need to get back to the citadel before the whole colony lands on our heads!"

He nodded. A passageway lay open right before them. As her eyes grew accustomed to the gloom again after the dazzle of outdoors, Annja could make out that it led back to what seemed a jog or juncture, for dozens of yards. They ran down it.

From all around them came the sound of fighting. They heard it through the makeshift walls and ragged filthy hangings all around—the ringing clash of metal on metal, shots, curses, the screams and groans of the wounded. Annja wondered how many fighters the Promessans had infiltrated into the camp.

A figure appeared in front of them. His eyes were wild in a skull-like face. He pointed a sawed-off single-barreled shotgun at them.

Dan shot him twice in the chest. The short slight man fell backward, discharging his weapon into the ceiling with a crash that brought a cascade of dust, rank with mold spores, raining down on their heads.

"The gangs are starting to fight with each other," Dan said, as if discerning Annja's thoughts of a moment before. "Like packs of jackals fighting over a waterhole—just flashing into rage because they've blundered into each other. This is all getting way out of hand."

They ran on through the cramped, gloomy, reeking space. As they reached the end of the passage to find themselves in a dogleg right they heard a whomp and instantly smelled gasoline burning. Annja had seen for herself the energy pistols were poor fire starters, especially in this waterlogged environment. But now she heard the greedy crackle of flames, smelled cloth and wood burning, as well as petroleum.

"Somebody threw a Molotov," Dan said. "Or maybe

one of those lasers set off stored gas. Either way, we've got to get out of this maze quick or fry!"

Around the dogleg they faced more claustrophobic corridor with doors or rough hangings to either side. *Maze* seemed about right. Despite bad light and head-long flight Annja had the impression that rather than one big purpose-built building, they ran through a war-ren of shacks that had simply sprung up together, fol-lowing some obscure logic of the builders or none at all. The ceiling changed level, from flat to pitched to slanting at a crazy angle as they rounded random jogs and junctions and stumbled over thresholds of varying heights. The passage twisted and turned without per-ceptible plan.

"It's like a bad wooden model of someone's intes-tines," Dan grunted.

A shot bellowed behind them. The bullet gouged a furrow in a plank by Annja's shoulder before punch-ing out. Dan spun to shoot back as Annja's ears rang from the noise.

Smoke had begun infiltrating the weird, winding passageway, hanging at head level. As Annja coughed, three figures materialized in front of her. From their hard, fit appearance and athletic posture she saw at once they were Promessans, not starveling colonists. One held two two-foot sticks of polished black wood. The two in front carried machetes.

Summoning the sword, she rushed them. The pas-sageway was only wide enough for two people to pass abreast, no higher than a couple of feet above Annja's head. It wasn't the most cramped stretch they had run through but left little room to swing a weapon. Fortunately the same limitation applied to Annja's attackers.

Once again her opponents were surprised at seeing a broadsword appear from thin air. Annja took her advantage. With the hilt in both hands she hacked through the machete of the man on her left. The one on her right recoiled in surprise, bumping into the stick-wielding man behind. Annja slammed her hilt against the side of the first man's head and side kicked him through a decayed hanging.

The second machete-wielding man struck for her head. She was out of position to chop through the short, broad blade. She brought it up before her face. The cut was a semifeint. The wide machete kissed off her sword with a sliding ring and then swung back down in a cut at her hip.

She managed to drop her hands fast enough that the machete clacked against the cross-shaped guard. She swung her left foot up and around in a roundhouse kick to her opponent's right short ribs, exposed by his low attack on his left. He was good—he got his right elbow down, fouling the blow and absorbing most of the fierce hip-turning kick, although a bit of air chuffed out of him as her shoe's reinforced toe drove the elbow into his side.

To block the kick he had to hunch forward, bringing his machete with him. Annja tipped her sword back over her right shoulder and cut down, as always putting her hip into it and driving with the legs. It wasn't a long cut but a very powerful one. It sliced almost effortlessly through his clavicle, right beside his muscle-corded neck, sank deep into his chest.

Gunfire roared like constant thunder in the passageway behind. Annja's shoulder blades kept trying to crawl together in anticipation of a bullet between them. She realized late she should have ducked into a side chamber herself. But her blood was up—and apparently Dan was mainly keeping the gunman pinned.

As long as his magazine held up.

Her stricken opponent slumped across the corridor, blocking the man behind him. The first machete wielder erupted from the chamber into which Annja had kicked him. He swung a small wood crate at the back of Annja's head.

She spun into him, kicked high, almost into a vertical split. Her painful hours of gymnastics-style limbering exercises paid off. The rotten-wood crate shattered. The Promessan blinked as splinters and dust fell into his eyes. She brought the heel of her foot crunching down in an ax kick that mostly by good fortune hit him square on the left wing of his collarbone and snapped it loudly.

He went down in a heap, moaning in pain. It was impossible for him to raise his left arm.

She faced back the way they had come. Yellow muzzle-flame dazzled her. A bullet cracked past her head, struck the ceiling a few yards farther down. At once Dan popped out of a side door and fired four rapid shots as the dimly glimpsed gang gunman ducked back in turn.

She heard a scuffle of rubber sandal on wood. Annja had been hypnotized by the firearm, which appeared to be a rifle or carbine, going off almost in her face. And now the stick fighter had gotten past the dead man in the hallway and was about the crack her skull open with one of his batons….

Holding the sword diagonally upward, she twisted her torso counterclockwise. At the same time she let herself fall to the floor. It gave her the split second she needed. Ebony wood clacked against the sword's flat blade three inches in front of her nose.

The man knew how to use the sticks in combination attacks. As the first, held in his left hand, kissed off the blade, he aimed the second for the crown of Annja's head. Her shoulders slammed the wood floor. She rolled into him fast. The stick smashed into the uneven planking as her long legs slammed against his.

It wasn't any kind of proper sweep, just desperation. But Annja was tall and strong and her opponent had sacrificed balance to strike at his falling foe. He went down in a tangle across her legs.

She lay on her belly with the sword trapped beneath her. Fortunately it had already been flat against her body; otherwise it would have gashed deeply into her rib cage.

The stick fighter was good. He reared upright, straddling her thighs, raised his right stick for a shot at her unprotected neck.

The sword was an impediment. She let it go back to the otherwhere. Then with all her strength she whipped her body clockwise, pushing off with her left hand, lashing out with her right.

The stick fighter's nose broke with a crunch of cartilage. He reeled back, blinking in agonized surprise as blood covered his upper lip.

She wrenched her right leg free, drew back the knee, pushed hard. The stick fighter stood almost upright. He slammed against the far wall of the corridor. His head cracked back against the planking so hard the wood split vertically. He groaned and sank to his knees.

From back up the corridor, she heard the heavy ringing slam of the gang member's carbine. Dan grunted.

A body thumped on the floor. Annja heard her partner moan, "Oh, shit," in a ghastly voice.

23

As Annja rolled back to face him, the gang member strolled from a doorway on the right as if he wanted to give the appearance he was going for a walk in the park.

Annja jumped to her feet. The rifleman ignored her. She summoned back the sword, knowing already it was futile.

Smiling, the man raised the stock of his rifle to his shoulder, sighting down the barrel at Dan, who had slumped out into the corridor doubled over his knees, a knot of helpless misery.

Suddenly he twisted sideways, bringing his gun up in both hands, thrusting them out to extend his arms fully in an isosceles triangle. The handgun cracked twice.

Dust flew from the rifleman's grimy shirt at belly and breastbone. He reared back, more in surprise and shock than pain. The metal butt plate slipped from his shoulder.

Dan rotated to a sitting position. He fired again. The man's head snapped back. He fell backward in a lifeless sprawl.

"Fell for it, asshole," Dan snarled, getting a knee up and starting to stand. He turned a grin of triumph toward Annja.

It froze. "Look out!" he shouted, bringing the handgun up again. It seemed to be pointing right at her face.

Annja's eyes widened. She was looking straight down the black muzzle.

Flame blossomed in her face. Hair that had fallen loose at the left side of Annja's face stirred as if brushed by careless fingers. Shock waves of the bullet's supersonic passage slapped her cheek with surprising force as its miniature sonic boom temporarily deafened her left ear and filled her head with ringing.

She spun. The stick fighter stood behind her. Or rather, he was falling away from her, weeping scarlet from where his right eye had been.

Whatever else he was, Dan Seddon was a hell of a combat handgunner. Accomplished herself, after considerable training, practice—and real-world experience—Annja could scarcely have done better herself.

Dan stood. "Nifty piece of cutlery," he said, looking at the sword. He had punched the magazine release and was pulling out the old box. He held a full reload, retrieved from an inner pocket of his vest, clipped between a couple of fingers. Annja had been meaning to ask why he encumbered himself with extra clothing in the unremitting wet heat. Now she knew. "Where'd you get that?"

"Tell you later." Her voice shook. Relief flooded her body and caused her legs to tremble.

Catch a grip, she told herself sternly. The smoke was a bit thinner but flames cackled madly not far away. And she still had no idea how they were going to get out of the strange warren alive—much less the whole monstrous desolation of the colony.

"I'll be sure to ask," Dan said. His eyes snapped past her. "Behind—right!" he shouted.

She wheeled, not right but left, counterclockwise. It allowed her to lead with the tip of the sword, gripped two handed and held horizontally to her left.

A warped wooden door had opened a yard behind her. A young man had emerged, bare chested, with a red cloth band holding hair back from a handsome Indian face.

The sword punched right through his sternum, through his heart. Fixed on hers, his dark eyes widened. They stared a final question into Annja's eyes. Then the light faded from them and he slumped. In sudden sick horror she banished the sword, as if that could unmake the wound. But life had fled the body huddled at her feet.

"He—he was unarmed," she said.

Dan gripped her hard on the shoulder. "Suck it up," he said. "He was one of them. See? He doesn't look anorexic."

She was shaking her head in desperate denial. "He wasn't armed. I killed him."

"He was an enemy. He ran up on you. And one thing you've got to learn about the real world, sweetheart—you can't make an omelet without breaking eggs."

She turned an agonized look on him. Tears blurred her eyes.

From behind them rang hoarse shouts. Ahead flames suddenly ate up another entry curtain and billowed out into the corridor.

"Choose now," Dan said. "Move or die."

She nodded. He turned and raced out ahead, weapon grasped in both hands. He didn't even flinch from the flames that lashed at him and filled the corridor with a hellish orange glare.

She followed. Dan vanished to the right around an unseen corner. She passed through the fire. She felt it sear her upper arm. The pain was like a penance.

It snapped her back to the situation. Batting at smoldering hair, she turned the corner and found herself facing another long corridor. Blessed daylight shone at its far end, a dazzling white oblong a good twenty yards away. She saw no sign of Dan.

But a figure blocked her path. It was short and unmistakably feminine. In spite of the way the flood of photons over her retinas blurred it to shadow, Annja recognized her antagonist.

"Xia!" It was half surprised exclamation, half curse.

"Annja Creed," the woman said in English, "you don't know what you do."

"I'm fighting to break free the secrets you're selfishly withholding from the human race," Annja stated, striding forward. "If you want to call that neocolonialism, go right ahead. But your murderous ways have shown you aren't fit stewards of whatever power you hold!"

"I see you've been talking to Isis," Xia said. Her tone was conversational, almost light. "She can be a bit strident. I hope you didn't damage her too badly. She has a good heart and great promise."

"If she's the tall black woman with the green headband, she was alive when I left her," Annja said tautly, "if not feeling too well. But what you'd know about a good heart I haven't a clue."

"If you keep on this path I must fight you," Xia said with what sounded like regret. Feigned, Annja was furiously sure.

She held her arm out to the side, started to form her hand into a fist to pull the sword from its special place. Then she let her hand drop to her side.

Treacherous as Xia and her people were, Annja felt she had sullied the sword—sullied her soul. She would not give in to damnation by deliberately striking down an unarmed person. No matter how deserving.

She charged. Size and strength were her obvious advantages over her foe. She hoped they sufficed to overcome whatever skill Xia possessed. Closing on the much shorter woman, Annja realized Xia was fuller-figured than she'd looked in her exquisitely tailored suits in Belém and Manaus. She wore a dark green wrap around heavy breasts and a loose brown skirt like a sarong around full hips. Her belly was a dome of muscle like a belly dancer's.

Annja expected the woman to try to sweep her legs, tackle her or kick at her belly or pelvis. The low line was the strongest attack against a taller foe. Instead Xia leaped straight into the air. Her rump-length hair formed a dark nimbus around her head.

Unable to stop, Annja ran right into her. Xia wrapped her legs around Annja's belly as her arms tried to tangle the taller woman's. The hair enveloped their heads like a cloud.

Annja fell heavily on her back. Air exploded from her lungs, driven by Xia's hard-muscled butt pounding into her solar plexus.

For a moment they were nose to nose, completely enclosed by Xia's amazing midnight hair. The Promessan smelled of sweat on clean female skin, and her hair like jasmine. Her nose was snubbed. Her big almond eyes, their jade-green hue visible even here, reminded Annja irrationally of the eyes of the golden *onza* she had seen on entering this hellish maze. That had been hallucination, she told herself.

Xia's hands were like steel clamps pinning Annja's wrists to the floor. The wood was slimy and irregular beneath her. She felt ancient ooze seeping through her clothes at shoulder and butt.

"It's not too late for you, Annja," Xia said. "You have been misled—"

"By you!" Annja shouted. Planting her feet, she violently arched her back.

Though Xia held the advantage—and, like Annja, her body was well packed with muscle—she had not managed to pin Annja's hips. Rather she sat astride Annja's flat belly just below her breasts.

Annja used her strength to buck the smaller woman off like an angry rodeo bronco.

Xia went tumbling down the passage. The way to outside lay clear. Annja doubted she could make it without her opponent taking her down from behind. And her nature rebelled against fleeing, though she knew it was the right thing to do.

She rolled over and jumped to her feet. Xia was already up, clearing a curtain of heavy black hair from her face with a flip of her head. She grinned at Annja.

"Not bad," she said.

Annja advanced. Not headlong this time, but behind a flurry of kicks and punches.

Xia blocked or redirected them with apparent ease and a remarkable economy of motion. Even as Annja struck for her in dizzying combinations, she marveled at the other's skill.

Annja's breath came in great gulps. Strength ebbed from her like blood from an opened vein. Along with total physical exertion loading up the lactic acid in her muscles came unrivaled mental tension.

Xia, her oval face serene, looked as if she could keep this up for a week.

Gasping raggedly, trying not to reel, Annja decided to try power where technique had failed. She threw a quick quartet of punches at Xia's face—all blocked by scarcely visible movements—then shifted weight to her back foot to fire a side kick.

But she had barely lifted her right foot to chamber the kick when Xia flowed toward her and slammed a palm heel into her sternum.

Floorboards slammed her in the back. The air fled her body. A dark figure rose above her. It was Xia, hair flying around her again.

From down the hall a noise erupted. Even with Xia suspended above her, Annja's eyes were drawn away, back down the hall. A gang member stood in a crouch, firing a Kalashnikov from the hip. The brilliant yellow muzzle-flare illuminated a face screaming almost in ecstasy.

The dancing flame went out. The banana magazine was empty. Annja looked up, wondering why Xia hadn't heel stomped on her sternum.

The air was empty of all but roiling smoke and drifting motes of dust and spores. The hallway between Annja and the door to the outside world was a roaring hell of flame.

The Promessan woman had vanished.

It was time for Annja to do likewise. A hint of light showed beneath a blanket hung in a doorway to her right. She rolled through it into a tiny room as a fresh burst of automatic gunfire chewed up the planking where she had lain an instant before.

A tiny off-square window let sunlight filter vaguely into the room through yellowed newspaper taped across its crossed slats in lieu of glass. Annja coiled herself and jumped through it. She carried with her not just the window but a good patch of rotted-wood wall.

She put a shoulder down as she landed and rolled clear of the wreckage. She got herself to her feet by sheer willpower and desperation and bouncing off the walls to both sides of the narrow alley. Speed was her only slim chance at life.

Coughing from the smoke she had inhaled, Annja tried to force her mind clear, assimilate surroundings and circumstances. She was alone in a tiny space that initially seemed to have no outlet. Then ahead of her she noticed the outward-leaning wall of the shack to her right didn't quite meet that of the hovel beyond.

She also noticed all the buildings around her were in flame to a greater or lesser extent. If she lingered another minute she'd best pray the Kalashnikov gangbanger blasted her from the blown-out window. Only that would save her from burning to death.

Annja raced around the almost hidden corner. Running through coils of brown-and-dirty-white smoke, she saw ahead of her, thirty yards away beyond a cross alley, two men fighting.

Dan. Looming over him was Patrizinho.

She shouted. Smoke clawed at her throat. Dan, barehanded, launched a savage one-two combination, left hook and right cross.

The punches came at their target from the sides, outflanking most attempts to block them. Patrizinho leaned back away from his opponent, slipping the blows. His bare brown upper torso gleamed in the sun

as if oiled. His dreadlocks, held back from his handsome face with a golden band, flew like a Medusa tail
of serpents about wide shoulders.

Dan's right hand went behind him, came up with the
handgun.

"No!" Annja screamed. She reached the crossing
alley. Firearms and energy weapons crackled to both
left and right through the roar of flames.

Patrizinho flicked the 9-mm pistol with the back of
his left hand. It fired. The muzzle-flame must have
seared his left biceps; unburned propellant and primer
fragments must have peppered his bronze skin. Paying
no mind, he stepped into Dan, dropping his weight and
driving a compact vertical punch straight into Dan's
chest above his heart.

Dan did not go flying back the way Annja had from
Xia's palm-heel strike between her breasts. Instead his
body seemed almost to balloon away from the blow, up
and outward. He staggered but stayed on his feet.

"No!" Annja shrieked again. This time Patrizinho
looked straight at her. His beautiful long face seemed
full of infinite sadness.

The black handgun dropped from Dan's fingers.

From her left, green beams flickered, crossing
Annja's path. Automatic fire answered invisibly from
her right. Disregarding both, she plunged on, across ten
feet of open death ground.

No energy beam or bullet struck her. But flames
suddenly roared from both sides and met in the middle, an orange wall. Just inside the cover of the far

alley mouth Annja was forced to stop, safe from the firefight but unable to proceed to the aid of her friend.

The flame curtains parted. As through an opened gate, Dan walked unsteadily toward her. There was no sign of Patrizinho.

Annja ran to him. His face was horribly pale, his lean cheeks ashen beneath his fine two-day beard. He scarcely seemed to breathe.

"My...heart," he explained. "It's my heart."

He staggered, went to his knees in the foul alley muck. One hand spasmodically clutched the front of her shirt. His pale eyes were wide.

Then he smiled. It was the sweetest smile Annja had ever seen. It would haunt her dreams so long as she lived.

"I see it all so clearly now," he said as he died.

24

The massive double doors, oaken, stained dark brown, polished as mirrors, swung open violently to Sir Iain Moran's shove. They would give me permission to enter, would they? he thought savagely.

Beneath a chandelier like a wedding cake of light and crystal, deep in the bowels of a little-known château perched high in the Bernese Alps, there stretched a long, massive table of oak, dark stained and polished like the door. Around it sat a dozen men.

They were old men. Sir Iain was junior in the room by a good two decades or more. Their hair was silver or white or absent, their clothes exquisite, with the unobtrusive perfection rendered by masters of the tailor's art.

These men brought unobtrusiveness to an art. Their names were unknown to the public, or only incidentally so. They sat on no thrones, in no cabinets, held no chairs in any corporate boardroom. No ties connected them to any government or corporation or recognized institution—visibly. They were as far above such things as eagles over ants.

But every single person who served a government or multinational, no matter how low or high his rank, served one or another of them indirectly.

Look at them, Publico thought with contempt, these self-anointed masters of the world. Withered old vultures is what they look like. But he knew them for what they really were. Jackals.

The ancient at the table's far end raised a head of hair like spun glass. On a face liver spotted and sagging with the weight of years, he adjusted his glasses. Like the presence he projected—even seated, even tethered by plastic tubes from his nostrils to an oxygen tank discreetly hidden behind his chair—the piercing blue eyes made no concession to age.

"Sir Iain Moran," the old man said in a high voice, upper-class English accent piping with outrage. "What is the meaning of this intrusion?"

"I meant to correct a most unfortunate oversight on your part, gentlemen," he said, his baritone Irish brogue at once rough and rolling. "You seemed to believe you could make me wait upon your pleasure like a lackey."

The chairman drew his head back on his skinny, wattled neck.

"What do you think to gain by storming in here like this, young man?" a stout man halfway down the table's right side demanded with Teutonic heaviness. He had white eyebrows that stuck out ferociously.

"My rightful place," Publico said.

"That has to be earned, friend," said a man across from the bristle-browed German in an elaborate Texas drawl. It was fake, Publico knew. The man in the pale gray suit and bolo tie with an immense silver steer head for a clasp had been born in Massachusetts and educated at Princeton and Georgetown.

"Ah, but have I not earned my place and then some?" Sir Iain asked. "I've served you well, gentlemen. I've done your bidding and more."

"Do you imagine," the chairman asked, "that we hand out memberships to the most exclusive council in the world like crackers at a child's birthday party? You have served well, it's true, Sir Iain. But you have likewise been well recompensed."

"You think to hire me like a tradesman, then?" His tone was silky.

They said nothing. They simply sat and stared at him. They showed no discomfiture. Security in the château matched that of a thermonuclear-warhead assembly plant. No matter how robust and agile he was, he posed them no physical danger. At the least aggressive movement he would instantly die.

Even the volcanic force of his own presence, his reproach, made no impression on them. They were men of necessity long inured to shame. And likewise to injustice.

He leaned forward and dropped his big, scarred knuckles on the immaculate wood with a significant thunk. If he could make no overt threat he could still emphasize his very potent presence.

"Some of you have lived even longer than your visible decrepitude would indicate," he said, continuing to speak in the softest voice his scarred vocal cords could manage. "Your relative anonymity, thanks to your control of the world's media, ensures that no one notices anything unusual about you. I know there are others. Members emeritus. Who yet have a voice in affairs."

He straightened, allowed his volume to rise. "Those of you who sit here today, sinking into the decay of your advancing years, do so because you either have physiological resistance to the current generation of treatment, or because you fear to step away from the table of power for long enough to undergo the full extent of rejuvenation. I know that at your level there is no friendship, no loyalty, no brotherhood. Only fear and interest—and your fellowship is that of a pack of wolves, always looking to rend the weak."

"Do you think to force us to admit you to our ranks by insulting us?" the German demanded.

"I might," he said, sticking hands in pockets and grinning, "if I thought you capable of being insulted. Any more than you are of feeling shame."

"Pray you are correct in that, Sir Iain," said a Frenchman who sat closest to Publico's right. "We might not make the truest of friends. But as enemies, we are dauntless!"

Publico showed him a frown, then he glared about at the council members.

"If you will not make a place for me at your table, gentlemen," he said, "I shall be compelled to force one open."

"Others have tried that before, Sir Iain," the American said with heartiness as false as his accent.

"But never I."

Again, there was no reaction. A lesser man might have quailed at the utter certitude their blandness showed. But such a man would never have pushed his way in there in the first place.

"Do you deny," Publico said, "that you have discovered the means, not just of life extension, but life renewal?"

"Why should we bother?" said the Chinese member who sat at the chairman's left. He was a large stout man with a fringe of white hair around the rear of a globelike head. His build and manner and blunt peasant's face projected almost as much physical force as Publico's weight-chiseled frame. "Or affirm, for that matter? We have no need to answer to you, Sir Iain."

"Do you really think not?"

"You think your billions impress us?" the Frenchman sneered.

The American laughed. It was presumably meant to be a guffaw. It came out a raven's croak. "He doesn't even know where they are!" he exclaimed.

"Ah," Sir Iain said. "But I do. Don't forget—I'm a man of deeds. You know I put my body, my very life on the line when I was a lad. Since then I've done as much in half a hundred less publicized ways. Of course, you gentlemen are well aware. I've made my mark upon the world. I've taken actions. Some on behalf of this august if nameless council.

"And I've a following. When I speak, tens of millions listen. *Hundreds* of millions. From the scruffiest street activists to crowned heads and corporate gods."

"Do you honestly think," the German chortled, his jowls aflutter like slabs of gelatin dessert, "that we don't control as much and more?"

"They may dance to your tunes, Sir Iain," the Chinese member said, "these masses and ministers and monarchs. Even march to them. But will they kill and die to them, as they do ours?"

"Do you honestly want to find out?"

"Enough, Sir Iain!" The chairman's thin voice rapped like a schoolteacher's ruler on a blackboard. "You err grievously if you believe mere wealth—or vulgar repute—can gain you entrance into our councils. You are permitted to leave now, Sir Iain. I will stress this word, *permitted.*"

Publico stood as erect as a soldier at attention on a parade ground. Then he turned and marched briskly from the gleaming chamber.

Out in the corridor he stalked, emanating rage. His hands were buried in his pockets. His great leonine head was thrust forward on his bull's neck.

Right, he thought. That's their last chance, then. The thought came with as much relief—satisfaction, even—as anger.

25

The water of the Amazon was ocher.

Annja Creed stood in the riverboat's blunt bow. One walking shoe up on the gunwale, the other on deck, she gazed up the course of the river.

The far bank, the left, was visible only as a green thread along the yellow flow. On the right the forest loomed over them so close that the outer limbs almost overhung the tubby, run-down vessel.

The trees were full of monkeys, screeching and hooting at the invaders and their engine, its mechanically monotonous regularity as alien to the surroundings as spiders from Mars.

Other primates lined the starboard rail—mercenaries of the small platoon of twenty-five men and an officer Sir Iain Moran had arranged to accompany Annja on her journey to find the nine-boled tree and the long held trove of secrets of the descendants of escaped slaves.

Whether they had been brought to Feliz Lusitânia especially for the task or recruited from the ganglike internal-security forces, Annja neither knew nor cared. They were heavily armed and showed every sign of ruthlessness. That was all that mattered to her now.

She was bound on a mission of justice. She needed hard tools. These men were that, at least.

She would not have chosen many of them herself. Half a dozen of them were perched precariously on the rail, all shirtless, a couple wearing nothing but shorts, hooting and screaming back at the furious monkeys.

A flight of blue macaws erupted from a tree, flew off over the ship and headed upstream. The ship was about sixty feet long and twenty wide. It had a modest deckhouse extended forward by a corrugated tin canopy and by a tentlike awning astern. There were also cabins below, stinking, close and crowded.

Annja had chosen to pass the first night alone on deck, under the tin shelter of the elevated wheelhouse for protection from the rain that drummed down half the night. The cabins offered a modicum of privacy. The captain, a short Belgian with a silver fringe beard, had offered his own, probably by prearrangement rather than gallantry. But even the captain's Spartan deckhouse quarters reminded her too much of the hopeless hovels of the lower circle of Hell she had known at the colony.

A tall blond kid from upper New York State

crouched atop the deckhouse, wearing only shorts and bulky combat boots and what seemed to be a T-shirt wrapped around his head. The skin stretched over his washboard ribs was fish-belly white. It was already changing to boiled-lobster red on his back from the sun. If Annja's extensive field experience was any guide he'd be writhing in agony by the early equatorial nightfall. But like the rest, he loudly claimed vast combat experience.

He cradled a long black M-16 rifle across his knees. He wanted to hunt monkeys, he said.

He was getting visibly more and more frustrated. The monkeys were shrewd. Watching the dense transition undergrowth and low-hanging trees along the banks, Annja could catch only flashes of their dark-brown-and-white-furred bodies.

She didn't much care. To the extent she paid attention to her surroundings she hoped her companions would exhaust their masculine energies in their dominance fight with their unseen rivals. Some had begun casting not-so-professional glances her way the moment they shoved off from the Feliz Lusitânia dock upstream of the river-dredging operation the day before. The looks kept getting hotter eyed and longer; she expected trouble by tonight.

She was ready for it. She was ready for anything. Perhaps things she never would have considered before.

SOMEHOW SHE HAD MADE her way back to the citadel after Dan's murder. Maybe it was the sword she carried naked in her hand. Maybe it was the look in her eye.

She had somehow found the presence of mind to put the sword away before approaching the heavily fortified gate through which they had exited that fateful morning.

She was recognized and admitted quickly. She knew her pale skin counted little and her U.S. passport even less—if she crossed the powers-that-be in the camp she wouldn't be the first American citizen to end her days in the cage, nor the first American woman. But whatever his relationship with the mining camp and its warring directors, Publico's patronage was a powerful shield for her.

She had been forced to leave Dan's body behind. There was no way to carry it while she threaded her way through the maze of hazards back to the central compound.

Gomes had assured her his bosses would recover the body. He scoffed at the notion there was any part of the camp the security forces dared not go, although privately Annja was inclined to believe Lidia. But she suspected the main gangs of that part of the colony had temporarily exhausted themselves, fighting each other, as well as the intruding Promessans, and would hunker down licking their wounds rather than oppose a patrol of official enforcers.

It all meant little to her.

Dr. Lidia do Carvalho had paid her a visit in her chambers as she packed for the trip's final leg. Each expressed pleasure the other had made it out alive. The doctor asked if Annja might please help her young daughter. Although she obviously felt constrained in what she said, supporting Annja's suspicion the rooms were bugged, Annja got the strong impression the little girl was being held hostage for her mother's compliance.

Annja felt genuine sympathy. Yet she had to tell the doctor there was nothing she could do for the child until she had finished what she was doing now. Lidia, though obviously disappointed, thanked her for her kindness and left.

Annja wished she could help. But Dan's death had sealed her, it seemed, to his viewpoint. She felt Lidia's pain. But Lidia and her daughter were only individuals. How could a the welfare of single individual or even two be weighed against the common good?

The Promessans had committed grievous crimes, against all humankind, as well as Annja and Dan. By withholding their knowledge they caused enormous suffering.

Now Annja would wrest the secrets forcibly from the Promessans' grasp or die trying.

And in return she would give them retribution.

THE MERCS ALONG THE RAIL grew impatient with the would-be hunter. They stopped screeching at the still-unseen monkeys and began to chant, "Bil-ly, Bil-ly," as Lieutenant McKelvey, a nervous American probably in his early thirties but with the receding hairline, lined face and stress-sunk eyes of a middle-aged man, ran around trying to bring them back to some kind of order.

Billy shouldered his rifle. Still no targets presented themselves. He held his fire. As if to assert his own dominance, he brandished his rifle above his head, miming triumph. Annja stopped straining her eyes at walls of green—always seeking the tree with nine trunks—to watch the proceedings. She felt a mild stirring of professional anthropological interest.

The chanting subsided. Annja was unsure why. Billy shook the rifle and grinned at his comrades below him. Annja raised a brow. That teeth-baring display was certain to be interpreted by the monkeys as a threat, and Annja wondered how they would react.

Nothing prepared her, or any of the hard men on the riverboat, for what streaked out of the dense green brush like a line of shadow.

Annja heard it hit, a distinct thump, with a slight crunching sound like gravel beneath a boot. Billy's grin froze on his sun-reddened face. He glanced down at his chest. The butt of an arrow stood a handsbreadth from his sternum. The fletching was black as crows' wings.

"An arrow?" he said in a puzzled voice.

He pitched forward. His body cleared the rail by a couple of inches to plunge into the reeking, tannin-stained water, raising a greasy splash to wet the chests and legs of his comrades, who stood gaping with an utter lack of comprehension at what had just happened.

Billy bobbed back to the surface. He floated on his

back with his arms outflung, eyes staring sightlessly at the hard blue sky. Red stained the yellow water around him. The arrow jutted up from his chest like some defiant banner.

With a furious scream a mercenary raised a machine gun and emptied the big box of .223-caliber ammunition clamped to its side into the undergrowth. Instantly the others joined in, blasting the greenery on full-auto with assault rifles and light machine guns and the shotguns.

Lieutenant McKelvey shouted himself hoarse trying to get them to cease fire. The boat groaned low in the water from the weight of ammunition as much as other supplies for the small expeditionary force. But in a serious fight those crates could be used up quickly.

In the end he drew his own side arm, a Springfield Government Model .45, and fired it in the air in an attempt to stop the mindless explosion of firepower. What stopped them, though, Annja thought, was simply that they'd exhausted their magazines.

The fury ebbed from the men as they broke out empty magazines and replaced them with full boxes. In part it was because of the utter lack of response to their bullet storm. Some wood splinters flew, some branches fell, a green flurry of leaves flew up in the air to settle on the slow flow of the river. A flight of small scarlet birds rose twittering hysterically from a nearby tree and flew inland in a colorful cloud.

Otherwise, nothing. No screams. No bodies. Not even more arrows. When the hammering racket of the gunfire ceased, the silence was complete.

The boat chugged on. Bellowing orders, the captain got the helmsman to turn the wheel over hard to port and swing the stubby bow back toward the middle of the broad river.

Billy's body was left bobbing in the wake. No one seemed inclined to get the captain to halt the boat or make any effort to reel in the body.

Annja had avoided interaction with the hired guns as much as possible, aside from their none-too-effectual lieutenant. She didn't want them to notice her, even though she knew they had been instructed to follow her orders instantly and without question. But now she turned to one who stood near her holding a big shotgun tipped over a camo-clad shoulder.

"What happened to never leaving a man behind?" she asked.

"He lost. Let the gators have him," the man said.

NO MATTER HOW IT FELT the heat was probably not greater at night, Annja thought. She tried to sleep. Only the crush of fatigue had driven her at last, long after sunset, from her self-appointed lookout at the *Marlow*'s bow. She had exacted promises from Captain Lambert and Lieutenant McKelvey that they would detail men to keep watch throughout the night for the nine-trunked tree.

The heat where she lay on her thin pallet before the wheelhouse, unallayed by the rain that had fallen earlier, made sleep hard to find. The mosquito netting she had formed into a sort of pup tent above her restricted such airflow as there was from the boat's slow, steady passage upriver. And when sleep came, the images she saw were anything but soothing.

She came awake to great weight pressing down on her body and stinking breath filling her nose and sinuses. Her eyes snapped open.

A beard-stubbled face loomed inches above hers. The mosquito netting had been stripped away. Starlight gleamed in pale slitted eyes. The mercenary smiled.

"We're gonna have us some fun, honey." She felt the hot kiss of steel against her throat. "Scream and I'll cut you."

26

For a moment Annja stared into the man's narrow and hard face. Then she sighed and went limp.

"That's right, honey," the man said in his Midwestern accent. "Just take it easy. You'll like it. You'll like it so good you'll think you never got it before."

He laid the flat back of his combat knife between her breasts, slid its tip into her thin blouse beneath the top buttoned button. "Once you do Ranger," he said, "you won't never be a stranger."

Annja moved like a viper striking. Her left hand shot out to seize his knife wrist, shoving it and the big blade, gleaming in starlight, to the side. It cut loose her blouse button as she whipped it away.

His eyes widened. His smile turned nasty.

"So you want to make it interesting—"

He sat astride her belly. He was too far up to control her long, powerful legs. With her foot flexed she snapped a kick against the back of his head, hard.

His head whipped forward. He reared back upright in reaction, waving the knife wildly. He had come up onto his knees, taking most of his weight off her. She whipped up her legs. Her feet went around his neck. She locked ankle over ankle.

Tucking her arms like a boxer's, clenching her fists, clenching her whole body to aid her effort, she rolled to the right with all her strength and weight.

The man's neck broke with a nasty sound.

The motion threw his body off her. It flopped like a fish in the scuppers in a final spasm.

She jumped up. Her nostrils were flared, her eyes wide and furious.

She had an audience. At least a dozen men were gathered around, standing or squatting to watch the show.

She swept them with a glance like lasers.

"Anybody else want to play?" she challenged them.

If they rushed her she was ready to summon the sword. But in a way she already had. The mystic steel had entered her spine, her soul. The fires of its forging blazed through her eyes.

One by one the men slunk away.

AT ABOUT TEN the next morning a French man the others called Taffy stood leaning over the starboard rail trailing his fingertips in the swelling yellow wake of the boat. Annja was in the bow doing some stretching in the limited space. The former paratrooper was perhaps twelve or fifteen feet from her. Sudden movement drew her eyes. An object like a blunt arrow broke the yellow swell. It was a huge black caiman.

The alligator-like reptile's mouth was open wide, showing pale yellow-pink lining and lots of teeth. It slammed shut like a bear trap on the Frenchman's arm. The broad, tapering head enveloped the limb to within six inches of his shoulder.

The Frenchman screamed in a clear falsetto. With a wrench of its huge body the caiman pulled him over the rail and into the water with a foam-edged splash.

Another shoot-out instantly followed. The mercs seldom strayed far from their weapons by choice, and doubly so since the arrow had come out of the green blankness of the woods. They emptied their magazines again into the roiling water. Annja wondered if they remembered their comrade was in there with the caiman, or whether they wanted to save him from a horrible death. Maybe they just didn't give a damn.

MORE ARROWS FLEW from the shadowed bank when the boat wandered near in late afternoon. All fell short, disappearing into the river. With none coming near and McKelvey glaring at his men with a hand on the butt of his side arm, the mercenaries did not respond with a storm of fire. Instead they gripped their weapons hard and watched the jungle edge with hot, straining eyes. The boat scuttled back out toward the middle of the river.

Lieutenant McKelvey tried to strike up a conversation with Annja. He seemed diffident, more than half-ashamed. Perhaps he felt embarrassed by how little control he had over his men, who squabbled often and violently now, and seemed to refrain from falling on and killing each other solely because of the imminent prospects of easier prey.

She wondered how such an ineffectual man could find himself in charge of such predators in human form. She saw no better reason than that the mercenaries' masters, back at the gold camp or beyond, had decreed him so. The mercs with regular military experience, she knew, were massively conditioned to obey anyone their superiors told them to.

Mostly Annja tuned the lieutenant out, as she tuned out the bugs that swarmed and buzzed and bit incessantly. He was a tool to the great purpose she felt called on to serve. Not a good tool, particularly—and he and his men were likely too many or too few for what lay ahead. But they would serve well enough if the dangers of their quest wore them away instead of her, so long as she was left to face the final and greatest challenge.

In the end it was her task alone.

THAT NIGHT A SCREAM awakened her.

She rolled off her pallet. Somehow she got out from under her mosquito netting without tangling herself in its folds. She was on her feet in a crouch in an instant, the sword firm in her hand.

She saw a flicker of motion from the top of the wheelhouse. A head with terrible incurving teeth flashed down to grab the upturned screaming face of a young man. Then coils as thick around as a truck tire slid down and around him, glistening in the light of the just risen moon. They seemed to move slowly, inexorable as fate. Yet by the time she reached him, sword raised to sever those thick brown-on-bronze loops of muscle, he was wound about three times.

His right arm, pinned against his body, couldn't reach his weapon. Annja saw the peristaltic action of the great serpent's body as it contracted around him, even as its weight bore him over the rail and off into the water.

The little round Belgian captain was out in a nightshirt, holding a big flashlight and screaming at the helmsman. The crewman had dozed at his wheel, and a trick of the current had drawn the boat under the overhang of trees on the banks. The anaconda had simply dropped down on the deckhouse from a branch and awaited prey.

In between barrages of abuse at his crewman she heard the captain wondering aloud just how the current could have so moved the boat when its slow, faithful engine was driving inexorably against it. As he vanished into the wheelhouse to take over the helm himself, Annja looked around to find the deck crowded with the surviving mercenaries. Instead of emptying their weapons into the waters that had claimed a third - comrade, they all stared at her with big, round eyes.

"I was too late," she said. "Sorry." She walked forward. The mercenaries standing between her and her comfortless pallet melted from her like mercury from a fingertip. She made no mention of the sword.

Annja smiled a big smile. Grumbling, the others turned away. Presumably their work had inured them to horrors. These were new horrors, but, in the end, just horrors.

What force could make the boat stray from midstream like that? she asked herself as she ducked under the netting once more.

All might be explained by superior technology. That was what she had come for, wasn't it?

She lay back down. The gauntlet had been thrown. She would face her enemies boldly, unafraid.

She slept solidly the rest of the night, untroubled by dreams.

As the sun's first light poured forth, pursuing them upriver, the *Marlow* lookout's call roused Annja. Blinking and fuzzy she crawled out from beneath the mosquito netting to stand upright in the bow.

Ahead, just where the great river bent to the right, its base obscured by mist as if it floated on cloud, a vast tree or collection of trees with nine trunks wound somehow together leaned out over the mighty Amazon.

27

Their beachhead was a natural clearing filled with shoulder-high grass. Natural seeming, Annja realized, when she saw that what she had taken for a driftwood raft caught on the bank, another hundred yards or so past the nine-trunked tree, was actually the remnant of a wooden dock, slumped into the water.

As the *Marlow* approached shore the men gripped their weapons and stared fixedly at the landing site. Annja thought it was professionalism belatedly asserting itself. A distressed-looking McKelvey disabused her of the notion as he removed his crumpled boonie hat to wipe sweat from his forehead.

"This is a bad place," he said. "We better pray your man Moran gets plenty reinforcements in to us pretty quick, like he said he would."

"Why is that?" Annja asked.

"A logging party got ambushed ten, twenty klicks back upstream from here, not three months ago. They had a whole security company with them, 120 men or more, with armored cars, machine guns, mortars, everything. Another two or three hundred workers, bulldozers, the whole nine yards. The Indians, just wiped the jungle with 'em. Total massacre."

"Why didn't I hear about it?" Annja demanded. It seemed to confirm they were in fact within reach of her goal. It also confirmed the level of danger.

"It wasn't the kind of thing that'd go on FOX News, ma'am," he said. "Not everything that happens even gets on the Internet, especially when it happens way out here in the back of beyond. A few survivors made it back to the gold camp. Some of Bull Campbell's boys heard the bosses. Sounded like a real horror show."

"What happened to the survivors?"

The lieutenant shrugged. But Annja noted his eyes slid away from hers. The Amazon camps were an ultimately Darwinian environment. And the big cage in the river always needed new gold panners, she reckoned.

Ashore, the men moved with self-confidence seemingly restored by familiar tasks. They unreeled rolls of the same German razor tape that topped the fence around Feliz Lusitânia. They set up curved plastic tablets whose convex face was stamped with the legend Front Toward Enemy. They erected little stands of equipment. It was all a very solemn ritual.

Annja had already knocked about the world enough in her young life to be familiar with most of it. The knife wire was suitably nasty. So were the Claymore mines. And the infrared detectors and infantry radars were undoubtedly far keener at night than plain low-tech human eyes.

Any stray capybara that chanced to wander out of the bush was certain to meet a swift and horrid fate.

As the activity got well under way McKelvey came to Annja, standing near the water. He seemed pleased. "We've got it under control now," he said. "We're doing what we do. We shouldn't have any trouble now."

"That's what we thought all along. And you've lost three men," she said.

His worried expression came back. "Well, I know there are Indian attacks all the time...."

"In the backcountry, on mining and logging camps," Annja said. "Tourist and trade boats come up and down this river all the time. They don't get attacked by Indians. Why your men now? With all these other incidents? And how many cases of anacondas attacking people have you heard about?"

"Well—there's those movies...." His voice trailed off as he realized too late how lame that sounded.

"There are documented accounts," she said. "A few. But three fatal attacks? You think that's coincidence? Something doesn't want us here, Lieutenant."

"Rationally—"

"Yeah. That's what I want to believe, too. But how rational is that level of coincidence?" Annja surprised herself with the question.

"Well…that's what all the guys with guns are for, aren't they?"

She resisted an urge to pat him on the cheek. "Sure, Lieutenant. And they'll probably even be some help."

He smiled and nodded. "Lucky there's a clearing here, huh, Ms. Creed? Helps a lot."

"I'm not so sure it's luck. I suspect this is an old, abandoned rubber plantation. The jungle takes longer to reclaim some fields than others."

"Huh," he said again. "You really know a lot about this place, don't you, ma'am?"

Annja scanned the surrounding trees. There was a break to the northeast. Beyond it she glimpsed more grassland. "Not as much as I intend to, Lieutenant."

ACCORDING TO PLAN the mercenaries, having secured an initial perimeter, moved beyond the gap Annja had seen into the open grass to create a landing strip. The night before setting out from Feliz Lusitânia Annja had spoken briefly, almost robotically, by the camp radio-phone to Publico. He said he had finished his urgent mission overseas. He would join the party when they found the nine-trunked tree.

She had not asked him what his connection was to the camp and its evils. It no longer seemed important. Her quest consumed her utterly.

As the men set to work hacking and trampling the high grass, Annja decided to have a look around for her-self. Walking off through a stand of trees along what she suspected was an old road leading northwest, she waved off the lieutenant's worried question, "Don't you want an escort, Ms. Creed?"

She still wasn't sure whether the mercenaries would prove more help than hindrance. She knew, ultimately, that what must be done, she must do alone. And after two days crowded on the boat with the surly, boisterous men, she wanted little more than to be left alone.

Unless it was a hot bath. But that would have to wait.

Emerging from the trees, she saw a cluster of buildings standing at the edge of the clearing a couple of hundred yards away. Guessing one was the old plantation house, and feeling the archaeologist's urge to explore abandoned human habitation, she struck out for them.

She kept an eye out for any of the numerous types of poisonous snakes that could be lurking to bite her. She kept her eyes moving all around, in fact. There were other dangers that never realistically threatened ecotourists—such as native arrows, anacondas and, of course, golden *onzas*. Not to mention the odd green energy beam.

As she walked along a rutted track through more high grass she wondered what other defenses the Promessans might have in store. Whether or not this was the actual border of the settlement known as the Quilombo dos Sonhos they were near to it—she was sure of it.

"I guess we'll find out soon enough," she said aloud.

Small gold-headed blue birds flew up from the grass and away from her as she walked toward the buildings.

As she drew closer she could see that they had fallen into ruin. The main building's walls, of stone or brick— either of which had once been expensively hauled all the way up the Amazon by shallow-draft steamboats— still mostly stood. Smaller outbuildings, presumably of wood, had mostly slumped into overgrown mounds.

She went into what had been the plantation house. Climbing vines veined the walls. Their suckers had torn away the whitewash in irregular sheets. Inside she found the upper floor and ceiling had fallen in. She could see the sky above, blue with clouds beginning to close. It would likely rain soon.

The floor was a jumble of broken beams and furniture, much covered by vines and grass and even brush growing through the floorboards. She wondered at the totality of collapse. Had the house been burned down?

Looking up at a jut of beam from the wall right above the entrance, she saw rippled char on its end that seemed to confirm it had burned through. That led her to new speculation—did it burn by accident? Lightning? Arson? Had the plantation been overtaken by the collapse of Brazil's rubber market, as Manaus had? Maybe it had been a front for the *quilombo* and the Promessans, as River of Dreams Trading Company was today, and had reached the end of its usefulness.

The Promessans, she thought, had a brisk way of dealing with things that outlived their utility. People, as well as artifacts, if the fates of the anonymous man in Feliz Lusitânia and Mafalda in Belém were any indication.

She backed out and went to the other sizable building. It was a chapel. Its walls of gray granite and even its arching slate roof were largely intact. The forest had grown right up against it.

Inside was bare but for broken pews and a layer of jungle litter on the flagstones. Buttresses mounted up the walls. Green lianas climbed them, as did chittering monkeys. Little blue ground doves pecked around the hollow altar. The windows had been broken out.

Annja wandered deeper into the chapel. Dry leaves skittered from her feet. Small creatures stirred unseen beneath drifted debris.

"Annja Creed," said a voice behind her.

She spun. The sword appeared in her hand.

"You won't need that," Xia said.

Her black hair, bound by what looked like a thin jade band around her temples, fell around her shoulders. She wore a sleeveless top of shimmering green, and what might have been a green suede skirt, leaving her firmly muscled stomach bare. The straps of sandals twined up her bare legs like serpents.

At her side stood Patrizinho, his arms crossed over his muscular bare chest. He wore loose brown trousers with gold trim and low boots with no visible seams or fastenings. Figured golden armlets encircled his forearms. His dreadlocked golden-brown hair was swept back into a brush at the back of his head by a gold cloth band. Neither bore weapons that Annja could see.

"I think I do," she said. To her surprise her voice did

not shake from her anger, or the force she was exerting to keep it under control.

"Do I even have to point out that if we wanted you dead you'd be dead already?" Xia said. Her tone was mild, conversational. Annja understood that sociopaths were often accomplished actors. "Or that we can escape at will?"

"If I'm alive," Annja said, "I presume it's in your selfish interest to keep me alive."

Patrizinho's face split in a huge grin. It tugged at her heart. He was so beautiful she *wanted* to believe in him.

"She almost gets it, doesn't she?" he said to his companion. "I told you, there is hope for her."

"We shall all know very soon," Xia said.

Annja laughed. It was a harsh sound. The laugh of a stranger. "You think I'm gullible because of how easily you tricked me before," she said. "I may be a naive and spoiled North American. I may not be as streetwise as I like to think I am. I may not even be that smart. But I am capable of learning."

"Good," Xia said, smiling and nodding tightly. "Because time is short. So learn fast."

"I already know all I need to about you."

"Do you really believe so?" Patrizinho asked. He almost sounded surprised.

"You know *nothing*," Xia said. "You have been misled, lied to at every turn."

"By you!" Annja couldn't keep the metal out of her voice.

"No," Xia said.

"Even now, if you look deep into your heart you can see the truth," Patrizinho said. He held out a hand. "Please."

"You risk compromising your destiny," Xia said. "You are betrayed. Now you risk betraying yourself and all that you stand for."

"How dare you talk of me betraying what I stand for!" she demanded. "What do you know about my destiny?"

Gripping the sword in both hands, she charged toward them. In blind, weeping rage she cocked the weapon back over her shoulder to strike.

Xia and Patrizinho stepped backward out of the doorway and stepped to the side.

When she ran out after them they were gone.

They must have gone into the underbrush, she assured herself. Though she could see no sign of it—no branches asway from being displaced, no stirring of growth deeper in, no birds startled into flight by human passage.

There was no point in pursuing, she knew. This was their forest. They could ambush her or evade her at will.

This proves we're in the right place! she exulted to herself.

From the southeast came the mosquito whine of airplane engines.

THE FIELD HAD BEEN VETTED for relative flatness and firmness by the mercenaries. It was nothing the little aircraft, and a seasoned Brazilian bush pilot used to landing on rough fields, couldn't handle.

Mladko and Goran emerged wearing loose long-sleeved shirts and tan trousers. Their shaved heads were covered in Panama hats. They winged out to each side of the aircraft door and stood with thick arms crossed.

A similarly attired Publico emerged. McKelvey, alerted to the plane's approach by radio, snapped to attention and saluted. Sir Iain acknowledged him with an airy tip of a forefinger off his craggy forehead.

Then his blue eyes lit on Annja, walking crisply toward him across the field. His face seamed in smiles. "Ah, Annja my dear. Just the person I want to see. Carry on, Lieutenant. You're doing a splendid job."

As mercenaries crawled into the plane between Goran and Mladko to unload Publico's luggage, the man himself walked to meet Annja. "Come," he said, taking her by the shoulder. "Walk with me. Talk with me."

She nodded. For some reason she was too suffused with emotion to speak.

"You've done well by me," he told her, as they walked back in the general direction of the plantation house.

Annja held an internal debate as to whether she should tell him what had just happened in the ruined chapel. Before she came to a resolution he said, "I've a proposition for you, Annja. You're a remarkable young woman. You've achieved great things. And you're really very beautiful, you know. So here's my offer—become my consort, and we'll rule the world together."

She laughed. He frowned. To her utter astonishment he seemed genuinely annoyed.

"I thought you meant to give the whole world the gift of immortality," she said half-facetiously.

"Are you daft? To hold such power, only to give it away? I'd have to be a fool."

It was her turn to frown. "You can't be serious."

"I'm deadly serious," he said, although he smiled once more. "You've put the power of the ages into these hands." He held them up before her.

"Why me?" she asked, to give herself time to think. Or more accurately, to try to bring her whirling thoughts into something resembling order. "What you said about me is very nice. But I don't have any illusions I'm anything special. Especially in the looks department. You've got to see that. You have beautiful women throwing themselves at you all the time."

"Don't sell yourself short," he said, not bothering to deny her assertion. "Your appearance is quite striking. And intelligence as incisive as yours is an aphrodisiac. That and tenacious will and competence such as you've displayed. They'd set you apart from a sea of pretty faces, if those eyes and those cheekbones didn't do the job."

He stopped. They stood at the border of field and brush. A stand of trees stood between them and a derelict field that adjoined the old plantation house. He ran the back of his right hand down her left cheek.

She thrilled to the contact. There was a magnetism to the man, she had to admit. And yet—what he was saying went beyond bizarre. If he meant it, it was monstrous.

But she couldn't believe. Wouldn't believe. Surely we didn't go through so much—surely Dan didn't die, for some kind of B-movie megalomaniac?

She reached up, took his big hard hand, pulled it gently but definitely away from her face.

"What are we really talking about here, Sir Iain?"

"With the secrets we're about to wrest from these selfish holdouts come power. Infinite power. With it, quite frankly, I shall force the world to put me in charge."

"You really think—"

"Who better to lead the Earth into a new era than an immortal philosopher king, an undying humanitarian? I shall use the carrot of eternal life—and the stick of denying it—to make myself undisputed ruler of all humanity. And then—"

He shrugged his broad shoulders. "Well, the human race wants paring back. The Earth demands no less. It will all be for the best. You'll see."

"You mean you'll promise the masses immortality," Annja said, "and not deliver?"

"Oh, bloody hell. Of course I won't. It would be like giving an infant an automatic weapon. The height of irresponsibility."

"So all this happened—all these people died—Dan died, he died in my arms—" for a moment the words clotted in her throat, choking her, but she shook tears from her eyes and plowed on "—just for your *ambition?*"

"If you care to reduce it to such sordid terms."

"You lied to me."

He shrugged. "You can't make an omelet without breaking eggs."

"I'll stop you."

He raised an eyebrow. "Please, dear child. You're a girl alone in the wilderness. I have a squad of armed men at my back. Don't let my glowing assessment of your capabilities go to that pretty head!"

She stepped back. The anger was ice within her now, not fire. The sword sprang into being in her hand.

"I have capabilities you've never dreamed of," she said.

He laughed in her face. Then before she could react he flowed forward, quicksilver, and punched her in the sternum.

She was stunned for a moment. Her back slammed against a tree. The wind was blasted from her lungs. The sword had vanished as consciousness flickered.

Publico stood twenty feet away, grinning a wolf's grin.

"So have I, my dear."

It was agony to breathe. The effort sent hot needles through her chest. She didn't know if she had broken ribs. She felt broken. She slumped like an abandoned rag doll at the foot of the tree.

He strode up to her. "I may not have the secret of rejuvenation yet," he told her. He reached down, grabbed her beneath the chin, raised her up, sliding her back up the tree's rough bark. She grabbed his forearm to try to ease the pressure on her windpipe. It was like grabbing a steel tube.

"But as I think I've hinted, love, I *do* have access to certain technologies you've been told were decades in the future—if they were possible at all. Among these are the means to give a human extraordinary strength and speed and endurance, temporarily. How very fortunate that, unsure what I might be flying into out here on the very fringe of the enemy's domain, I thought to dose myself right before landing."

She kicked him in the crotch.

Evidently his wonder drugs didn't armor him there. Nor render the target impossibly small, the way steroids were reputed to. He doubled over with an entirely human—and entirely satisfactory—gasp, clutching at himself with both hands.

The sword, she knew, was more powerful than all of treacherous Sir Iain's wonder drugs. But not even it could shield her from a couple of dozen mercenaries with automatic weapons. They were boiling out of their riverbank cantonment now, weapons ready. Goran and Mladko were running toward her from the aircraft with guns in their hands.

She turned and ran. Through the underbrush and the stand of woods, out again into the long-fallow field. The soil beneath her soles was black—the black Indian earth, so rich and mysterious, in a realm where no natural topsoil existed.

Ahead of her rose the jungle, shore of a green sea that stretched unbroken as far as the eye could see. If she got into the dense brush of the transition zone she could lose herself. Clumsy Western mercs and Croat war criminals could never match her in the bush. She'd eluded such before.

But she could not outrun bullets. As she reached the far side of the field, the green refuge mere tantalizing steps away, a sledgehammer force struck her back. Only then did she hear the rippling snarl of the shots that hit her.

Momentum carried her on into the brush. She crashed through. She fell down a short slope, rolled. She felt nothing. She scrambled up. Her limbs obeyed reluctantly, almost at random, like a newborn foal's.

Another burst of gunfire. She felt another powerful impact low in her back. Lightning agony flared through her right side. She got up, ran up the far side of a small gully with a trickle of stream down the middle, into more brush.

She ran and ran, desperate, incapable of thought. Until she ran head-on into blackness, and knew no more.

28

Annja opened her eyes. "I'm not dead," she said.

"Not yet," Patrizinho said with a wide smile.

He and Xia sat beside her bed. Both wore long loose robes. His was maroon in the center and black down the sides. Hers was shades of blue in diagonal swirls. Her hair was twisted into a complicated knot atop her head, and she wore large turquoise earrings. His dreads hung loose about his shoulders.

Annja sighed. "Are you going to say 'I told you so'?"

"No," Xia said. "We only *tried* to tell you so."

Annja sat up. A moment later she felt the bed press itself gently against her back, mold to her ever so slightly, so as to continue to support her. She raised an eyebrow.

The bed lay at one side of the room, in a sort of alcove. The floor and bedspread were deep maroon. The walls were pale tan that showed a pearlescent undertone in the sunlight streaming in the pointed-arched window. Rain forest plants, or so she took them for, sprang up in profusion about the room. It was comfortable, warm rather than hot. For the first time in what felt like forever she was aware of not being oppressed by a humidity a percentage point or two less than the bottom of a swimming pool. Yet the window apparently stood open—gauzy cream-yellow curtains moved slightly in a breeze, and the air smelled fresh.

She let herself relax back into the bed. "How?" she asked.

"How is it you're still alive?" Patrizinho said. He crossed one long leg over the other. "We healed you, of course."

She sat bolt upright.

"Relax," he said with a smile, holding up a pink palm.

"But, my God! They shot me! I'm—I'm sure I felt bullets hit."

"Not to put too fine an edge on it," Xia said, lounging like a cat in her chair, "you were mortally wounded."

The bed had not angled up to meet her this time. She let herself fall back to what she realized was a very comfortable angle, one that didn't put undue pressure on her lower back and tailbone. "Smart beds," she said softly. "This is what Moran was willing to kill for?"

"Very possibly," Xia said. "Among other things, I'm sure."

"How long have I been here?"

"Three days."

"Three *days?* I must be dosed to the eyeballs on painkillers!"

"No need," Xia said. "Patrizinho told you—we healed you. You might feel some residual pains. We can block those. If they keep recurring, we can teach you meditation techniques to make the pain go away. But you should feel no lasting effects."

"But that's—"

"Impossible?" Patrizinho looked at her blankly for a moment. Then he laughed.

After another moment she laughed, too. She had to. He just had that kind of effect.

"How did you ever get me out alive? I know they chased me into the undergrowth, the mercenaries. Did I just pass out and fall into some bush where they overlooked me?"

Xia laughed softly. "We ambushed them about the time you dropped."

"The old plantation is in what you might call a buffer zone," Patrizinho said. "It gives us room to maneuver on familiar ground against intruders without letting them in among our crops and homes."

"Okay," Annja said. "You know, it's really hard trying to prioritize the questions. They're all crowding toward the turnstiles at once and it seems important none of them gets trampled."

"Take your time," Xia said. "We have a little breathing room."

"All right. Why?"

"Why?" Patrizinho made a gesture beckoning her to elaborate.

"I was going to ask why you saved me. And that's probably what surprises me most. But it's all suddenly starting to land on me—why did you bring me here?"

The two Promessans looked at one another and laughed. "In part for the reason you just demonstrated, Annja," Patrizinho said. "Your remarkable agility of mind."

"When you don't let your habitual skepticism bind you," Xia said.

"Well, perhaps I'm jumping to conclusions—I guess it does kind of verge on paranoia—"

"The way it's starting to bind you now," Xia said. Annja piped down.

"Why did we bring you here?" Patrizinho said. "I take it you don't just mean why we spirited you away from the place where you fell wounded."

"No. I meant what you thought—why did you permit me to find you? Or lead me here. Whatever."

"Why do you suspect we led you to us?" Patrizinho asked.

"Is he always like this?" Annja asked Xia.

"Except when he's worse," Xia said. "That's why he's laughing all the time. It makes it harder to throttle him for being such a pain."

Annja looked back at the tall and muscular Promessan. She thought anyone would face quite a challenge trying to throttle him. She forced from her mind an image of his crushing Dan's heart with a blow of one of those fists, so relaxed now it seemed they'd be hard-pressed to do anything more militant than pet a kitten. She had a great deal of assimilating to do. And she sensed there was going to be a great deal more to as-similate. She knew she probably didn't have much time to process everything.

"We kept conveniently finding just one more scrap of evidence that led us up the river," she said. "I began to suspect in Manaus that Moran knew more than he let on—"

"He did," Xia said. "Our poor friend Herr Lind-müller was able to remember enough to provide him a general idea of where the city lies. Enough so Moran felt compelled to kill him to keep him from telling any-one else. Our mental techniques are not infallible, sadly—he should never have had those dreams."

"You brainwashed him?" Although it chilled her to hear the claim Moran had murdered his friend Lind-müller, she realized that the germ of suspicion had en-tered her mind in the River of Dreams offices, where the representative mentioned he had fallen to his death—supposedly rock climbing, despite his fear of heights.

"We conditioned him," Xia said, "as he agreed to before he was ever brought here. That was our bargain. He could come here, make deals—highly profitable to both sides—and even receive various restorative treat-ments. But in return he had to give up any memories of our existence."

"So what did Publico need *me* for?"

Patrizinho smiled again. "Amazonia is vast. And Sir Iain obviously guessed we had means of preventing detection from above. So he needed your skills to pin down our location. He had no way of knowing where along the way you might pick up the vital clues. But he did act, subtly, to keep you moving in the right direction."

"Also," Xia said, "it appears he was auditioning you, so to speak. Testing your suitability for his larger plans."

Annja felt her cheeks get hot. "You eavesdropped on us at the airfield?"

"Of course we did," Xia said. "This is our land. We do what we must to defend it."

Annja pressed her lips together. So many questions. "I keep coming back to why you brought me here," she said, after brief hesitation.

"We may have much to teach each other," Patrizinho said.

"Your sword," Xia said. "We sensed it had been restored."

"You sensed it?"

"It's an artifact of tremendous power," Patrizinho said. "When such an event happens—when something so powerful is made whole again after such a long time broken—the world rings like a bell for those who know how to listen."

Annja frowned. She opened her mouth to argue then shut it quickly. She realized the sword's existence was going to be a sticking point to any attempts at debunking she might make. "Is that what you want?" she asked, suddenly suspicious. "To get the sword away from me?"

After a moment she relaxed slightly. "Fact is, if you did want to take it from me I might just say, go ahead. But you don't want that, do you?"

"Not at all," Patrizinho said.

"Forgive me, please," she said. "I'm tired, all of a sudden."

"We said 'we' healed you," Xia said, "but it would be more accurate to say we helped your body—and mind—to heal yourself. And that took a great deal of work on their parts. Get some rest."

"But what—what about Publico? Is he gone?"

Patrizinho's laugh was sad. "Him? No. He smells the prey now. The sickness of power is upon him. He'll never give up, short of success or death."

"He's got reinforcements," Xia said. "Specifically, he's mobilizing some members of the Brazilian army and air force against us, under the pretext that our *quilombo* is a terrorist stronghold."

29

"I still find it a pretty thin pretext for Publico to use," Annja said, "that this is some kind of summer camp for terrorists."

It was another day. She thought—hoped—it was the next. She had slept soundly after her chat with Patrizinho and Xia.

She thought of them as her friends. Although she and they had fought. Yet they seemed to consider her their friend, too. It was another mystery of the place. It was filled with them.

"Let us show you what some of your North American news programs are saying," Xia said. She and Annja sat on comfortable chairs. The third woman in the room preferred to stand, a thunderous expression on her dark face.

Xia gestured to a wide-screen television.

A man with eyes little mean squints behind round glasses was shaking his jowls. "This well-known nest of terrorists," he was saying. Frothy saliva flew from his lips in his vehemence. "Only the bleeding-heart liberal traitors have kept our forces from wiping them out!"

The ebony-skinned woman standing beside Xia smiled bleakly.

Annja's glance at her was quick and tight-lipped. Her name was Isis. Annja had last seen her lying in the muck on the floor of the death hut in the gold-camp colony, where Annja had just broken her jaw. She was cleaned up considerably, strikingly beautiful, and obviously Promessan healing techniques had served her as well as they had Annja. She was visibly struggling to contain her anger.

Annja shook her head. "I'm sorry. But I have no control over what our media say."

"If it's any consolation," Xia said, "I doubt the United States government will act directly against us."

"But you do bear responsibility," Isis said to Annja. "For bringing their attention upon us. Not to mention the attentions of the armored cars and strike airplanes of the Brazilian armed forces—which are even less welcome."

Annja sighed. "Yes. I thought I was doing the right thing."

"And you feel that excuses what you actually *did?* Your pious intentions?"

"Please, Isis," Xia said. Her voice was like satin—over steel. "Don't badger my guest."

The thin lips compressed further. The handsome

face did not soften. "I apologize to you both for allowing my self-control to slip. I will leave you now."

She went out. The door slid open to her approach and slid shut again behind her.

The door had likewise opened to Annja's own approach. She was not being held prisoner. Her wandering had, however, been circumscribed by her weakness, her having no idea how to get around the place—and her concerns about meeting others, like Isis, who did not seem as blithely unconcerned as Xia and Patrizinho over Annja's having fought and killed several Promessans.

"I'm sorry, Annja," Xia said quietly. "I had hoped she would forgive you. It appears she has more of that particular spiritual path to walk yet."

Annja looked puzzled. "You killed her lover," Xia said matter-of-factly. "Hoatzin Nest. The man who visited you in your hotel room in Belém to try to warn you away."

Annja felt her body go numb as if with cold. She tried to speak. The words stuck in her throat.

"I know," Xia said. "Patrizinho killed your lover in Feliz Lusitânia, as well. You killed several of us, in Manaus and the gold camp. You wonder why we would forgive you. You wonder why you don't hate us."

"Yes," Annja said.

"We'll try to make it clear to you," Xia said. "Soon."

Annja rose, went out onto the balcony. The floor, which looked like tile, gave slightly beneath her sandaled feet. She wore a green T-shirt and blue jeans. She

wasn't too surprised they fit her, although she had yet
to see anyone inside the City of Promise itself wear any
such garments. Her belongings had all been left behind
with the mercenaries.

She had wondered at her own uncharacteristic lack
of adventurousness. Usually her response to someplace
new and different was an irresistible urge to poke
around. But she was off balance, suffering, as closely
as she could reckon, from massive information and
cultural overload.

The doors to the balcony opened as quietly and automatically as the door to the corridor outside. Annja
stepped out into a bright morning nowhere near as
muggy as she'd expected. The city spread out before
her.

The first surprise, when she had finally mustered the
strength to get out of bed that morning and peered out
the balcony doors, was that it had levels. Not just mul-
tistory buildings but actual relief.

That struck Annja as unusual. The Amazon Basin
downstream from the Andean foothills was flat as prai-
rie farmland. Moreover the water table was so high it
was hard to build anything lasting. The plantation house
and attached chapel had presumably been constructed
on enormously deep foundations of stone or concrete.
In a few decades they'd show signs of serious sinkage
into the underlying muck. To build an entire city was remarkable.

In front of Annja's building lay a large, sunken plaza.
Its terraced levels followed flowing organic contours

rather than the usual strict rectilinear lines of most city squares she'd seen. Fountains played in broad pools. Masses of greenery formed irregular islands in the multilayered pavement. There were so many brightly colored flower patches that it looked at first glance as if the city had been bombarded with paint balloons from orbit.

She saw no vehicles. Plenty of people walked about or simply sat on benches and fountain-rims. Dozens of children, mostly wearing brightly colored smocks, raced here and there among the adult pedestrians. She heard the sounds of their laughter.

The buildings themselves particularly fascinated her. Their walls seemed slightly sloped. The general pattern suggested Mesoamerican architecture. Some buildings incorporated or were themselves outright step pyramids, the buildings truncated and broad topped. The structures that crowned some buildings came to near points.

She saw rounded features, as well, like towers of a Medieval castle. The city had a more graceful, less oppressive—or clunky—aspect than most excavated Central American buildings she had seen. The ancient Indians had been constrained by the limitations of available building materials, and by the fact that the rulers who built the great public structures wanted them to be oppressive—to remind all who saw them, whether potential invaders or their own subjects, just who was boss.

She also thought to see elements, strangely, of Nepalese and Tibetan architecture, in the odd dome or stepped tower or building with pagoda-like sweeps to the eaves. Disparate as the elements were, all fit together with wonderful harmony.

"It's beautiful," Annja said. "It looks like nowhere else on Earth."

"It reflects our influences. The tribal cultures of Africa and Amazonia, the scientific and rationalistic cultures of the West, the spiritual learning—and millennia-old science, that Westerners always like to overlook—of India and China," Xia said.

"How is that possible?"

Xia shrugged. "From our very inception, our predecessors realized the value of information. So we've spent centuries gathering all we can, whether through our own researches or trading for it from others. We take what serves us, and use it." She gestured toward the door. "Come on. Let's get out in it. You can stand to stretch your legs."

"That's the truth," Annja said.

30

They found Patrizinho in front of the building, which seemed to be a sort of dormitory or apartment. He stood by a fountain surrounded by children. He held a laughing little boy up in the air and laughed with him. He smiled happily to see Annja and Xia, put the child back down, tousled his hair.

"Thank you," he said to the boy. "Now I have to go play with my other friends."

"Okay," the boy said. He and his half-dozen little friends ran off laughing.

"Why did you thank him?" Annja asked.

"For sharing his laughter with me."

"It was sweet of you to take time to play with them," Annja said as they began walking down into the sunken plaza.

He grinned. "It's part of my job."

"It helps to realize," Xia said, "that along with playing, he was teaching them basic physical science concepts. Here we teach our children from the start to regard learning as a form of play, rather than making it into a form of torture, the way they do in your world. But then, the goal where you come from is to instill habits of obedience. And after all, an eager curiosity and propensity to ask questions is quite counterproductive from that outlook, isn't it?"

Frowning, Annja opened her mouth to defend her society and its education practices. But all the arguments that came to her mind struck her as feeble at best.

"You've got many questions," Xia said. "We haven't got much time. Choose your questions carefully—then ask them, Annja."

Again, the questions thronged forward, jostling each other. Annja found her tongue tied when it came to the most important. So she skirted it.

"You always seem to be armed," she said. "Is there danger to defend against on the streets of Promessa?"

Patrizinho smiled. "There's danger everywhere humans are, Annja," he said. "Surely you of all people know that."

"It's a tradition," Xia said. "With practical roots. We had to fight to escape. We had to fight to stay free. We had to fight to survive. And after three centuries we must fight the greatest danger in our history." Annja didn't have to ask what—or why.

"We're no pacifists," Patrizinho said. "I know you've noticed that."

"Did you kill Mafalda?" she blurted.

"Not personally," Xia said. "Did Promessans kill her? Yes."

"And if you wonder whether we approve of the killing," Patrizinho said, "the answer is, reluctantly, yes."

"But what was she doing to you?"

"It was what she had done," Xia said. "She betrayed some of our people abroad. Sold them. They had to suicide to escape torture. Publico is not the first or only party to learn enough of our secrets to be willing to use extreme measures to learn more."

"And the man in Feliz Lusitânia?"

"We went to bring him home," Xia said, "not kill him. He was exiled for certain crimes, but none so dire that he'd be denied the mercy of dying among friends."

"Most people who leave the city do so because they choose not to participate in our culture," Patrizinho said. "The tiny number who are exiled for cause submit to having their memories suppressed, as do most outsiders allowed to visit here. As Reinhard Lindmüller did."

"Advanced as our mind science is, it isn't perfect. Sometimes the conditioning slips. Thus with our brother in Feliz Lusitânia," Xia said.

"Why do you even take the risks of dealing with the outside world, then?" Annja asked.

"Trade both in goods and ideas is our lifeblood, as it is of all humankind," Xia said.

"And it's a means whereby we can parcel our knowledge out to humankind as a whole—against the resistance of the powerful of the world, whose political and monetary power are based upon scarcity," Patrizinho said.

"You mean you're not deliberately withholding your knowledge? That's what Sir Iain believes."

"Is it?" Patrizinho shook his head. His smile was sad. "Don't you suspect he knows exactly what the truth is?"

"Yes," Annja admitted. "I guess I do. He told me at the airstrip, just before he tried to kill me. He wanted your secrets to use to bring himself power." The memory made her stomach churn.

"Annja," Xia said, "information is more than just a commodity to us. It's *life*. It's always been our life, our mainstay—as well as the source of our wealth.

"In the first days, when our ancestors ran away from their self-proclaimed owners, our brothers and sisters taken from the cities of West Africa pooled their knowledge of the arts of civilization. Their tribal cousins contributed knowledge of warfare and survival, the arts of wilderness. Later we traded our knowledge with the Indians for theirs."

"What about the Indians? Didn't they regard you as invaders?"

"Some did. And in truth not all of our ancestors were eager to embrace them—bigotry is a many-headed beast, and no people has a monopoly on it, or totally lacks it, or ever has. But necessity forced us to learn to get along with the natives of the land. Eventually we began to meld together."

"You never fought them?"

Patrizinho shrugged. "Sometimes we did. Especially those of us driven from Palmares in 1694. After our Dutch trading partners betrayed us to our masters, the pioneers who founded the Quilombo dos Sonhos determined to put as much space as possible between themselves and the colonials. As they pushed up the river some of the tribes contested their passage, though they tried to keep to the river as much as possible and make no mark."

"What about the Indians here?"

"Our ancestors sought a completely receptive environment," Xia said. "The land, the water, the creatures and the people. We found the proper combination here. The local tribes agreed to cede us land in return for our protection and our knowledge. The arrangement continues to this day."

Annja sighed. "I've got a lot to learn."

"Yes," Xia said. "And not much time to learn it. So why not go ahead and ask the question that's really on your mind?"

"Such as why you do not hate me," Patrizinho said. "For which I am thankful, by the way."

She shook her head. She wasn't ready.

"I'll go ahead and play the bad guy," Xia said, "and tell you the truth about your friend Dan."

Annja looked at her with a mix of dread and eagerness.

"He branched out early on from violent street protests into extortion and the odd assassination," Xia said. "The latter came after Sir Iain scooped him up and provided advanced training. He was an apt pupil, you might say.

"As Moran told you, Dan was his troubleshooter. I gather he didn't fill in many details. Among other things, despite his tender years Dan served as advisor in such matters as the campaign of genocide against nomadic peoples certain African governments are waging, with the complicity of the UN and the West. Not unlike the way the Brazilian government is trying to destroy the Indians of Amazonas—and us—by wiping out the rain forest upon which we all depend for survival. Except the African governments cloak their crimes in the name of the Earth. The Brazilian government uses economics as its pretext."

Annja walked between the magnificent buildings, hugging herself tightly. Her reflex was to reject all this information as slander.

Didn't I notice disquieting things about Dan from the very outset? she asked herself. I suppressed them, in the heat of our shared cause.

"He was…a good man," she said. "In his way."

"But too angry," Patrizinho said.

"Why—why would he take part in mass murder?" she asked.

"He did care deeply about his fellow humans, I think," Patrizinho said. "What he saw they were capable of doing to each other disgusted and confused him. It became easy for him to rationalize anything, I suppose, as long as he believed it served his cause. I think that was largely what Sir Iain told him it should be."

"So you're saying he did terrible things *because* he was a good man?" Annja asked in confusion.

Xia shrugged. "The passionate best—or those who believe they know best—always commit the greatest crimes. For those who believe they serve some ultimate good, the sky's the limit."

"I regret that it came to pass that he and I fought," Patrizinho said. "In that we did, I do not regret I killed him."

Annja drew in a deep breath and exhaled. "I understand," she said in a shaky voice. "I feel the same way about the people I killed." She looked at them with tears blurring her eyes. "Why don't you hate me, for killing your friends?"

"Some do," Xia said. "Isis isn't alone."

"Yes," Patrizinho said, nodding, for once unsmiling. "But we each walk our own path. Those whom you killed accepted the possibility of their own deaths the instant they set foot upon the warrior's path."

"As for responsibility for their deaths," Xia said, "we bear our share. We chose to bring you here."

Annja stopped and stared at them. "You're saying you influenced Sir Iain to hire me?"

"Not at all," Patrizinho said. "Once we knew he had recruited you, though, we made our decision. Xia, myself, certain others in the city. You have the potential to be an enormous force for good in the world, Annja. You carry the sword. We wanted to help you learn a bit about what that means. We also wished to try to show you how to avoid…certain pitfalls."

"If it seems as if Patrizinho's skating around the subject," Xia said, "it's because he doesn't want to point out just how easy it would be for the sword to turn you into a monster."

Annja looked down. "I know. There were times on this journey—"

She stopped and raised her head to stare at them. "Wait. You set this up as a test, didn't you?"

"You had to earn your way here, Annja," Patrizinho said. "If we gave you gifts without your proving worthy, we would compromise not just your destiny but our own."

"So you set up your own people for me to kill as a means of testing me?" Her voice rose with outrage.

"Blame me if it makes you feel better," Xia said.

"You weren't the only one being tested, Annja," Patrizinho said. "Those whom you fought had their own tests to pass. Some did not. If that horrifies you, it saddens me, but so be it. We did not survive this long by making things easy on ourselves." He smiled. "Don't let our beautiful surroundings mislead you. We have provided comfort for ourselves. That is part of the reason we must continually test ourselves. That, and the desire to expand our understanding."

They had halted by another fountain. Annja walked a few paces away from her escorts. Her thoughts were a turmoil. She was fighting against a feeling of overwhelming relief combined with guilt.

She sat down on the lip of the fountain and wept bitterly into her hands.

When she had cried herself out she raised her head. Patrizinho held out a hand to her. "Now—let us do what we can, while we can," he said.

31

Away off in the night, a sudden nova flamed. Aircraft-engine whine turned to the scream of tortured metal as the plane plunged out of control. A comet of yellow flame arced down behind black trees to the east. A flash lit the sky. A column of cloud rose, underlit by a dancing orange glow.

"Attack airplane," Xia said. "They're flying out of a base near Lake Aiama."

The forest and fields were quiet. The rumble of nearby battle had suppressed the normal nocturnal sounds. The Promessans and their Indian allies fought a hit-and-run battle against the Brazilian forces Publico had brought in. Even the bugs were quiet, except for the irrepressible buzzing of the small, and not so small, biting insects. Nothing except the city limits of Promessa daunted them, Annja had found.

I wonder what this war will do to Publico's peace-activist image, she thought. Probably nothing, she had to admit. If word of his involvement ever got out, which was doubtful in itself, Sir Iain Moran employed phalanxes of expert spin doctors. For evidence she had only to recall the news broadcasts Xia had shown her several days earlier. Never had she heard mention of his name.

"That sounded like a propeller plane," Annja said, puzzled.

"It was," said Xia.

"You're kidding. I thought Brazil had a pretty modern air force."

"It's the very latest thing in the Brazilian air force," Xia said. "Embraer ALX, light attack fighter variant of the Super Tucano."

"You sound like an enthusiast."

Crouching there at the verge between jungle and another abandoned rubber field, Xia shrugged and grinned. "A girl has her hobbies. Even in Promessa."

"Don't they use jets?"

"They're mostly too fast," Patrizinho said. "Prop planes can fly slow enough to really see and hit smaller ground targets." He shrugged. "Like us. This aircraft is designed to murder helpless native people on the ground, such as so-called insurgents, guerrillas and bandits," he said.

She cocked an eyebrow at him. "Helpless? You shot it down! What was that, some kind of death beam?"

The dozen or so Promessans of the infiltration force

laughed. "You want them to nuke us, outsider?" Isis asked. Her voice, not surprisingly, was not friendly.

"Shoulder-launched modern man-portable air-defense missile. Russian made. We tweak the nitrogen-cooled indium antimonide seeker head to give it all-aspect tracking capabilities against reciprocating engines—meaning, prop planes. They run lots cooler than jets. Another reason they're better for close air support," Burt, a young Asian-looking man who was one of their team of twelve, said.

"Our capabilities, advanced as they are, aren't anywhere near sufficient for us to take on the whole world," Xia said. "Not even the U.S., which still boasts a big chunk of the world's military capacity. We're using our energy hand weapons sparingly, because they're not really anything that couldn't be duplicated and we don't want to announce to the world that, here we are, lost city with supertechnology, just waiting to be plundered. It'd be a feeding frenzy."

"And that," said Burt, "would be why we're off on a good old-fashioned decapitation strike."

ANNJA WAS UNSURE how far they had hiked. She knew Promessa lay well inland of the main river, although lesser streams skeined the land as they did most of the whole basin. She guessed it was at least twenty miles away; she didn't know the *quilombo*'s full size. Xia and Patrizinho and the others she had met the past few days had smilingly refused to answer questions about specific locations.

Along with Annja and Xia and Patrizinho the group included Burt, stocky and round faced with his hair in a long queue down his back, and a pair of young women, Lys and Julia. Lys was blond and slender, a few inches shorter than Annja. Julia was average height, sturdy and broad shouldered, brown skinned and eyed and with short black hair. Everyone spoke English around Annja. Lys spoke with what sounded to Annja like a Midwest American accent.

Everyone was dressed in practical combat gear. She was told the specially developed fabric used the wearer's own metabolic energy to optimize their body temperature. It was also waterproof, as the diminutive and very dark armorer explained as they were fitted for the suits. Likewise the combat suit resisted cuts and bullets—though was far from bulletproof—as well as fire. The clothing reduced the wearer's heat signature, although since the team wasn't using any kind of face masks or shielding, infrared detectors would see their heads as bright balloons bobbing above the ground. No one else seemed bothered by that, so Annja didn't worry about it.

A lot was not being explained to her, she knew. Some was because she didn't have the referents for it. Some was because what she didn't know she couldn't tell. She had not been taught the willed-suicide technique of the Promessans—her head had been stuffed too full of knowledge in too short a time as it was, and she wasn't even sure how she felt ethically about using it.

For the same reason she had also refused any kind of suicide pill. She hoped she didn't regret it. If Publico thought she had any information that might serve him, she didn't doubt he was capable of handing her over to his local allies for torture.

She also refused the treatment some Promessans going out in the world took. The chemical injection turned their bodies into incendiaries or bombs in case of death. Hoatzin Nest, Isis's lover whom Annja had killed, had taken the former route. Upon his death, his body had spontaneously combusted and burned Mafalda's shop to the ground. Annja had to admit part of her found that idea appealing. But she'd never be able to rest for fear the stuff would accidentally go off while she was still alive. Or even cause her to die of some horrid hitherto-unknown cancer ten or fifteen years down the line.

"AND HERE I WAS THINKING you two were otherworldly spiritual types," Annja said once they started moving again. All of the team wore harnesses of some dark, tough synthetic over their midnight suits, with light packs on their backs. Each carried a weapon that vaguely resembled a modern bullpup carbine. Over each Promessan's shoulder rose the hilt of a short sword.

What seemed to be a derelict field turned out to be a bog. Warm water squelched to just above Annja's ankles. It made her very glad for their special suits. She knew what kind of things lived in Amazon waters. Not that the creatures crawling through the leaf litter ubiquitous on more solid land were any friendlier or more reassuring.

"Did we give that impression the last couple of days?" Patrizinho said. He chuckled. "Forgive it, please. The spiritual part of what we had to teach you in such short time was the greater. Your physical skills are already superb."

"Haven't you figured it out yet?" Xia said. "We're in the same business as you, Annja—defenders. Physical combat in all its aspects is only part of our jobs. But it is a major part. And like anyone you're likely to encounter among us, the jobs we do are the ones we're most attuned to."

The sky lit with a flickering white glare to the accompaniment of a snarling thunder. Though Annja, like the others, wore small buds in her ears to dampen the supersonic harmonics of gunfire and explosive blasts, she could tell the noise was savagely sharp.

"Twenty millimeter machine cannon," said one of Isis's team they had joined up with on the ground. He looked like a pure Amazonian Indian, short, spare built but broad across the shoulders, with long black hair tied back from his handsome face.

They advanced into more dense forest. The two squads walked roughly parallel, staggered so that no one walked exactly behind the person in front, apparently to reduce the likelihood of a single burst of gunfire that would take them all out at once. Annja, in the middle of her group with Patrizinho's comforting pres-

ence behind her and Lys in front, tried to walk as soundlessly as the others. She didn't find it as easy as the others seemed to not squelch in muck, rustle in leaf-litter
or swish and crackle through branches.

Each of the midnight suits had a small panel on the
breastbone and between the shoulder blades that
glowed faintly, a different color for each team member. The others had laughed at Annja's vocal alarm
at having an illuminated target right over her heart,
front and back. No one not on the team, Burt explained, could see the panels. How that was even
possible Annja had no clue. The Promessans offered
no explanation.

Isis led the second group. Despite her barely
shielded enmity toward Annja, Annja had to admit she
seemed quietly competent.

The chief of the strike team was named Marco. Instead of the harness the others wore, he sported a web
utility belt heavily loaded-down with instruments.

Xia held up her hand. The two squads came to a halt
in the midst of a particularly thick stand of underbrush.
A small figure materialized soundlessly as a shadow
right by her left elbow. He grinned at her with teeth
bright white in a black-painted face. He was no taller
than Annja's shoulder, with a bowl haircut and a
skimpy loincloth. He also had a Kalashnikov assault
rifle almost as long as he was tall.

Xia conversed in low, fluid syllables with the small,
nearly naked man who suddenly crouched beside her.
Annja couldn't understand a word. It was obviously a

local Indian dialect. The crouching man answered softly, nodded, stood. Then he simply became one with the night.

Xia turned back, beckoning the others to gather near. "We've got our allies passing word we're coming through so they don't bushwhack us," she told the team. "They say the invaders are patrolling very aggressively."

"Aren't they bushwhacking *them?*" Burt asked.

Xia nodded. "The commander is showing the degree of regard for human life you'd expect. They care about their own troops only a little more than they do about us. The only real difference is, they actively want us dead."

"So it is in the Third World," Patrizinho told Annja softly. "Life isn't cheap to the people. It's the rulers who don't value the people's lives."

"They're getting ready to make a big push," Isis predicted.

"At night?" Burt shook his head. "No way."

Xia held up a hand. "Not our concern. We just have to be ready for anything."

They moved on again. Twice they stopped and crouched immobile as enemy patrols crashed by. The first spoke in semimuffled Portuguese. The second was mostly being harangued in English by somebody with an unmistakable American accent. Annja wondered if it was one of Publico's mercenaries.

In both cases the patrols blundered within a few feet of Annja and her friends without showing any evidence of suspecting they were there. Annja could smell the sweat soaking their fatigues—and smell the fear in that sweat, as well as traces of the alcohol and tobacco they'd recently consumed.

The noise and glare of battle increased as the team proceeded. Mortars and grenades sounded. Automatic weapons popped and snarled. Tracers arced against the sky. Annja couldn't tell how much, if any, fire came from the defenders. The invaders let off rounds in truckloads, whether against actual targets, or to suppress suspected enemies or simply to make themselves feel better, she couldn't tell. It occurred to her that her group risked getting hit purely by accident.

Gradually they moved beyond the sound and light show of the ongoing firefight. The invaders pushed to the west-northwest, angling inland from the river. Xia had led her infiltration team north and east, swinging wide around the main thrust.

Now they turned back toward the river and the headquarters the Brazilian commander shared with Sir Iain and his men. They began to advance by impulses. One squad hunkered down, rifles ready, covering as the other moved. Then the group that had just advanced would go to cover and keep watch while their comrades leapfrogged out ahead of them.

Xia raised her hand. Her five followers sank into a stand of brush. Annja raised her rifle and snugged its padded butt to her shoulder as Isis got her people up and led them forward.

Annja peered through her sights. She had been

checked out with the weapon at the armory that afternoon. It fired semi- or full-automatic, quite silently. It
reloaded from the top with blocks of fifty projectiles.
The chief armorer told Annja the rifles used electro-
magnetism, whatever that meant in this context.

Atop her rifle, conventional night sights glowed
ghostly in the darkness. With a pressure of her right
thumb she was provided with infrared vision.

At once she saw big blobs of yellow so bright they
were almost white, right ahead. "Isis, get down!" she
hissed, knowing the communicator woven into the fabric of her suit would transmit the warning.

The night was ripped apart by white fire and horrific
noise.

32

Helpless, Annja watched as a pair of Isis's squad members, silhouetted against a colossal muzzle-flare, were shredded by a burst from a machine cannon. The rest of the armored car's 20-mm shells cracked over the heads of Annja's squad to rake the jungle line forty yards behind them.

Lesser flashes lit the night as soldiers fired their assault rifles. A second armored car opened up from thirty yards or so to the left of the first.

"Stay down," Isis seemed to whisper in the back of Annja's skull. "They're not shooting at us."

She was right. The shots all passed over the heads of the now totally prone Promessan team. Isis's two people had been blown away by a cruel accident, by a foe who had no idea they were even there.

Diesel engines throttled up with a noise like dragons

clearing their throats. The armored cars rumbled forward.

A curious buzzing sound passed over Annja from behind. A brilliant flash lit the wedge-shaped snout of the vehicle that had shot up Isis's team. The vehicle stopped. A moment later orange flame roared from the driver's and cupola hatches. A figure wrapped in flames climbed screaming from the cupola, fell to the ground and rolled. Smaller white flashes started strobing through the black smoke pouring from the stricken machine like firecracker strings as the ammo storage went up.

"Here they come," came Patrizinho's voice in Annja's skull. It soothed her back from panic's raw edge. "Stay low and don't move unless you have to."

Two vehicles rolled on, a dozen yards to either side of the wreck. In the garish light of the flames Annja saw soldiers coming toward her, heads hunched forward beneath their camo-mottled boonie hats, prodding the night before them with their rifles.

The skirmish line passed. One man came so near to Annja she might have grabbed his right ankle as he went by. Not daring to breathe, keeping her eyes slitted, she tried to remember the lessons Xia and Patrizinho had given her the past two days on stealth, among a myriad subjects. Try to think as little as possible. Envision yourself a part of the landscape—a fallen log, a bush. Breathe shallowly but remember to breathe. Never look directly at an enemy. He'll sense you.

Men she had known who had seen combat, especially special-operations troopers, had told her exactly the same thing, about trying to think like a bush and never looking straight at anyone.

The hardest part, she found, was remembering to breathe.

Then the oblivious enemy was past, shouting and shooting. But to Annja's renewed terror a fourth armored car appeared, swerving around the blazing wreck. It headed straight for her.

She stared at it. It got bigger, big as a moving mountain. Its three independently suspended right tires would all roll over her in series if she didn't move. Yet she was terrified of moving prematurely, lest the crew spot her.

The metal monster loomed above. She tried to roll left, out of its path, only to fetch against the stout central stem of a bush. Panic blasted through her. The bush refused to yield. The cleated front tire crunched toward her face. With a desperate heave she rolled to her right.

The backward-sloping lower plate of its snout brushed her shoulders. She moaned aloud in fear as the car rolled over her, blotting the stars. Its tires crunched deafeningly mere inches to either side of her.

After it passed, Annja lay quivering. She felt a touch on her shoulder and gasped. She struggled to bring up her rifle.

A strong, gentle hand caught her arm. "Easy, easy," said Patrizinho, kneeling beside her. "You're okay, yes?"

She drew in a deep breath. Then she nodded convulsively.

He touched Annja's shoulder again. "Let's go. "We're almost to the real danger."

The uproar of the Brazilian advance or patrol or whatever it was, receded as the strike team's surviving members moved on. The Indians who had ambushed the soldiers with an antitank rocket and rifle fire had long since melted into the jungle.

After the Promessans had gone twenty or so yards a pair of explosions behind them, unnoticed by anyone else in the awful night's battle sounds, marked the self-destruction of their dead friends' bodies.

As they crouched they could see the nimbus of light above the trees cast by the base camp the invaders had established near the ruined plantation house. It marked their objective. There waited Publico and the Brazilian army officer in command. And there also lay tents and trailers containing the invaders' command and communications gear, as well as stations monitoring the enemy's sensors.

If the Promessans and Annja could destroy that equipment and kill the leaders, the whole invasion would lose momentum and quickly mire down. Annja didn't believe that could win them any more than a temporary reprieve. But her friends assured her that a little breathing room was all they needed to secure the safety of their city and its tribal allies. All she could do was swallow her doubts and do her best.

To Annja's surprise the invaders had not occupied the plantation buildings. The main house she could understand—it was a wreck. But surely with all that manpower they could have cleaned out the largely intact chapel?

"They fear ghosts," Julia matter-of-factly said when they halted in the scrub near the empty buildings, still a hundred yards from the enemy perimeter, when Annja voiced the question in her mind.

She was a bit surprised at the Promessans' seeming cold-bloodedness. They had just seen two of their comrades torn apart. Yet no one showed any reaction.

"Remember," Xia said softly to her, crouching down at her side, "we have fought for centuries for everything we have—starting with our lives and freedom. There'll be forever to mourn afterward. For those who make it back."

"I TELL YOU," the Brazilian commander said, "we should wait until the assistance promised us by the North Americans gets here." He was a tall, fat, sweating man.

"Surely your men can handle a few naked natives, Colonel Amaral," Publico said.

"These natives whom you call 'naked' have modern antitank and antiaircraft missiles, as well as automatic weapons and apparently endless supplies of ammunition. Savages they are, but naked they are not!"

The billionaire rock star half turned toward Amaral. "You command a regiment. That should be ample to crush any resistance you're likely to face."

"Only half of my troops are on the ground," Amaral reminded him. "And we are far, far up the Amazon. It will be days before my regiment is up to strength. That being the case, why not wait for the Americans?"

Publico slowly smiled. "Because an unimaginable treasure awaits us up ahead, Colonel. You know that."

33

Annja crouched beside the fence encircling the invaders' base. Within no searchlights moved; the banks of generator-fed lights, though bright, were spottily placed, leaving plentiful shadow pools for them to skulk through. Once they got inside.

"What about this fence?" she asked Patrizinho, who squatted beside her. "You forgot to teach me to levitate."

"That's an advanced course," he said, and laughed. "But we don't go over. We go through."

He reached behind himself and withdrew wire cutters from his pack. With little musical pings the wires parted in a line four feet from its top to the ground. Patrizinho made two cuts outward from the slit, each about a yard long. Then he pushed the wire open. "After you," he said. "We'll fold it back in place when we're through."

Annja nodded. Bent over she slipped through the instant gateway in the chain link. She kept her weapon at the ready, scanning back and forth as she slipped right, toward the cover of a tent obviously protecting a stack of supplies.

She had no qualms about using her sword. Not tactical, moral or even in terms of letting out her great and dangerous secret—any survivors of tonight's bloody work would have memories so confused and chaotic that any interrogator would simply dismiss out of hand any wild tales about a tall white woman wielding a broadsword like an avenging angel. It was one factor she had found worked consistently in her favor—the natural conservatism of the human mind, that saw mainly what it expected to see, and overlooked or edited out what didn't fit.

But the sword was a weapon for face-to-face combat. If she had to engage any guards at a distance she wanted to be able to just shoot them. And hope she shot well enough that they died as silently as her Promessan weapon fired.

The team had coalesced and then split into two groups different from the initial squads. Nobody spoke of it and Annja didn't see fit to question. Xia had taken Burt and a woman named Reed and gone off circling the wire perimeter to the left, to infiltrate closer to the river. The compound had grown up inland of the beachhead, not on the Amazon bank. Someone had been cagey enough to worry about enemies infiltrating by water, as well as the possibility of the river's unexpected rise. The ground inland was clearly not subject to regular flooding or the plantation would never have been built where it was, and where it had obviously ruled for decades before its abandonment and decline.

The landing area had been transformed into a separate compound ablaze with light day and night to unload supplies from relatively fast diesel riverboats. Likewise the bigger airstrip was blasted from the jungle and improved with perforated steel plating to allow cargo planes to fly in and out.

Xia's group went to destroy generators and the trailers where sensor inputs and communications were processed. Marco hung back by the chapel, his wonders to perform. The other six survivors had been split into two fire teams of three each. They would aim to hit the command tent, right in the middle of the several-acre compound, from two directions simultaneously.

Up against the intimidatingly large compound it all seemed hopelessly ambitious. But Annja was determined to try. And die, if necessary. The thought of what Publico would do if he succeeded was all she needed to keep her going.

She reached the supply tent and squatted. A moment later her fire team's other members joined her—Xingu and Isis. As promised Patrizinho had smoothed the slashed wire back into place, so deftly Annja couldn't see the cut from a few yards away. He took Lys and Julia and vanished into shadows to the left.

Isis clearly commanded this team. She acknowledged Annja with a simple nod. Whatever Isis har-

bored in her heart toward her, Annja felt confident it
would in no way affect what she did here inside the
wire. The life the Maroons had chosen to live was quite
Darwinian, for better or worse. Those who indulged
their emotions at the wrong time died.

Annja didn't know what criteria had been used to se-
lect the team. She didn't even know who did the decid-
ing, since Promessa had no visible government, and
seemed more a tribal collection of clans than anything
else. But she had no doubt her comrades would be professional in action.

They slipped to the tent's far end. Isis did a three-
second lookout, then gestured for Xingu and Annja to
advance while she covered.

With Xingu on her right Annja moved into the open.
There was still shadow, thanks to the haphazard place-
ment of the lights. But she felt naked anyway. Worse,
they would have to transit a good ten yards of brightly
lit open space to reach the huge multiroom tent where
Publico, according to their Indian spies, held court.

From the right came voices. Male, young, full of
boisterous energy, although held fairly low to keep
from attracting the ire of their superiors. They spoke
Spanish. Xingu held up his hand. Annja froze, wondering if stopping in the open was a really good idea.

Xingu carried two projectile weapons. Slung behind his back, barrel down for ready access, rode his
compact electromagnetic rifle. He held a second weapon, about half its size and with a single pistol grip, in
both hands. It had a bulbous body and a long narrow

barrel. He snugged it to its shoulder and aimed it toward the voices.

Two men in cammies strolled out from around the
corner of another tent ten yards away. They were so engrossed in their clowning that neither so much as
glanced toward the two people crouched in plain view.

Not until it was too late, anyway.

Xingu shot the man on the right in the throat. His
weapon made no sound. The merc dropped instantly.
The other faltered in midstep. Annja could see the look
of baffled surprise come onto his lean young features.

He started to turn, reaching clumsily for the M-16
slung over his own shoulder. But Xingu calmly shot
him under the right ear. He folded like an empty rain-
coat.

"Curare-derived toxin," Xingu told her as they scuttled for the cover of the tent the two had emerged from
behind. "Rapid propagation. Death instant." They were
the first words she had heard the young man say.

Once at the tent they covered as Isis joined them.
"Why don't we just use that, then?" Annja asked.

"Clothing stops projectiles. Have to hit skin," he
said.

They held position as Isis ghosted on right and in-
ward, to a pile of crates covered with olive-drab tarpau-
lins. They kept working their way toward the command
pavilion from its end. Such action as was visible was
all going on to the river side of the camp, where a
stream of trucks came through the gate and off-loaded.
As Annja and Xingu darted around the end of a dark-

ened tent from which snoring emerged in several keys, Annja dared hope they'd make it undetected.

Then the door to a latrine to their right opened and a geeky guy with glasses came out fiddling with the fly of his camo pants. His eyes and mouth flew wide.

"Alarme! Alarme! Alarme!" he shrilly screamed.

Xingu shot him twice through the open mouth with two curare darts from his high-tech blowgun. By then it was too late, of course. The soldier got what his last words called for—alarms fired up all over the camp. It flashed through Annja's mind how all her special-warfare buddies would sagely nod their heads—another flawless op ruined by a totally random event.

She darted for the cover of the latrine, a long shack walled with what looked suspiciously like prefab fence sections from Home Depot, with a slanting roof of corrugated tin. A heavy weight hit her from behind.

The world exploded in flame and noise from scarcely fifteen yards away.

Even as she was falling she felt impacts, heard grunts. But the impacts weren't on her. Rather they were transmitted through the lithe, strong body that had hit her in a flying tackle. They landed. Isis's forehead slammed hard against the hard-packed earth beside Annja's face.

Annja rolled the woman off her. She was limp. She was surprisingly heavy for one so lean. Like Annja herself, she apparently packed lots of muscle on a rangy frame.

The anthracite eyes focused on Annja's face. "Do what you must," Isis said.

Annja's heart fell into her stomach. Life fled the Promessan warrior woman's eyes. Her head lolled to the side.

Looking up through tears that threatened to blind her, Annja saw Xingu running to her, firing his electronic rifle toward where the terrific light and noise had come from. From beyond the latrine came more bright flashes and crackling explosions, full of supersonics that seemed to go through her skull like needles despite the sound dampers in her ears. She expected to see the man shot down.

Instead he dived down beside her, intact and breathing hard. Annja low-crawled to the corner of the latrine to risk a look around.

Fifteen yards away a huge Hummer was going up in flames. A big pintle-mounted machine gun sprouted from its roof. Fire jetted straight up through the mount. Men bailed out the doors, screaming, shrouded in flames.

Annja dropped to her belly, stuck her rifle out with her left hand, fired two quick bursts. The screams cut off. The men dropped. She wasn't sure whether it was an act of mercy or to ensure they didn't somehow extinguish themselves and come after the infiltrators again.

She ducked back and looked at Xingu.

He patted his rifle. "Selective load," he said, almost apologetically. "Explosive shells."

She started to demand to know why she hadn't been told about that feature. She stopped herself before wasting the time and breath. She had gotten the basics she needed to fight. It was for the best and she knew it, no matter how badly she wanted to resent the fact.

She got up on her haunches, transferring the rifle back to her right hand. She looked down at Isis. The woman seemed at peace. She had fought her best and died the death she had chosen. She might even be envied.

She had also displayed inhuman fortitude to be able to so much as talk. The Hummer had mounted a .50-caliber machine gun. The special suit was no protection—it was probably all that kept her being blown to pieces.

Annja reached down her left hand and closed the staring eyes with a quick motion of her first two fingers. "We have to go," she told Xingu. He nodded.

The camp was alive with shouting, shooting men. They all seemed to be blazing away at random. Looking back across the compound, Annja saw two men go down, apparently hit by friendly fire.

By unspoken consent she and Xingu both took off around the latrine shack's far end, ran between it and the burning Hummer despite the big machine-gun cartridges cooking off inside the inferno. There was no point in any fancy bounding overwatch now. Their only hope of reaching their goal was speed.

Once inside—well, they had to get there first.

They almost made that final dash. Then a burst of gunfire, from what direction Annja couldn't even tell in the pandemonium, raked Xingu's torso from the left. He sprawled on his face.

Annja glanced back in an agony of indecision. She burned with desire to go back to help her wounded comrade. But that would doom her and the mission. She could not let herself die and fail.

Xingu heaved himself up. The grin he showed her from his dark, handsome face would have carried more reassurance had it not been crimson with his own blood.

A single shot punched through his temples left to right. He fell on his face in the dirt.

Annja turned and sprinted for Publico's tent. Letting her rifle hang by its sling, she summoned the sword.

34

Inside the big tent Sir Iain smiled as he heard sirens howl and guns speak.

"Annja, dearest girl," he said. "I've been waiting."

He reached into an interior pocket of his linen jacket, produced a small object. It was blue plastic and shiny metal and resembled an asthma inhaler.

"What's that? Drugs?" Colonel Amaral demanded from across the tent. The color had dropped from his plump, dark-olive face, leaving it ashen behind his beard and moustache.

"Transformation," Publico breathed as power rushed through veins and nerves like a shock wave from a bomb.

A flap at the tent's rear flew open. Eight men charged into the room. They were tall men, wide men. They were made even wider by the bulky olive-and-

earth-tone-painted suits of bullet-resistant polycarbonate armor they wore. They carried curved polycarbonate shields on their arms, and held yard-long shock
batons in gauntleted hands.

"Who are they?" Amaral demanded, gaping in
amazement.

"My bodyguards."

Fat jiggling above his too-tight web belt, the colonel
tried to force his way into the protective circle the armored
men formed around Publico. They thrust him rudely back.

"Sorry, Colonel," Publico said. "They're for me,
not thee."

Amaral's dark eyes bulged. Publico laughed, a huge
roaring laugh that rattled the tent walls. The drugs always had that effect on him—filled him with the sense
of invincibility.

And why not, he thought, when my enemies are
bringing everything I desire right to me?

A ripping sound from the weatherproofed fabric behind Amaral made him turn. His right hand clawed at
his holster flap.

Something silvery flashed in out of the humid night.
There came another sound like tearing cloth. He felt a
burning sensation at his throat.

Amaral spun back to face Publico, visible past the
armored shoulders of his guards. Then he dropped to
his knees and pitched onto his belly, as blood drained
from his gaping wound.

A young man, at least six-four and built like a grey-
hound, stepped into the tent. His midnight-blue body-

suit fit his muscle-rippling torso like skin. Chestnut dreadlocks hung about his shoulders. He held a Japanese-style short sword naked in his hand.

He stepped over the colonel's shapeless lump of body. Ignoring the huge armored guards, his eyes fixed like golden spotlights on Publico's blue ones.

"Welcome, my friend," Publico called to him as a slender blue-eyed blond woman stepped in quickly to the young man's left.

Moran held up a huge hand and beckoned. "Come on and die."

ANNJA SLICED a six-foot vertical cut in the tent and stepped through.

The pavilion's main room was a good ten yards long and six or seven wide. Despite its size it was crowded.

In the center of a circle of enormous men in bizarre plastic armor carapaces painted in camouflage patterns, Patrizinho was slashing at Sir Iain Moran with his sword. The big Irishman was easily dodging the serpent-fast sword cuts and laughing uproariously, as if he were having the time of his life.

Annja's eyes narrowed. No normal human could have evaded Patrizinho's attacks so fearlessly. Sir Iain was into his chemicals again.

On the far side of the wall of goons Annja glimpsed blond hair. She heard a hailstorm sound. Lys was shooting her noiseless electromagnetic rifle, trying either to chop a path clear or drop Sir Iain, their most vital target. But the big men just held up their Roman-style shields. The projectiles rattled off them as harmlessly as Ping-Pong balls.

Three of the thick men charged Lys. She let go her rifle and whipped out her sword. She uttered a falcon scream of challenge.

Publico darted in to rock Patrizinho's head back with a fast straight right. The Promessan staggered back. Blood streamed from his nose.

Annja charged. Shield to shield, two of the bulkily armored men advanced to meet her. She swung the sword overhand at the one on her right, figuring to break or even sever the man's shield arm.

The blade bit right through the upper rim of the shield, cut deep. But after a bit more than a foot the blade stopped.

Grinning behind the faceplate of his helmet, the man on her left jabbed his stick toward Annja's ribs. He had a big brutal face. She thought to recognize either Goran or Mladko.

She pulled on the hilt of her sword to yank it free of the shield. It stuck fast. Belatedly she realized why the cut had stopped—it wasn't that the tough polymer material of the shield defeated the sword's edge. It was because the plastic sides of the cut had gripped the flat of her blade tightly as a vise.

She released the sword and danced to her right. Goran, as she chose to think of him, didn't have a lot of range, trying to reach around the big shield. He could not stretch far enough to hit her.

The man at his side yelled in surprise as the sword simply vanished.

Annja smelled ozone. She realized the batons were tipped with electric leads. If Goran's had struck her she would have received an incapacitating shock along with any other damage the blow might do.

She scampered back to reassess the situation. Patrizinho was battling with Publico. The rock star stood with his head tipped forward, his lightly silvered dark blond hair framing his face. Two other bodyguards were stomping something on the floor. To her sick horror Annja realized she could no longer see Lys.

The two men closest to Annja, having absorbed the fact that one way or another the woman in front of them was now unarmed, glanced toward each other and charged as one. Annja was fairly certain the second was Mladko.

She lunged toward Goran on her left. Turning sideways, she slammed into his shield. Taken by surprise, he rocked back onto his heels. Then he swung the shield outward with all his strength, hoping to fling her to her back, where she'd be helpless against a baton thrust.

But Annja had grabbed his shield's upper rim with both hands and let all her weight hang from its inch-thick polycarbonate. Adding her weight to the momentum Goran had imparted caused the shield to swing open to his left like a gate.

Before an almost equally surprised Mladko could strike at her Annja had swung past the business end of his baton. She found herself right between the hulks.

With her right foot she kicked hard at the back of Goran's left knee. It wasn't a blow that could break the joint. But it did buckle it.

Already overbalanced Goran dropped to that knee. Annja got her feet beneath her, stood. She glanced quickly over her right shoulder to make sure none of the other bodyguards was trying to club or zap her from behind.

But they had clearly been ordered to stay surrounding Publico at all costs, in case more would-be assassins turned up. Patrizinho and Publico continued their death dance, oblivious to the world. For the moment she was clear. And a moment was all Annja Creed needed.

She let her weight fall back again, locking out Goran's shield elbow. Mladko had turned toward Annja. He thrust his baton at her. Her latest move caused him to ram the tip of his baton against the inside of his partner's shield instead.

Goran's armor could not prevent Annja's using legs and hips to torque the shield and pop his elbow joint with a nasty crack. He bellowed in agony and pitched forward onto his face.

Mladko pulled his shield between himself and Annja. She grabbed its top as she had his partner's. He was ready for that. He braced and stood like a rock.

She was ready for that, too. Jumping and pushing hard with her arms, she scaled the shield as if it were a solid wall. So strong was the polycarbonate that the cut she had made didn't open a millimeter. As she came over the top Annja bounced a shin kick off the side of Mladko's head. His helmet took the force of the blow—most of it. But it gave her the split second she needed to scramble astride his shoulders like a monkey behind his head.

Roaring with rage, he teetered in a circle. He tried to reach her. The armor bound his joints, rendering him clumsy. He slammed himself in the faceplate with the upper rim of his shield, stunning himself enough for Annja to catch hold of his baton right behind its live tip, use the leverage advantage to twist it from his hand and fling it away.

He had turned 180 degrees. Still riding Mladko's shoulders, Annja saw Publico lunge toward Patrizinho. Instantly Patrizinho's blade flashed in a backhand slash for his enemy's eyes.

Patrizinho was fast and skilled. But in the grip of his drugs Publico was faster. He reversed motion, bending backward like a limbo artist. The short sword's razor edge clipped a lock of hair from his head before swishing harmlessly past.

The outward cut left Patrizinho totally open. Publico snapped forward and seized his foe. His right arm went beneath the Promessan's left. His left hand caught the biceps of Patrizinho's outflung sword arm.

Patrizinho tried to head-butt him. Publico buried his face in the juncture of Patrizinho's right arm and neck, jamming the attack. With his right arm clamped up at an angle between his opponent's shoulder blades for leverage, Publico pushed back on the trapped arm with all his augmented strength.

Patrizinho groaned as his shoulder joint was forced from its socket.

His sword fell to the floor of the tent. Everything froze. Mladko stopped ineffectually trying to bat at

Annja, momentarily more fascinated by his boss's fight than his own seemingly comical predicament. Sensing the climax had arrived, the other guards had turned to watch their master's combat.

It all burned itself into Annja's brain—the guards, faces obscured by visors. The sad crumple of Lys in a pool of blood at the tent's far end, pathetic as a kitten hit by a car. Beside her an armored bodyguard lay on his back, unmoving arms outflung. The woman had not died without exacting a blood price of her own.

And then Annja's vision contracted to a tunnel around Patrizinho's beautiful face, contorted with agony and effort as he still strove to break free.

Reaching up behind Patrizinho's head, Publico grabbed a handful of his dreadlocks. Then with all his strength he yanked down. Although the muscles stood out like columns on Patrizinho's powerful neck, his head was whipped back.

Annja heard his neck break.

35

Publico let Patrizinho go. The beautiful young man fell back dead.

"*No!*" Annja screamed.

Fury rose in a flood through her body, her mind. She summoned the sword. Reversing it, she drove it point downward toward where Mladko's thick neck joined the swell of his trapezius muscle.

Through the neck hole of his armor the blade plunged. Mladko gurgled, then he dropped first to his knees, then onto his face.

Springing free, Annja tore loose her sword. As nimbly as they could, the guards to left and right sprang to form a new wall between her and Publico.

Goran had struggled to a sitting position. He somehow managed to disengage his shield from his ruined

left arm. He reached with his good hand for the gun hol-
stered on his right hip.

Reversing the sword again, Annja slashed at his head
left-handed. The helmet was not thick enough to trap the
blade as Goran's shield had. Nor was it strong enough
to resist being neatly split by the powerful weapon.

He went down for good.

Three of Publico's remaining armored guards stood
between Annja and the billionaire, who stood astride
Patrizinho's corpse grinning at her. Two others hung behind him, still guarding against reinforcements. Utterly absorbed in events inside the tent, Annja wasn't
even aware if the sabotage charges the other team were
supposed to set had detonated yet.

She wouldn't have counted on reinforcements—had
she been capable of thought.

Screaming, she feinted right, then lunged left. The
men were big and strong and obviously practiced in
their armor. But it still rendered them clumsy—and
disrupted their sense of balance.

The left-most man had fallen for Annja's feint,
stepped forward with his left foot and committed his
weight to it. Before he could shift his balance back,
Annja had run past his right side. His unshielded side.

As she went by she slashed backhanded at the small
of the guard's back. He shrieked as the end of the blade
bit through the soft flesh between hips and ribs.

One of the guards standing behind Publico charged
past his master, drawing his baton for an overhand
strike. Annja tipped the blade of her broadsword back

over her own right shoulder and thrust the pommel straight for the angry gray eyes behind the visor.

Reflexively the guard raised the shield to protect his face. Then just as automatically he lowered it to clear his counterstroke.

But Annja hadn't swung her sword—merely feinted with the hilt. Taking the sword in both hands she swung it around, up, down.

It came down in the center of his helmet just as the rim of the thick shield dropped to expose it.

There was a hideous squeaking crunch. The guard dropped.

Another guard charged from her right. She ducked under a horizontal swing of his baton and slashed him across his right shin. He howled and fell with a tremendous racket.

"That's enough." Sir Iain Moran did not shout. But his voice filled the tent like the report of a grenade going off. He hadn't been a professional performer for a quarter of a century without learning to project.

His two remaining men stopped in place. Even the man whose tibia Annja had just slashed whimpered more quietly, rolling to his side and coiling into a knot of agony.

"I'll handle this from here," Publico said in a softer voice. "You want a piece of me, don't you, Annja?"

He had shed his jacket. His fight with Patrizinho had torn his shirt open, revealing his powerful torso. In his right hand he held one of the long black shock batons. In his left he held Patrizinho's sword.

"What good do you think those will do you?" Annja said. "Whatever happens, even if you try to surrender now, I will kill you. I swear it!"

"Talk is cheap, dear girl," Publico said. "Cheaper even than your friends' lives. Show me what you've got."

If he'd meant to taunt her into a blind-angry attack he failed. She couldn't be any more focused. She took up an *en garde* position like a modern fencer, left hand on hip, sword thrust toward his face.

The baton clacked against the flat of her blade. She was already withdrawing the sword, coiling her legs for her real attack, a slash to take the legs right out from under him. Instead he spun toward her. Whirlwind fast he came out of it slashing with the blade in his left hand at the unprotected left side of her head.

She had no graceful defense for the unexpected move. She only escaped by flinging herself in a dive to her right. She was able to get her shoulder down, rolled and snapped up to her feet with her back to the tent wall.

Publico stood with his stolen short sword held out before him and his baton tipped negligently back over his right shoulder. "You see, Annja dear, at the end of the day you're just an ordinary girl who's happened to luck into possession of a fascinating sword," he said. "An exceptionally resourceful girl, not to mention athletic and alarmingly skilled at combat. But still just a girl."

Annja had worked her way away from the wall to

give herself some room to fight. Obedient to their master's command the two armored men still on their feet had pulled back to the rear of the tent to clear the floor. They had dragged the injured man with them.

Publico grinned a wild grin and launched a whirlwind two-weapon assault. He was fast. He might have defeated her with sheer strength. But for all his speed and power Publico had one very serious problem—his drug did nothing for his weapons. All she had to do was get an edge on one and she'd chop it off like a skinny dry twig. So he was forced to pull his blows unless he was certain they'd connect with either Annja or the flat of her blade.

Like a skilled boxer, she managed to keep moving in a circle rather than backing straight away from him. She was fit, and knew how to use her resources in combat. But if all she did was defend and give ground he would sooner or later get lucky or just smash down her defenses. And she knew with terrible certainty that one solid hit would incapacitate her.

But he made an amateur's mistake. He tended to fall into predictable patterns. And his timing was regular as clockwork.

Annja's blade flicked out. His reflexes saved him. He danced back with a red line across his left cheek that slowly blurred downward as it bled.

He laughed, but it rang hollow. "You're good," he said, "I'll give you that." He couldn't help his words turning to a snarl at the end. He had obviously not expected to get stung.

Annja wasn't cocky about drawing first blood. She had aimed for his forehead. She'd intended either to split his skull and end it, or more likely, to open a cut that would fill his eyes with blood and blind him. As it was, she knew she was lucky to have tagged him at all.

Nonetheless when he roared back to the attack his strikes were that much clumsier. They came faster, though. The sword sliced through Annja's tough suit and her skin just below the short ribs on her left. The pain was bright as a camera flash. But she didn't let it distract her. Adrenaline quickly dulled its edge. And Publico's days as a street-fighting man lay decades in the past. She'd been hurt in battle a lot more recently than he had.

His minor success led him to redouble his attacks. That came at the expense of such technique as he had. In a moment she translated the rebound energy from blocking a transverse stroke of the baton into a quick cut down and left that caught the flat of his sword with her edge.

With a high, pure note her sword cut through the other blade two inches from the round handguard.

"Ho-ho!" Publico shouted, dancing back just in time to avoid being eviscerated by a whistling horizontal stroke of Annja's sword. "Well done!"

He tossed away the useless stub. Then he took up his own exaggerated fencer's pose, right side on to Annja. The contacts at the tip of the shock baton were aimed straight at her right eye. His left hand was held up behind him.

She thrust toward his eyes. The baton parried with a clack. She thrust again, stopped short in a feint, thrust for true. With the prodigious strength of his wrist he whipped the baton in a tight circle around her blade, outside to in. Then he knocked the hard sword to Annja's right, throwing wide her arm and leaving her open.

Laughing he swung the baton high and charged to club her down.

And again lack of skill at this kind of fighting played him false. Vulnerable as she was, a strike could have taken her down. But Publico raised the baton high overhead as if winding up to split a log.

She just got the sword up, hilt gripped in both hands. She had to catch the blow on the flat. She feared that with his speed he could jam the stub of his baton into her belly if she chopped it off.

It was like parrying a falling car. The blow's incredible power drove her down. She had to use her back leg, her left, as a shock absorber, bending it until the knee touched the floor.

Publico leaned far over her. "I knew you'd come, Annja dear," he told her. "And I knew that everything I desired, you would bring to me. You wouldn't consent to surrender now, and save yourself some pain?"

She went limp.

As she let herself fall toward the floor she thrust her left leg between his feet. Crossing her legs she stuck her right foot just to the outside of his right calf. She landed hard then, shoulders first, then whiplashing her head into the plank floor so hard she saw sparks behind her eyes. Undeterred she rolled hard to her left.

The scissor sweep twisted Publico's legs right out from under him. He went down hard.

Annja leaped to her feet. He had lost his shock baton. He lay on his back, with his shoulders held just off the floor.

His eyes were wide as they stared at the sword tip just six inches in front of them.

"Why not finish it, then, Annja?" he said. "You were filled with self-righteous bloodlust a moment a moment ago."

"I can always kill you," she said. "For now—"

She heard the click of plate on plate as a guard prepared to intervene to save his master, and turned a glare on the men by the back wall.

"Stand back or I'll open his third eye!" she snarled. Both bodyguards stepped back and raised their hands. The effect was almost comical, like cartoon robots surrendering.

Like a rattlesnake striking, Sir Iain moved. His left palm slapped the sword away. His right hand dived behind his back.

Screaming in frustrated anger, Annja raised the sword to cut him dead.

He raised a Taser and shot her in the belly. Chained lightning flashed through her body. The pain was unbelievable. She found herself on her knees.

The sword had gone. When her concentration broke it had returned to its otherwhere.

"Call it back, my love," Sir Iain said, climbing to his feet. "I've got plenty of charges in this little beauty. And I do love to watch that lovely face when the current hits you!"

He loomed above her like an ancient colossus. "Not only do I get the hidden city with all its secrets. But I've discovered a beautiful woman running about the world fighting evil with a magic sword. How very sweet."

"You can't believe everything you see," Annja said. She thought furiously, seeking a course of action. Nothing suggested itself. With Moran's enhanced reflexes he would shock her insensible with laughable ease if she brought back the sword. Nor did she think she was quick enough to rip the barbed contacts out of the skin over her ribs before he triggered the device.

"Feel free to go ahead and kill me," she said dully. "Then you'll never get the sword," she said, not sure if that was even true.

He looked past her. His smile broadened.

"In any event," he said, "I won't need to try any such desperate measures."

The tent flap opened. Two of the huge armored guardsmen entered. They held Xia by her arms between them. Her long black hair had been torn loose and hung in her beautiful face. Her hands were bound behind her back.

"Splendid work, gentlemen. The others?"

"Dead," a guard said.

Xia stared at Patrizinho's body. He lay sprawled on his back, just a few feet from the man on her left. She raised her face slowly to look at Publico with chilling hatred.

"Your lover?" Publico shrugged. "I'm sorry I had to kill him."

"At least spare us the crocodile tears," Annja snapped.

He laughed. "But you do wrong me, my dear! You see, I know you don't fear death. And I suspect you'd show the most wearisome resistance to torture. The martyr type, clearly.

"But you've a glaring weakness." He turned a meaningful look to Xia.

Annja felt all the blood drain from her face.

"I only have one of your friends captive—for now. It's only a matter of time before I capture more. As well as the city called Promise itself, with all its wonderful, wonderful trove of secrets.

She looked sideways at Xia. Seeing her former enemy, now friend, so vibrant and resourceful, held helplessly captive by these thugs, forced to look at the body of her friend—her lover—broke Annja's heart.

Xia caught her eye. She winked.

Patrizinho's body, Annja thought.

She turned to look her tormentor in the face. "Torture's a lousy way to get actual information, Publico," she said. "Surely your intel pals have told you that."

"Well, field research has confirmed what common sense told me," he admitted, "that a subject being tortured either says nothing or tells her torturers anything she thinks they want to hear in hopes of making the pain stop. But when I torture this exquisite creature before your helpless eyes—cause her to suffer unendurably, not just for hours, but for days, for weeks—how long will you be able to bear *her* agony, Annja Creed?"

Patrizinho's body burst into flames.

Publico looked at the sudden conflagration. The guard holding Xia's left arm gaped in astonishment. Then, glancing down, he saw that the left leg of his armor had caught fire. Blue flames raced up his side. He let go of Xia and began to beat at himself, screaming in terror.

Annja was already in violent, decisive action. No sooner had Publico's eyes flicked from her than she called the sword back to her hand. As he stared, utterly dumbfounded, at the fiercely burning corpse of his foe, she leaped to her feet. Holding the sword with both hands, she brought it up beneath the two wire leads of the Taser.

They parted with no more resistance than cobwebs.

She spun in a circle. Sir Iain turned back toward her.

She whirled into a lunge and rammed the sword through his belly to the hilt.

He doubled over. His handsome face clenched like a fist in agony.

Annja looked down into the blue eyes of Sir Iain Moran. They looked very surprised, staring up at her from the floor where he lay dying.

EPILOGUE

Annja Creed sat back in bed with her knees propped up, tapping contentedly on her laptop. She felt as if she could lie in the air-conditioned comfort of the Belém hotel room forever. The television rattled away in the background, unheeded—electronic wallpaper, synthetic companionship.

It had been a wild ride.

The television suddenly drew Annja's attention. With a start she realized she was seeing an aerial shot of the camp near the old plantation.

"Just days ago rogue elements of the Brazilian armed forces," an announcer was saying, "apparently bribed by renegade billionaire masquerading as philanthropist Sir Iain Moran, attempted genocide against a tribe of peaceful Indians of the upper Amazon. This crime against humanity was foiled when the aggressors fell to fighting among themselves. They killed their officers and Moran before surrendering to the indigenous defenders. High civilian and military officials are under arrest this hour in Manaus and Brasília, and the U.S. has joined Germany and Russia in an emergency session of the UN Security Council in calling for a worldwide investigation into the so-called humanitarian empire of the man who called himself Publico...."

Annja sat up. With the remote she turned up the volume. The Brazilian news went on to report on the latest disappointments involving the national soccer team.

Intrigued, Annja clicked around the channels. In short order she turned up a broadcast from a North American news network.

"—back to talk about how the late rock star Publico's bizarre New Age beliefs led him to madness and mass murder. And how, ironically, he might have done a final humanitarian work greater than all the previous ones for which he had become so famous. Here to tell us about it is Dr. Frederick Mobutu of the World Health Organization."

From the host with the wild hair and heavy-framed glasses the camera switched to his guest, a stern, dark man wearing an embroidered cap like a fez.

"Thank you, Charlie," Dr. Mobutu said. "The Yaraíma tribe, whom Sir Iain nearly succeeded in wiping out, has just entered UN-mediated negotiations with the government of Brazil, along with a consortium of pharmaceutical companies. All access to their lands will be most strictly forbidden, but they will happily share the cornucopia of hitherto unknown and fantastically potent medicinal plants Sir Iain Moran sought to take from them by force."

"For a price, I'm guessing," the host said.

"To be sure," the doctor said. "Royalties, it is predicted, will run to hundreds of billions of dollars within a very few years."

"And I'm guessing that, even before a penny is paid or a deal is fully in place, waves of lawyers have rushed forward to assist the victimized tribe," the host said.

"That is also true. We might perceive a silver lining even in that, though, Charlie. Between the lawyers and all the media attention there will surely be no further attempts, legal or otherwise, to steal the land and its treasures from its rightful owners."

Annja laughed even as tears rose in her eyes. They did it! she thought. The Promessans finally found a way to get more of their secrets out to a needy world.

It shouldn't surprise her, she realized. These were the same people, after all—or their descendants, anyway—who had hidden combat training from their masters in a dance.

She closed out the file she was working on, anthropological notes she was never, ever going to be able to publish, and shut her laptop. Laying it aside, she clicked off the television and the light and lay down to sleep. Her thoughts were jumbled. She knew she'd agreed to have her memory altered by the Promessans. She wasn't sure anymore what had been real or what she'd imagined. She was content to know she'd helped to accomplish something good.

THE PHONE SHOOK her rudely out of sleep.

"Hello?" Usually she snapped straight to full wake-fulness. *Maybe I still haven't healed as much as I thought.*

"Annja sweetie honey?"

"Doug?"

"The network wants extra shows," Doug Morrell, ir-repressible producer for *Chasing History's Monsters*, warbled in her ear. "We're starting back up early. I've been calling you for days and days and days. What, did you fall off the edge of the Earth?"

"Something like that," Annja said.